The Soldier's Impossible Love

One Night in Blackhaven
Book 3

MARY LANCASTER

ARE YOU SIGNED UP FOR DRAGONBLADE'S BLOG?

You'll get the latest news and information on exclusive giveaways, exclusive excerpts, coming releases, sales, free books, cover reveals and more.

Check out our complete list of authors, too!

No spam, no junk. That's a promise!

Sign Up Here

www.dragonbladepublishing.com

Dearest Reader;

Thank you for your support of a small press. At Dragonblade Publishing, we strive to bring you the highest quality Historical Romance from some of the best authors in the business. Without your support, there is no 'us', so we sincerely hope you adore these stories and find some new favorite authors along the way.

Happy Reading!

CEO, Dragonblade Publishing

Additional Dragonblade books by Author Mary Lancaster

One Night in Blackhaven Series
The Captain's Old Love (Book 1)
The Earl's Promised Bride (Book 2)
The Soldier's Impossible Love (Book 3)

The Duel Series
Entangled (Book 1)
Captured (Book 2)
Deserted (Book 3)
Beloved (Book 4)

Last Flame of Alba Series
Rebellion's Fire (Book 1)
A Constant Blaze (Book 2)
Burning Embers (Book 3)

Gentlemen of Pleasure Series
The Devil and the Viscount (Book 1)
Temptation and the Artist (Book 2)
Sin and the Soldier (Book 3)
Debauchery and the Earl (Book 4)
Blue Skies (Novella)

Pleasure Garden Series
Unmasking the Hero (Book 1)
Unmasking Deception (Book 2)
Unmasking Sin (Book 3)
Unmasking the Duke (Book 4)
Unmasking the Thief (Book 5)

Crime & Passion Series
Mysterious Lover (Book 1)
Letters to a Lover (Book 2)
Dangerous Lover (Book 3)
Lost Lover (Book 4)
Merry Lover (Novella)
Ghostly Lover (Novella)

The Husband Dilemma Series
How to Fool a Duke (Book 1)

Season of Scandal Series
Pursued by the Rake (Book 1)
Abandoned to the Prodigal (Book 2)
Married to the Rogue (Book 3)
Unmasked by her Lover (Book 4)
Her Star from the East (Novella)

Imperial Season Series
Vienna Waltz (Book 1)
Vienna Woods (Book 2)
Vienna Dawn (Book 3)

Blackhaven Brides Series
The Wicked Baron (Book 1)
The Wicked Lady (Book 2)
The Wicked Rebel (Book 3)
The Wicked Husband (Book 4)
The Wicked Marquis (Book 5)
The Wicked Governess (Book 6)
The Wicked Spy (Book 7)
The Wicked Gypsy (Book 8)
The Wicked Wife (Book 9)
Wicked Christmas (Book 10)
The Wicked Waif (Book 11)
The Wicked Heir (Book 12)
The Wicked Captain (Book 13)
The Wicked Sister (Book 14)

Unmarriageable Series
The Deserted Heart (Book 1)
The Sinister Heart (Book 2)
The Vulgar Heart (Book 3)
The Broken Heart (Book 4)
The Weary Heart (Book 5)
The Secret Heart (Book 6)
Christmas Heart (Novella)

The Lyon's Den Series
Fed to the Lyon

De Wolfe Pack: The Series
The Wicked Wolfe
Vienna Wolfe

Also from Mary Lancaster
Madeleine (Novella)
The Others of Ochil (Novella)

Prologue

"WHY ARE YOU looking so worried?" Leona asked her twin brother.

It must have been half an hour after their successful family meeting, and the Vale twins had agreed that all the right elements were set in motion to shake up Julius, their eldest brother, and keep Lucy, youngest of their sisters, safe. But while Leona scribbled in her notebook, Lawrence was peering out of his bedchamber window, a frown on his face. Usually, the twins contrived to look younger than their fifteen years. But sometimes, now, Lawrence's rare scowl made him look older, almost...manly.

"Roderick," he said.

Leona stood and went to join Lawrence at the window. Major Roderick Vale, second eldest of their siblings, marched rather than strolled in the untamed part of what should have been a formal garden. Even when not in unform, Rod looked like a soldier, upright and efficient in his every move. Except there was no purpose in his march.

He broke out of the garden and strode toward the wood. It would be dark soon.

"He will go to the ball, if only to keep an eye on Lucy," Leona said.

"Yes, but will it do him any good?"

"We can't solve all their problems in one night," Leona said. "And, in fact, I'm not yet sure what Roderick's problem is—except that the war was not good for him in the end."

Roderick had fought under Wellington all through the Peninsular campaign and the invasion of France. He had always been a rare but welcome visitor in the twins' lives, right up until the peace of 1814. But after the great battle at Waterloo, he had been different. Quiet, moody, his speech varying for no obvious reason between harsh and gentle, his temper erratic, though he was never unjust or even unkind.

Julius, their eldest brother, had given up the sea, retired from his outstanding career in the Royal Navy, in order to make a home for himself and his siblings here at Black Hill, the old family estate situated a few miles from the town of Blackhaven. It was a good decision, but in making it, Julius seemed to have lost his passion, almost as though he had retired from life as well as the navy. The twins would not allow that, which was why they had talked the rest of the family into making sure he went to the Blackhaven Assembly Rooms Ball.

Roderick was almost Julius's opposite. Some sort of passion or grief seethed silently behind the façade of normality.

"As if there is only a very fine thread binding him together," Lawrence said slowly.

"Something happened during the Waterloo campaign," Leona said.

Lawrence nodded.

"Well, at any rate, going to the ball in Blackhaven won't do him any harm," Leona said. "In fact, it will take him out of himself, let him worry about Julius and Lucy. And he might even meet someone himself."

Lawrence turned to her. "Well, that's really one of his problems," he said ruefully. "He already has someone, and I'm not convinced she is good for him."

"Lawrie!" she exclaimed. "How could you keep that from me?"

At least he had the grace to look sheepish. "Sorry. Thing is, she isn't exactly respectable. Which is why we don't know her."

"But she is why he goes so often to Whalen?"

Whalen was the next town along the coast. Although Blackhaven now rivaled it in size, it still had a deeper harbor and a more stable, working population, where Blackhaven relied on visitors taking the fashionable waters for their health.

Even in her twin, Leona knew she would come up against the male sense of honor, of keeping unrespectable women quite apart from their family, even in speech. There was no point in her asking questions about Roderick's lady.

"Then really," she said, "we want Roderick to meet someone else at the ball. Someone fun and kind, who will eclipse this other female in his mind and heart." She frowned. "I'm beginning to think we will *have* to be there."

Lawrie shook his head. "No, we'd inevitably be discovered, and that would distract them and spoil everything. With Rod, we'll just have to hope." His frown smoothed. "Or speak to Felicia, so that she is sure to introduce him to lots of charming people."

"Lucy is a better judge of character," Leona argued.

"Yes, but she needs to have fun without worrying about Rod."

Leona nodded reluctant agreement. "Felicia, then. And a good deal of luck." Now it was her turn to frown. "What if he just needs peace?"

"He has peace here," Lawrence pointed out. "It isn't working. He needs an occupation and the right wife who will love him."

Leona smiled at him. "Sometimes you sound almost grown-up."

Chapter One

THE LADY IN green changed everything.

Major Roderick Vale attended the Blackhaven ball for three reasons. Mostly to support his brother Julius, who did not want to be there either, but who could do with an awakening kick, though Roderick also needed to help keep Lucy, their mischievous little sister, in line. His other motive had to do with personal boredom.

He did not particularly believe he would achieve any of these aims at the town's handsome assembly rooms. Until he forgot all about them the moment he saw *her*.

At first, he could not think why it was she stood out from the fashionable throng surrounding her, for although it was a provincial party, there were many wealthy and important people present. She wore an exquisite gown of a shimmering green so pale it was almost white. Her soft, glossy brown hair was in a style of such artful disarray that it looked natural. Her figure was perfect, slender and yet feminine, the gown draping it modest and yet hinting at the delightful treasures within. But it was her face that held his attention.

He did not know whether she was beautiful. He thought so, but her expression was more arresting. Even from the other side of the ballroom, he could see the contradictory mixture of haughty weariness and eager curiosity. As though she had shrugged off everyone surrounding her and was in search of something else entirely to interest her.

Rising to the challenge from pure instinct, Roderick set down his glass beside his brother's and rose, all his predatory instincts aroused. He felt as if he prowled across the room, stalking his prey. Oh yes, she was beautiful, clearly sought after...and different. Someone, perhaps, to intrigue his intellect as well as satisfy the lusts of the body. Although he would settle for the latter, he was surprised by the strength of his sudden longing for that meeting of minds to go with it.

Very briefly, Meg Maven flickered across his mind. Without any friendship, their relationship had grown cloying and dull. He did not regret ending it, but still, there were delights a man missed, and the lady in green...

The man beside her moved, allowing the candlelight he had been partially blocking to fall directly onto her face. It was like a dash of cold water.

It was true she had all the beauty he might wish for, and everything about her proclaimed she was joyously unafraid of life. But she could not have been more than eighteen years old.

To make it worse, she suddenly sensed his attention and glanced directly at him. Her gaze should have fallen at once. It did not, so he inclined his head distantly and kept walking, straight past her group of friends toward the young officers of the 44th huddled beyond.

Dear God, what had she read on his face? Shame? Disappointment? Certainly, he felt both rage beneath his skin. He could not have his imagination conjuring beautiful sirens out of very young, respectable ladies! Roderick had no interest in, and less fitness for, marriage. His tastes ran to women of experience and no commitment, who understood the game of dalliance and the arts of pleasure. Not to some innocent child barely out of the schoolroom. He hoped he would never have to meet her and remember this moment again. Ever.

LADY HELEN CONWAY, youngest of the Earl of Braithwaite's sisters, had entered the ballroom surrounded by her chattering family. Yet her gaze fell on the soldier almost immediately. And suddenly, she forgot to breathe.

In a vague kind of way, she registered that he was a stranger, not one of the familiar officers stationed at Blackhaven, that he was tall and lean and harshly handsome in his military uniform. But what stunned her, what caused the mad butterflies and the surge of longing and anticipation, was his face. She ached to paint it in all its pleasing contours and severe, oddly powerful features.

He did not even see her, so she had ample opportunity to observe him as he paused by a pillar and leaned one shoulder against it. He might have been watching the dancers, but she didn't think so. In his mind, he was miles away, in another, bleaker world than this bright, frivolous ballroom. As well as authority, she read darkness and suffering in his face, in the restlessness of his far-seeing eyes. A man of rigid self-discipline, she thought, with profound passions simmering just below the surface. For Helen, that made him exciting and curiously romantic. But mostly, she yearned to paint him.

To catch the shadows, physical and emotional, to somehow bring them alive in the handsome features she would immortalize on paper. Or on canvas...

Someone moved into the way, blocking him from her view, and a moment later he wandered toward a table among a group of other people. She was glad, somehow, that he was not alone.

"Oh look, Helen, Bernard is here!" her sister Alice said, pulling her over to sit with the rest of the family.

"Bernard is always here," Helen said sympathetically. If he was not escorting his old maiden aunt, he was escorting his widowed stepmother, always with uncomplaining cheer. All the same, she recognized Alice's surprise. While they had been away in London, the boyish Bernard had grown up. Or, more likely, he had grown up long since, and because they had known him forever, they hadn't noticed.

Well, they had grown up, too. Alice had had her first Season, and unless Helen could stave off her mother and brother, she would be next. And she was not looking forward to it. Black-haven balls were different. They were full of friends and folk she knew. London was a heaving mass of people and manners and pitfalls for all save the most obedient and conventional. Alice and Helen were neither, though to their surprise, Alice had known considerable success during the Season, being regarded as "original."

"I might even get away with being a professional musician and composer!" Alice had marveled.

It would not happen, of course. The only way Alice and Helen would ever follow their dreams, to be a musician and artist respectively, was to run away and lose themselves in Europe. Which might just be possible now that the war was over.

Helen danced with Captain Grantham, an old friend from the 44th, then greeted her old governess—once Miss Grey, now Mrs. Benedict—with great delight. But as other strangers joined them, shamelessly angling for an introduction to the Earl of Braithwaite's sister, she grew stiff and uncomfortable. Of all things, she hated to be courted, for no one was interested in *her*, only in her birth, her connections, and her dowry.

That was when she glanced around, looking for a quick escape, and again saw the officer she wanted to paint. For an instant, their eyes met, and her heart seemed to dive into her stomach. Unquiet, surely predatory eyes that saw *everything*. Right through her clothes to her skin, and beyond that to her soul.

And he looked as if he would devour it all with pleasure. He even moved like a hunter stalking his prey.

She should have been appalled, not so excited that she stopped breathing.

A mixture of panic and gladness held her spellbound, for he was prowling straight toward her. He was going to speak to her, ask her to dance, even though they had never met. Perhaps Caroline Benedict knew him…

He inclined his head in acknowledgment, and her heart nearly jumped out of her throat. And then he simply sauntered past.

He might never have seen her, except she knew that he had. She could not help following him with her eyes, and he did not go to another woman, but to exchange greetings with a few local officers before wandering onward.

He *had* been looking at her! And she was fiercely, triumphantly glad.

So why had he walked on? Had he taken fright?

No, a man with that face would not be frightened by a mere woman, however well born! In any case, why did she even want him to notice her?

Because just for an instant, she imagined he had seen *her*? Not Lady Helen Conway, the Earl of Braithwaite's sister, but *Helen* as she was. And she knew somehow from his face that he would never pretend an interest he did not feel.

Excusing herself from the company, she retreated back to Eleanor, her sister-in-law and official chaperone, and again looked around for the unknown officer. He was easily spotted, still roaming the edges of the ballroom, occasionally nodding to acquaintances or stopping to exchange a few words.

"Eleanor, who is that officer with Mrs. Winslow? He is not with the 44th, judging by his uniform."

Eleanor followed her gaze. "Oh, that is Major Vale, one of Sir Julius's brothers. There are about nine siblings, I believe, all staying at Black Hill now. In fact, we met two of his sisters earlier. Why?"

"No reason," Helen said vaguely. "There seem to be a lot of faces I do not recognize anymore. Nine Vales certainly accounts for some of them!"

She shifted restlessly. She had chosen to sit this dance out to speak to friends, and yet now she did not wish to speak to anyone. She wanted to draw Major Vale before the sharpness of the detail faded from her mind, before his expressions blurred.

She jumped up, barely even aware of the vague excuse falling from her lips. Unlike their mother, currently recovering from the journey north from London, Eleanor was not a high stickler. This was Helen's chance to escape.

It was her older sister Serena who had told her about the alcove in the shadows beneath the orchestra gallery. Serena, now happily married to the Marquis of Tamar, had been a handful in her day. Her exploits—and those of their eldest sister, Frances— were legendary among the youngest members of the family. No doubt Serena had flirted here—perhaps even with Tamar!—but it could just as well be Helen's temporary studio. If it was free.

She whisked back the curtain as though she had every right to be there, and, relieved to find the alcove empty, she slipped inside and let the curtain fall back behind her. Two straight-backed, upholstered chairs stood by a small, round table, on which a jug of water and two clean glasses had been left.

Helen threw herself onto the first seat, shoved the glasses aside, and stripped off her gloves. It was hard to draw well in even the finest of gloves, and besides, they would end up with lead stains. She wrestled her notebook out of her reticule with some difficulty, for she always brought the largest she could squeeze in there. By the time she found a clean page and held the small lead pencil poised over the paper, she no longer saw her surroundings, only the arresting, fascinating face of Major Vale.

She worked quickly, with no time for mistakes, for her family would notice she was missing. Alice would cover for her, if she had seen where Helen went, but one could never rely on peace at a ball.

Portraits were her new obsession. She had learned years ago to render an accurate physical likeness, but hinting at the expressions, the character, behind the features, was what truly fascinated her.

Her pencil flew over the paper in sweeping curves and bold, sharp lines, shading shadows and darkness. It was a small space to convey all that she needed to, but in this early stage, she barely saw her own work. It was his face she held steadily before her eyes, strong yet fragile, weary and yet yearning, the darkness unbearable, the light unreachable. But there was that second glimpse too, that instant of surely wicked desire. For her. She could not choose between the two glimpsed insights into his character. She just kept drawing, feeling her way deeper with each minute mark on the paper.

The moving curtain broke into her world like a gunshot. Her head jerked up and she stared at the real Major Vale.

She gasped, hot, guilty blood surging into her cheeks.

If there was a saving grace to the situation, it was that he looked as stunned as she.

"Excuse me," he said, with the faintest bow, and was already turning away when the small, inarticulate sound of distress escaped from behind her lips.

She did not know if it was alarm at her discovery, or disappointment that still he would not speak to her. Either way, she was appalled by the sound and jumped to her feet so quickly that the table rocked. She seized it just as the notebook slid to the floor. She froze.

His hand fell from the curtain. He glanced back, a faint frown tugging his brow. "Ma'am, are you ill? Shall I send someone to you? Your mother?"

"God, no," she said fervently. "She would scold me mercilessly. Fortunately, she is not here, but if word gets back to her, I shall be in disgrace."

His frown vanished. "You do not appear unduly perturbed by the prospect."

"Not really," she admitted.

"Dare I ask why you are hiding alone in here when the waltz is about to begin?"

"Why are *you*?" she countered.

"I'm hiding from my sister," he said, so unexpectedly that she smiled.

"Does she bring you prospective partners that you then feel obliged to dance with?" Helen asked sympathetically. "So do mine."

"Don't you like dancing?"

She considered. "Yes. But I very much dislike all the formalities and conventions surrounding it. I like to dance with friends, not with men who have no interest in me. Most of them don't even have interesting faces."

Reminded, she glanced down at the notebook beside her feet. Major Vale's recognizable face gazed up at her. She might have done good work there, if she could ever bear to look at it again.

"*Interesting* faces?" the real Major Vale repeated in apparent amusement. "That is an unusual requirement, is it not? What about handsome faces? Charming conversation? Skill on the dance floor?"

"I'm no judge of any of these things." Casually, she bent to pick up the notebook, but he was quicker, and she was forced to straighten without it.

She was afraid to look at him. What on earth would he think of her drawing him? Would he even recognize himself? It would say little for her skill if he did not, though it might be the best outcome she could hope for…

To her relief, his gaze remained on her face. He did not even glance at the open book in his hand as he offered it to her.

She dared not look at it either. Instead, she held his eyes with her own. They were slate gray, hard and wintry, but surely there was a hint of curiosity there, even if was mostly amused. Behind those surface expressions, they were deep, troubled, a little violent, a little desperate, full of infinite pain.

They distracted her, those eyes, making her too slow to take the book and shut it. She had only just closed her fingers over it when his gaze dropped.

Hastily, she tugged it, but his own grip had tightened, possibly involuntarily. His eyes widened, then, slowly, he released the book and raised his gaze to hers.

"Is that…me?"

He was not angry. He was not making fun of her meagre talents or her obsession. Instead, he looked almost…frightened. Which, for some reason, made it possible to speak, if only to reassure him.

She closed the book and dropped it into the open reticule on the other chair. "Yes. I'm sorry. I should have asked your permission, but I wanted to get the bones of it before I forgot."

His lips twisted. "Does this mean I have an interesting face?"

She smiled. "Yes."

A quick breath that might have been laughter. He bowed. "Then I am honored. I think."

"I won't show it to anyone without your permission," she said anxiously. "In fact, I probably won't show it to anyone anyway. It won't be good enough."

"I don't think that is your problem," he said. He stared at her, perhaps seeing her afresh. She wondered, ruefully, if that was good or bad. "My name is Vale," he said at last.

"Mine is Conway. Helen Conway."

His eyebrows flew up. "*Lady* Helen Conway? You are Braithwaite's sister?"

"The youngest," she admitted. "Do you know Gervaise?"

"I know *of* him. I don't think we've met. I don't go into Society much."

"Neither do I." She wrinkled her nose. "I'm not actually out yet."

He drew his breath in sharply, muttering something at the same time.

"I beg your pardon?" she demanded icily.

At that, the twinkle of amusement crept back into his difficult eyes. "Are you even sixteen?"

"Eighteen," she said glacially. And then, as his eyes never wavered, "In a couple of weeks. Alice came out this year, so I was saved."

"You don't want to be out?"

She shuddered. "I hate the whole idea of it."

"So do I," he said. "Though, fortunately, it's not a ritual men are put through so rigorously."

"And you can escape to university, or the army, or a year-long tour of Europe."

"Several years, if you play your cards right."

"How long were you away? Were you with Wellington? At Waterloo?"

A shadow passed over him, so briefly she might have imagined it. "Fourteen years, off and on. And yes to both. Lady Helen, may I ask you something?"

She blinked at the abrupt question. "Of course." She lifted her reticule off the chair and sat down. He moved toward her and sat in the other chair, leaning forward to meet her gaze.

"Why did you draw me like that?"

"Like what?" she asked, playing for time while the color seeped back into her face and neck.

He raked his fingers through his hair in some nameless frustration, then held out his hand, half a command, half a plea.

She swallowed, then reluctantly took out the notebook, turned it to the correct page, and passed it over to him. Although she had drawn it so recently, she was really seeing it for the first time. And she had worked so feverishly, it could have turned out really poorly.

With relief, she saw that she had indeed got the basic features right. It was recognizably Major Vale. She glanced up at him, peculiarly anxious. He looked...disturbed. "You don't like it?"

His frown cleared. "As a picture, a portrait, of course I do. You clearly have considerable talent. I think, rather, it is me I don't like. Like *that*."

She gazed at it more closely. She had caught something of his expression. Unsure whether to draw him tortured or predatory, she had managed to merge a little of each. The result was too raw, too troubling. But the very masculine desire was clear in his mouth and his eyes, and she should not even be aware of such things.

"I'm sorry," he said awkwardly. "I seem to be much more of a rough soldier than a civilized gentleman. Please believe I meant you no disrespect."

So he knew he had been looking at her like that. Otherwise, he would not have apologized. For a moment, she was afraid he would leap up and run.

"I saw no disrespect," she said. "I sketched one instant—Well, two. I could draw a hundred others."

He blinked. The faint, disarming smile began again in his eyes. "A hundred? I cannot believe my face is *that* interesting. May I?" He had paused, his finger and thumb ready to turn the page.

She hesitated, then nodded once. If she could not bear criticism, she would never improve. Tamar had taught her that years ago.

For a while, he looked in silence, flipping from page to page, and occasionally back again.

"These are people you love," he said, running several through his fingers.

"My family," she said. "Drawing them helps me to really see them. My mother… So fierce and stern she used to frighten me. But she would die for us without a second thought. Gervaise, my brother, looks haughty, and yet he is anything but. My sister Alice…" The fear that she was losing Alice shot through her again, closing her throat.

"And this?" he asked.

She smiled. "My brother-in-law, Lord Tamar. He teaches me."

Major Vale looked impressed. Tamar had made a name for himself, even in London. "You like him, too."

"Everyone likes him. You will, too. He and my sister Serena are on their way north now. They will be here in time for the garden party."

"And these gentlemen?" He paused at two sketches on facing pages.

Helen wrinkled her nose. "They are not interesting, are they? They were courting Alice, but neither of them was worthy."

He cast her curious glance. "Does Alice agree?"

"Of course. She would have been bored with either of them before the ring was on her finger. In fact, they are pretty interchangeable. You think me unkind, but one fortune hunter quickly comes to resemble another."

"Perhaps they saw your sister's beauty."

"They did not," she said flatly.

"They certainly don't look as if they did, but then, I blame the artist for that."

"I draw what I see."

"That is what worries me." He closed the book and stood up. "Thank you for letting me see your sketches. I admire your talent very much. And now, I fear, it is time for us both to face the music. Good evening, my lady."

With that, he smiled, bowed, and vanished behind the curtain.

Chapter Two

HE SHOULD HAVE left as soon as he saw the alcove was occupied. He should not have spoken to her, let alone looked at her sketches. But he felt guilty for startling her, and in any case, she had taken him by surprise with her mixture of artless innocence and mature insight. Her voice, low, clear, and strangely beautiful, seemed to shiver through him. As for her sketch of him…

She had read him like an open book. He was appalled to see his own selfish desire staring back at him. And yet it had not appalled her. She had seen it and blended it with the rest of him, without judgment. In fact, with a compassion he should have found unbearable and yet did not. He hadn't even been surprised to find the same kinds of insight in the rest of her drawings. The girl was wildly talented. And while she may have been young in years, she was much older in observation and understanding.

Intrigued, he had wanted to stay with her—and knew he should not for any number of reasons, including her reputation. Perhaps his retreat was a trifle ignominious, but he found he was smiling as he went in search of his siblings.

Lucy was dancing. So was Felicia. He could not see Delilah just at the moment. Cornelius appeared to be deep in conversation with a lady on the far side of the room. Julius… Where was Julius? Had the wretch sneaked away while Roderick was looking at sketches? In fact, Roderick had had the feeling that his eldest brother never had any intention of attending the ball, so he had been more surprised that Julius had come at all.

"You're too young and beautiful to cry into your brandy," he told his younger brother Aubrey, easing into the chair beside him and reaching for the bottle.

"Not crying, planning," Aubrey retorted. "What have you been doing to cast you into such a jolly mood?"

"Looking at pictures," Roderick said, pouring himself a small brandy.

Delilah sat down on his other side without saying a word. She was the sister closest to him in age, and he could tell instantly that something had distressed her. She was breathing too quickly. However, she had herself well in hand, and her expression was forbidding.

Roderick's fingers tightened on his glass. If anyone had slighted her…

Beyond Delilah, another, very different woman caught his attention. Dressed at the height of fashion and extravagantly jeweled, she was only just on the right sight of vulgar. A handsome and clearly devoted young man escorted her. Roderick, appalled that she had come here, wondered if he should also be offended that she had filled his vacant place so swiftly.

Certainly, he did not regret ending their affair, which had become both stale and cloying in the few short weeks he had known her. Meg had taken it well, but then, her affections were no more engaged than his were. In fact, for some reason, the whole relationship now seemed entirely distasteful.

"I think Julius has gone," Delilah murmured.

"I'm surprised he stayed so long."

"So am I, but at least he came."

"He danced, too," Aubrey contributed, "with a rather beautiful lady."

Meg had seen Roderick. She actually swerved, dragging her hapless escort with her, although after that, she made some effort not to look too obvious. Roderick was furious. He was with his sister, whom he would not introduce to Meg Maven.

She strolled toward them, smiling graciously as she inclined her head to Roderick. "Good evening, Major Vale."

Her use of his name was quite deliberate, to make it obvious that they were acquainted. There was no need for it. Since she had not avoided him, he would never have given her the cut direct, not in a public place like this where it would cause unlimited gossip. But if she imagined he would introduce her to his sister, she had misjudged her man.

He did not rise, for he would give her no excuse to stop. But he did nod distantly. "Madam," he murmured before turning back to speak to Delilah.

There was not the smallest hesitation in Meg's step. She walked on as though it was always what she intended. Perhaps it was. He had no reason to suppose she would pursue him now that their affair was ended. He was not such a coxcomb. And yet he had never seen her in Blackhaven before.

Well, he had only been in the area a few weeks.

"You don't know that young fellow, do you?" he asked Aubrey, nodding after Meg and her escort.

"No, but then, I'm more interested in how you know the lady."

"No, you're not," Roderick said pleasantly.

Aubrey took a drink. "Ha, and you call me a rake." As the music came to a close, he looked round Roderick to Delilah, as though he too had sensed her upset. "Want me to punch anyone's nose, Delly?"

"Only your own," Delilah replied. "Although you might fetch me a glass of wine first."

Aubrey rose lazily. "Your wish is my command, rudest of my sisters. Rod?"

"No thank you. I am enjoying your brandy."

"Goodness." Aubrey strolled past. "You'll be smiling next."

"He's foxed," Delilah said, frowning after him. "And ripe for trouble."

"He's four and twenty," Roderick said, "and it's the first time he's felt well enough for trouble."

"Well let's hope it's something we can bail him out of," Delilah said tartly.

"Is yours?" Roderick asked. "His offer was kindly meant, you know."

Delilah's gaze fell to her lap. "I do know. Perhaps neither of us needs nursemaiding. It becomes a habit. Ah, here comes Felicia with another partner for you!"

Roderick scowled. "How come she never brings any for you?"

"Oh, we have an agreement, Fliss and I," Delilah said, turning to smile at the approaching Felicia.

Sighing, Roderick was already rising to his feet to face the inevitable, when he saw that the young woman accompanying Felicia was Lady Helen Conway.

Fliss had probably brought her for Aubrey, who was much closer in age. But Helen's clear, direct gaze was upon Roderick, despite the tinge of color seeping along the delicate bones of her face.

"Allow me to present my sister, Miss Vale, and my brother, Major Roderick Vale. Delilah, Roderick, this is Lady Helen Conway, the Earl of Braithwaite's youngest sister. We first met in Hyde Park—feeding the ducks!"

"I think we fed them your luncheon, Mrs. Maitland," Helen said. "Though I didn't notice at the time! How do you do, Miss Vale?" She curtsied to Delilah first, despite her own higher rank, and Roderick held a chair for her to sit.

"Aubrey has gone in search of wine. May I fetch you something, my lady? Fliss?" he asked.

If his aim was to vanish and leave the field clear for Aubrey to dance with the earl's sister, he was foiled unexpectedly by his own sibling, who said, "Oh, nothing for me. I am promised for the next waltz."

Felicia's gaze met Roderick's only long enough for him to know he had been outmaneuvered. With a frisson of shock, he realized he did not even mind. He *wanted* to dance with Helen Conway.

"Dare I hope you are not already promised, my lady?" he asked her.

"I am not, but you need not feel obliged—"

"I never feel obliged. I would very much like to dance with you, if you would care to." He wondered if she knew how true that was. She had already proved alarmingly proficient at reading his expressions. Since the orchestra began the introduction to the waltz, he held out his hand to Helen, who flushed more deeply as she rose with his aid and walked on to the dance floor with him.

For Roderick, there was a novel pleasure in taking her in his arms. She felt light yet warm, all womanly curves and a beauty that took his breath away. She smelled of summer—flowers and fruits and innocence, and something utterly feminine and unique that could not be bottled. She invaded all his senses. And he let her.

She might not have been "out" yet, but she danced with a grace and elegance any woman might envy. Yet something bothered her. She danced naturally, without thinking, because her thoughts were somewhere else entirely.

"What is it?" he asked, and her eyebrows flew up in surprise. Did she imagine he wouldn't notice? Or not care?

She spoke in a rush. "I did not ask Mrs. Maitland to introduce us formally."

"I never supposed you did," he said. "Though I might wish it."

She frowned. "Why?"

"No one objects to such flattery."

"Then you *did* look at me…*so*."

Alarm bells rang in his head, but honesty won out. "I did."

"And then found me wanting?" she challenged.

"And then I found you too young and much too respectable

for dalliance," he said brutally.

Spontaneously, her eyes crinkled up at the corners and she laughed. The effect was breathtaking. "Don't be silly. My eldest sister was married by my age. Not that I am proposing marriage or any other arrangement with you, major."

"Just as well. Because behind this interesting face is a very uninteresting man."

Her head tilted. "I'm not sure I believe that. I think you have lived a life of adventure and courage and tragedy."

"Something of an exaggeration. I might be able to dredge you up a few funny stories about the Peninsular campaigns, but to tell you the truth, I can't actually remember any more which are mine and which are other people's."

"I don't believe that either. Are you trying to put me off in case I have any intention of pursuing you further?"

"I would love you to pursue me at all. It is you who would not enjoy it."

To his amusement, she appeared to think about that, too. "Actually, I don't think either of us would care for pursuit. It sounds a little demeaning."

He closed his mouth. "I suppose it is. Unless you dress it up in other words like *courting*. Or *seducing*."

Color stained her face, but still she held his gaze. "Are you trying to offend me?"

"No, I like you too much," he said candidly. "So far, we have nothing to reproach each other with. That is rare for me. So we *could* just enjoy the dance."

HELEN DID ENJOY the dance. Major Vale waltzed divinely, with grace and confidence and absolutely no self-consciousness. He told her amusing tales of balls in winter quarters in Portugal and Spain, as well as in Paris and Brussels. And she told him about her sister Maria smuggling herself and Alice into a masked ball when she was only fifteen.

She liked to see the smile in his eyes, for she suspected it was all too rare. It was definitely too attractive, especially when she waltzed in his strong arms and could smell his skin, all clean, fresh masculinity. She studied the texture of his lips as he spoke and lost herself in the depths of his eyes. She felt breathless and happy and afraid all at once, because the feelings were coming too fast, but she would not have given up those moments for anything or anyone.

Do I love him, then? Is love at first sight truly possible?

No, I am being ridiculous… And yet she ached with sheer emotion. *What do I do now?*

With sudden panic, she realized the dance was nearly over. He would escort her politely back to Eleanor and Gervaise, and the moment would be gone forever.

Perhaps he saw something of her disturbance, because as the music came to a halt, he said, "Are you quite well, Lady Helen?"

They stood by the French doors onto the balcony, and a welcome draft of cool air wafted over her nape and shoulders. She latched on to it as to a lifeline.

"I think I need a little air." Her heart thundering, she turned toward the balcony, and, of course, he held the door and stepped outside with her. It was only a small space, but it was blessedly empty. Instinctively, she moved to the corner where she could not be seen from the doors.

"There is nowhere to sit," he observed. "Shall I bring you a chair? Fetch your sister?"

"No," she said quickly. "No, thank you. I will be right as rain in just a moment."

He followed her, frowning in the glow of the outside wall light. Her heart fluttered because he looked so lean and handsome and stern.

"Actually, there is nothing wrong with me," she blurted, determined to be honest. "I just did not want to go back to my family, and I like being with you."

She could not read the expression that flickered across his face.

"I'm flattered," he said.

"No you're not," she said with a smile. "You think I chose you because you are safe. I don't want to be safe. Would you kiss me, major?"

She did not mean to say the last part. It just slipped out, probably because she was gazing at his mouth and wondering…

His lips curved, causing a funny little dive of her stomach. She knew he was going to refuse, and at that moment, she didn't care if that stemmed from chivalry or lack of interest. Except she had *seen* his desire. She had drawn it.

Without answering in words, he offered her his arm. She had little option except to be escorted inside. She laid her hand on his arm but then stood suddenly on tiptoe, reached up, and pressed her lips to his. They were warm and firm, parted in surprise.

"Thank you," she said breathlessly.

Abruptly, his eyes softened. He even touched her cheek. He parted his lips to speak before he changed his mind and lowered his head instead.

Helen melted as his mouth covered hers with exquisite tenderness. The kiss held for a magical instant, and then his lips moved softly on hers, deepening the intimacy, and she clutched his arms in wonder. Sensation flooded her. She only knew she wanted more, but just as she pressed instinctively closer, he ended the kiss.

"Be careful what you wish for," he murmured, and stepped back.

"Is that meant to be a warning?" she asked, somewhat shakily.

He made a sound that might have been a laugh. "Yes, but I wasn't talking to you. Let me take you back to your brother before he calls me out."

"WHEN ARE WE going to arrange our event in Whalen?" Alice murmured, just before the supper dance, as Helen walked with her around the ballroom.

"You still want to do it?" Helen asked in surprise.

"Of course I do." Alice cast her a frowning glance. "I thought we had agreed. Are you backing out?"

"I am not," Helen said. "But this is the first time you've mentioned it for weeks."

"I have had other things on my mind," Alice said impatiently, "but I have not forgotten."

Helen waited, but her sister did not elaborate. "The day after tomorrow," she suggested. She had already decided to go then alone, although it would be undeniably more fun and a better proposition with Alice. "That will be market day in Whalen, and we have an excuse to be there."

"It's a pity we couldn't do it in London," Alice said. "There just never seemed to be any time. But perhaps we are better beginning on a smaller scale. We can learn more, and there is less likelihood of being caught."

"True. And no one who knows us ever goes to Whalen for entertainment. I—"

"Oh, the *devil!*" Alice interrupted fiercely, veering sharply to the right.

Helen followed, bemused as to what had startled her sister. Before she could ask, a gentleman also veered from the opposite direction and came to a smiling halt in front of them, forcing Alice to stop too or give him the cut direct. He was a pleasant-looking young man with curly brown hair and an amiable, if somewhat eager, expression.

"Lady Alice," he said, bowing. "I so hoped I would meet you here."

"Why?" Alice asked rudely.

The young man looked a little rueful. "Forgiveness?"

Alice curled her lip.

Helen said bluntly, "What did you do that requires forgiveness of my sister?"

"Nothing," Alice said hastily, and changed tactics. "Helen, Mr. Glover, Lord Bow's son. Sir, my sister, Lady Helen. Mama invited Mr. Glover to the ball."

"I came early in the hope of seeing more of..." Perhaps he caught the ice in Alice's eyes, for there was a slight hesitation before he said smoothly, "The countryside. I am staying at the hotel."

"How do you do?" Helen said politely. "You will excuse us?"

He had no option but to stand aside.

"What on earth was that about?" Helen demanded as soon as they were out of earshot.

"Mama has decided he will be a suitable match," Alice said between her teeth. "Presumably she told him so, for he clearly believed he was permitted liberties he most certainly is not!"

"What did he do?"

"Kissed me."

Helen, flushing with the very recent memory of her own first kiss, almost did not recognize the crime. She said, "You don't want to marry him, do you?"

"I don't want to marry anyone! I want to play the wretched pianoforte!"

This spilling of a Season's worth of frustrations should have pleased Helen. For a moment, Alice was her best friend again.

Alice sucked in her breath. "Sorry. I was too rude to him. He isn't actually a bad fellow. I quite liked him, in fact, until the *incident*. I should have been gracious enough to forget it—after all, I scolded him sufficiently at the time, and he did apologize quite handsomely. But he took me by surprise. I never supposed he would turn up so soon."

"Perhaps he really loves you?"

"No, he's getting a head start on his rivals," Alice said cynically.

"Shall I contrive to speak him so that he understands and does not cause gossip by looking frightened around you?"

Alice let out a breath of laughter, before glancing at her sister with some respect. "Would you do that?"

"Of course. He does not seem…"

At that moment, Helen saw Major Vale again and lost her train of thought. There was no reason for the bump of her heart. He had not even noticed her, for he seemed to be deep in discussion with a group of men, most of whom she recognized. Just as she would have dragged her gaze away, he glanced up and caught her eye. His lips quirked into a spontaneous smile, just for an instant, and then he returned to his conversation.

A smile of response was still trembling on her own lips when a complete stranger said, "Oh, my dear, *please* don't be deceived down that road."

Helen glanced around in surprise to see a very beautiful woman glittering in the candlelight, smiling at her with inexplicable sympathy.

"I beg your pardon?" Helen said, bewildered.

The lady stepped closer. Her glitter came from the quantity of jewels in her hair, hanging from her ears and throat, and scattered about her flimsy gown.

"Roderick Vale," she murmured. "He flirts because he cannot help it, and it is true that he is quite charming. But I have seen too many like you fall into the trap of taking him seriously. He is more than a little mad, sadly. And besides, you should know he is engaged to a lady who can handle him."

Quite aside from any truth or otherwise in this confidence, everything in Helen revolted against the lady's manner, her language, her whole attitude to another human being, whom she discussed as if he were a difficult horse.

"How very unpleasant for him," she said icily, and walked away, taking Alice's arm.

"Who," Alice demanded, "is that?"

"I have no idea, and less interest."

"She seems to know the Vales. Do you suppose you should have been quite so rude?"

"Was I rude? Whether or not she knows the Vales, she most certainly does not know us."

Alice blinked, a hint of amusement entering her face. "Goodness. You will be haughtier than any of us! Mama will be proud."

This was when, a year ago, Helen would have dragged Alice away to a private corner and confided the whole story of Major Vale to her. But this was still too new to put into words, even to Alice. And Helen was aware that her sister was keeping her own secrets. Alice would never even have mentioned Mr. Glover or his advances had the man not accosted them. Until this evening, that reticence had hurt Helen. But perhaps there were times for privacy after all.

Chapter Three

W AS MAJOR VALE engaged to be married? And if so, was it to the jeweled lady? Helen hoped not, with a strength she had no right to. She might not like the woman, but she hardly knew Major Vale. And if he were betrothed, she certainly had no right to the feelings tumbling through her. She did not want to regret the kisses.

It was during supper that she noticed the major again, walking into the room with a girl of about Helen's age. Helen recognized her as one of his sisters, whom she had met briefly earlier on. Lucy Vale's cheeks were flushed with excitement, although Helen suspected the major had been scolding her, for the girl was doing her best to look submissive. It was a poor effort that seemed to amuse more than fool him.

While they chose from the remains of the excellent buffet, Helen, mindful of her observation being noticed so easily by the strange lady in the jewels, turned back to her partner, an old officer friend whom she had known since childhood. From the corner of her eye, she saw the jeweled lady again, with a handsome young gentleman sitting attentively opposite her. The lady herself was watching Major Vale, who strolled once more into Helen's line of vision, seating himself and Lucy beside their sister Mrs. Maitland, and Bernard Muir.

"Captain Greene, do you know that lady?" she asked impulsively.

The captain followed her gaze. "I think I met her once, though I can't quite recall her name. Maybury or something. Marston, perhaps. Marvin? At any rate, she is a widow. Lives in Whalen, I believe." His eyes refocused on hers. "Friend of yours?" he asked.

"Oh, no. She spoke to me, but I have no idea who she is."

"Not surprised," Captain Greene said with a hint of relief. "Not the top drawer, but she would like to be. Her husband left her a fortune from trade."

"I expect she considers marrying again," Helen said.

Greene regarded the youthful escort with some doubt. "Perhaps. So what are your plans now, my lady? Will you be at the castle all summer?"

"I believe so. We shall have guests arriving soon for the ball. Including Lord and Lady Wickenden, although I believe they will stay with the Muirs as usual. And my sisters, of course. Will you come to the garden party next week?"

"I'm hoping to, if Colonel Doverton gives me leave."

"Oh, good. We are still calling it a garden party, though, given the weather this summer, it is likely to be all indoors. But it should be fun. Eleanor—and even Mama—are ecstatic because they have apparently secured the elusive poet Simon Sacheverill. And a very fine Scottish pianist that Alice heard in London. We caught him on his way home. And, of course, Tamar has some new pictures to show, especially a new portrait of Gervaise and Eleanor that I have not seen."

"It all sounds delightful."

"I hope so. I like the garden parties. So much less formal than our balls at the castle. Although this year is to be another *masked* ball, so that will be amusing and mysterious."

"In Blackhaven? We all know each other too well to be able to hide behind masks."

"Oh, no," Helen insisted. "With a little imagination, you can disguise yourself from anyone."

He looked amused. "I'm sure you speak from experience."

Helen tried to look modest.

RETURNING TO THE ballroom after supper, Helen deliberately dropped back a little from her family, and went in search of Mr. Glover, who had so offended Alice.

Eventually, she caught sight of him wandering somewhat disconsolately toward the card room. His expression perked up when he saw her, though clearly he had learned from experience, for rather than accost her, he paused, giving her the chance to avoid him if she chose.

"Mr. Glover," she said, inclining her head.

"Lady Helen. May I fetch you some refreshment? Or would you care to walk for a little?"

"A walk would be pleasant." She laid her hand lightly on his proffered arm.

"She has not forgiven me, has she?" Mr. Glover said.

"Oh, I think she has, provided you don't repeat the error. She wished me to apologize on her behalf for any perceived rudeness. You took her by surprise, you see, and she does not like the idea that you might have pursued her here."

His expression, which had grown hopeful, fell. "She doesn't?"

"Sadly not. If...anyone gave you cause to hope otherwise, that person was mistaken. My sister knows her own mind, sir. She likes you very well as a friend, but she will tolerate nothing else."

She could see she was dealing him a blow, though he tried to hide it beneath a smile. "Your kindness is devastating, my lady. I am not a fortune hunter, you know. I hope Lady Alice is aware of that. She is...different to other young ladies of my acquaintance. She is so natural and honest and funny."

"She is, isn't she?" Helen agreed. "Also blunt to the point of rudeness. You would not like that in a wife."

He blinked, a mixture of realization and amusement flickering across his face. "Perhaps you are right. I was too hasty, was I not?"

"I expect it is your nature," Helen said kindly. "But don't let it lead you into trouble."

"I shan't. So tell me, now that I am in Blackhaven, what must I see and do?"

Helen told him about the local attractions, and places to avoid—like the tavern where apparently pockets were picked on a regular basis and one had to be quick on one's feet to avoid a fight. He appeared to take it all in, laughed at her jokes, and ended by asking her to dance.

Helen, glad to have done her sister this service, accepted. However, she found herself thinking more and more about what the jeweled lady had said to her about Major Vale. It was not so much the words—which she largely discounted—but the purpose behind them that bothered her.

Why would she tell a complete stranger that a man was both mad and engaged to someone *who could handle him*? There had been no kindness in the waspish voice, no respect. As though she wanted Helen to hold him in contempt. Why? Did he need to know he had such an enemy? Was he aware already? If she told him, would he regard her words as childish misunderstanding? Intolerable interference? Would it *hurt* him?

There was no one she could ask, except him. As her dance with Mr. Glover ended and she walked back toward her family, she mulled it all over in her mind. Part of her wished she could discuss it with Alice, or with Maria, or even Caroline Benedict. But that would *definitely* be betrayal. In any case, Alice, clearly, had a good deal on her mind, too.

Since everyone in Blackhaven wanted the chance to speak to the Earl or Countess of Braithwaite, their table was always surrounded, even during the dances. Helen found it quite easy to lurk on the fringes.

And when she saw Major Vale stride from the ballroom, she suddenly knew what she had to do. She stood up and followed him.

The foyer was quiet, the music muffled by the ballroom doors, and no one was about, save the servants clearing up in the supper room—and Major Vale walking toward the gentlemen's cloakroom.

"Major," she called, unwilling to have him disappear where she could not follow. He turned, his brows raised in surprise, then walked quickly back toward her. She hurried past the supper room door, which, only a moment later, slammed shut like a gunshot.

Major Vale threw himself at her, pushing her hard against the wall, his arms protectively over her head. Stunned, she thought for an instant that it was a highly improper joke. Indignation warred with secret, startled delight in his closeness, in the sheltering strength of his powerful arms and body. Until she realized his whole person was shaking.

His assault was not remotely amorous.

She peered up, trying to see his face, which rested on the wall above her. Then a movement beyond his left shoulder caught her eye.

The jeweled lady stood with her hand on the supper room door. *She* had slammed it. Deliberately. Her beautifully arched brows lifted. She smiled with the faintest shrug of her shoulders as though saying, *See?*

Helen could have struck her. Instead, ignoring the woman, she reached above her head and took the major's ungloved hand. Gently, she disengaged it from her hair, then tugged him with her the two paces to the meeting room door. He did not resist, which was as well, for he was far too strong to compel, and while the jeweled lady had turned on her heel and vanished, anyone could come through the foyer at any time.

She whisked them both inside the meeting room.

It was empty and dark, save for a shaft of moonlight shimmering through the window. Major Vale did not move, even when she slipped from his hold and felt for the tinder box and flint.

She lit the nearest branch of candles, some instinct warning her that he needed light. His face was frightening. Tears trickled down his cheeks. His eyes stared straight ahead, and yet he seemed to see nothing. He jerked from side to side, as though trying to escape something unbearable.

Helen did not know what to do. She acted from instinct, taking both his hands. "You are safe," she said, just a little shakily. "We are all safe. Major, come back…"

He blinked, and his eyes lowered to her face. He looked utterly disoriented. His fingers gripped hers hard, and then a shuddering breath shook him.

"Oh God," he whispered. "Did I hurt you?"

"No, no, of course not."

He pulled free of her hands, then dragged his fingers through his hair. They still trembled, but whatever nightmare he had been in, he seemed to have left it for now.

She said, "I…I think you were trying to protect me. A door slammed. It was terribly loud and startling."

He closed his eyes, then swung away from her, dashing his sleeve against his face. "I'm sorry," he said harshly. "I am not really fit for Society. In fact, I'm a bit of a mess. Would you—"

She spoke over him. "She did it deliberately. That woman slammed the door to show me your reaction. Why would she do that?"

He stared at her some more, but there was comprehension in his eyes. He did not even ask which woman she referred to. "God knows. Helen, you can't be here alone with me."

"It is becoming something of a habit," she remarked, mainly for something, *anything*, to say.

But to her surprise, his eyes lightened a fraction. His lips even twitched upward. "Go now. Please."

She swallowed. "Shall I send your brother or sis—"

"No!" He drew a deep breath. "Please, just go."

"I don't want to leave you alone."

"I *need* to be alone."

Anxiously, she searched his eyes. They were hard, uncompromising. He was holding in check whatever desperation bubbled below his surface calm.

"Do you know the ruined abbey?" she asked abruptly.

A look of incomprehension crossed his face and vanished. "Of course."

"I shall be painting it tomorrow afternoon," she said. "Believe it or not, it also has an interesting face."

She did not wait to see if he smiled. She knew her presence was unbearable. But as she slipped out of the door, she heard a breath that might just have been laughter.

MEG MAVEN WAS annoyed with herself as she swept back into the ballroom. She had misjudged the girl twice, first by speaking to her at all and incurring her haughty displeasure, and secondly by assuming she would scream the place down when Roderick exploded into a gibbering idiot.

But again, the girl had surprised her. Although little more than a spoiled and sheltered child, she had not gone into hysterics when Roderick shoved her against the wall. Instead, she had led him to privacy—with a gentleness Meg did not like, and a maturity that worried her even more. She was no milk and water miss but a dangerous foe. Perhaps. Forewarned, Meg now looked forward to the fight. And she would win. She might lose the odd battle, but she always won the war.

Roderick should have understood that, but he had dismissed her as though she were some private soldier. Well, more like a camp follower, considering...

She was so deep in her own thoughts—that in itself was rare, for Meg was always aware—that she swerved right without looking and almost bumped into a young gentleman heading for the door.

Fortune smiled upon her this time. This was the man she had seen dancing with the girl who was Roderick's latest flirt. He could almost certainly be used.

She smiled, gratified by the dazzled admiration showing so clearly in his face. "I am so sorry, sir! Woolgathering!"

"Entirely my fault, ma'am," he said civilly.

"No," she said, "but we shan't quarrel over it. In fact, sir, our meeting might well be fortuitous. Are you not a family friend of the lovely young lady in green? I'm sure I saw you chatting with her and her sister."

This might have been something of a shot in the dark, but it hit its mark.

His eyebrows flew up. "Lady Helen? Yes, I—er…I suppose I am."

Lady Helen? That was certainly a warning to be careful. She had to be the daughter of an earl at the very least, and one did not invite the enmity of the powerful with impunity. Even if one was far richer.

"Why?" he asked, which gave Meg the excuse she needed to tell him.

She leaned forward. "You might want to rescue her—discreetly, of course. I was in the foyer and saw her being persuaded into a private room by an army officer. He looked a bit…undisciplined, if you catch my meaning."

He clearly did, for he seemed appalled—as much, she suspected, by the responsibility she had just given him as by the danger to Lady Helen.

"Perhaps it would be indiscreet to worry her ladyship's family," Meg said. "But if you think the presence of a lady might help, you could escort me across the foyer?" She smiled her most soothing smile and offered her hand. "I am Mrs. Maven. Though not a native of Blackhaven, I live a few miles along the coast." It was true, and might well encourage him to believe her landed gentry.

He bowed punctiliously over her hand. "James Glover. Not a native of Blackhaven either. I have been invited to the castle…" He broke off, his gaze going beyond her, and she turned to see the girl in green—Lady Helen—walking back into the ballroom.

She did not look remotely distressed. Her face was aristocratically calm, her poise almost regal, hiding whatever shock Roderick had inflicted.

It was not what she had originally intended, but with her temper fading, Meg decided to go to him and pick up the pieces. And she had no objection to being discovered alone with him. Roderick might look down on her for her birth, but honor would compel him to do the right thing and marry her. And *then* she would be landed gentry. He was the gentleman, and she would buy the land.

She half turned toward the door once more.

"Would you care to dance, Mrs. Maven?" asked Mr. Glover.

She could not refuse. And perhaps the long game was better. She smiled, and graciously bestowed her hand upon him.

Chapter Four

THE MORNING AFTER the ball, Helen woke feeling *different*. It had something to do with kissing Roderick Vale. No one had ever kissed her before, not like that, and it was rather wonderful. Even the memory intensified the butterflies already playing in her stomach. But *everything* about him filled her senses, to the extent that she lay awake for ages, just thinking about him, before the maid, Jinny, disturbed her with a cup of tea.

Smiling vaguely as she sat up and took the tea, she had no idea what Jinny actually said to her. Was it just the way Major Vale looked that she liked so much? Certainly, it was what she had noticed first, before his expressions and the character behind them had begun to fascinate her. There was a hard, unreachable quality about him, and yet at the slamming of the door he had dissolved into another creature entirely. And now he was ashamed to have been exposed in front of her.

Was that what the jeweled lady had intended all along? Was she fending off what she saw as competition for Major Vale's affections? Showing Helen she was incapable of "handling" him?

Helen thrust the woman aside as unimportant to her, whatever she was to him. It was Vale who concerned her. Something was very wrong with him. He did not need pity or *handling*. He needed...

Her thoughts stumbled helplessly. She did not know what he

needed. She was too sheltered and ignorant.

He needs a friend.

Even that seemed a foolish realization. The man had nine siblings, including a Royal Navy captain, the amiable Mrs. Maitland, and the younger sister, Lucy, who had entertained him at supper. But sometimes one needed more than family. They were too close, knew one too well. Although if he had been away with the army for fourteen years, how well did any of them *know* him?

Would he come to the abbey today?

If she were honest with herself, which she always tried to be, she doubted it. Her glimpse of what he would see as his weakness probably made her unbearable to him now. Which brought her fresh pain, but she would go anyhow.

She rose, washed, and dressed in one of her old, comfortable gowns, and spent what was left of the morning with Alice, going through music and paintings. Then, avoiding a family luncheon, she informed her family she was going to paint, loaded up her poor mare like a pack animal, and rode out to the abbey.

On previous expeditions to paint the ruin, she had needed a sun shade. Now, she had a large umbrella, which she stuck into the ground to cover both her person and her easel and set out her watercolor paints. The ruined abbey could be beautiful in the sunshine, which turned the old stone a beautiful shade of gold. Now, for the first time, she saw it under dark gray skies, and it held a different kind of charm, one of age and atmosphere that was almost ominous. It reminded Helen of Gothic novels and made her fingers itch to paint.

As the afternoon wore on, she was always aware of Roderick Vale's absence. But she kept her mind focused on the painting, and that helped.

RODERICK HAD NO intention of going near the abbey while Lady

Helen Conway might be in the vicinity. In fact, when he could no longer bear being indoors, he set off deliberately in the opposite direction.

The nightmares were getting worse, not better. Last night had shattered his last comfortable illusion that there could be nothing at a ball to set them off. There were no fireworks, no thunder in the air, only relentless chatter, music, and dancing. At some point in the evening, despite Meg Maven's presence, he had even begun to enjoy himself, to appreciate the company and the conversation. If Helen Conway had much to do with that, he let his mind slide over the fact. She had everything to do with his agony now.

He did not know what he had done.

He had heard the explosion and reacted to save her, and suddenly he had been in the hell of the battle again. Reality… In truth, he did not know what was reality. He had found himself in a dim room, alone with Helen and with no idea how he had got there or what he had done to her. The pity and the fear in her eyes had been unbearable.

Somewhere he was glad that she had not appeared to be frightened of him, so perhaps he had not hurt her. She had said he had not.

But God help him, he was a danger to whomever he was with. He had accepted his colonel's insistence that he take leave after attacking two fellow officers with their own swords. An accidentally fired gun somewhere in the camp had set him off that time. He had thought home would be safe—if he stayed away from hunting and fireworks and locked himself in his room during thunderstorms. But if a slamming door could set him off…

Helen had said someone had done that deliberately. And it could only have been Meg Maven. She was the only one present who had witnessed his lapses. She had seen his wild overreaction to a tray of crockery crashing on the floor in her house. And she had seen him in the throes of a nightmare once when he had broken his own rule and fallen asleep in her bed.

Was that the real reason he had ended his relationship with her? Because her knowledge of him was unbearable? So she had taken her revenge, and now he could never look Helen Conway in the eye again either.

He should never leave Black Hill, never go beyond the garden. Except that would drive him insane, too. He had thought his long walks and the peace of the countryside were helping him. But apparently he was no better after all.

Deliberately, he drove all the past from his mind, absorbing only the present—the crunch of his boots on the ground, the fields and woods stretching before him, the glimpse of sea beyond. He liked the coolness of the breeze against his face, the soft patter of rain that couldn't quite make up its mind to be a proper shower. The earth smelled fresh and damp and sweet, and the only sounds to break the silence were those of the birds and the farm animals. He allowed the peace and the beauty into his world and wondered, vaguely, why it was not enough. Still, he was content to search for more.

Somehow, he was not even surprised when, two hours later, he recognized the tall ruins of the abbey rising up before him. Without being aware, he had circled right around and come upon it from a different path.

Perhaps, subconsciously, he had wanted to come, just to prove to himself that Helen would not be there, that a night's sleep and common sense would have drowned her pity and ensured she came nowhere near him.

He saw the horse first, a sturdy animal cropping grass, reins looped around a boulder.

Closer to what was left of the building, on the lower hill to his left, a female figure sat beneath a large umbrella. An easel was set up before her and she was painting. Although he could not see her face from here, he knew it was Helen. He recognized her posture—her body bent forward in eagerness, lacking just a little of the ramrod straightness dinned into girls of gentle birth.

He was sure she had not noticed him. He could walk away

before she did. And probably should. Yet now that he was here, to flee smacked of cowardice and avoidance. He would keep his distance so he would not frighten her, but he could wish her good day, perhaps even be allowed to see her picture...

He walked obliquely nearer, approaching between the ruin and where she sat on a small, three-legged stool. She might have known he was there before she looked. Although, frowning over her work, there was a hint of delicate flush in her cheeks. Did she wish him just to walk on?

He decided to do just that, and merely raise his hand if she greeted him. But quite suddenly, she said, "Oh, stop!"

It was half command, half plea, but not remotely frightened. He halted, looking directly at her, and she smiled in a distracted kind of way. Her brush flew over the paper, dipped and flew again while she spoke.

"Sorry! But please, will you not move? The light, or lack of it, is perfect, and I... Well, I'm either spoiling a decent picture or creating a masterpiece..."

Intrigued all over again, he kept perfectly still—something he had been incapable of even for a few seconds this morning—and watched her face as she painted. Her eyes darted between him, the abbey, and her easel. Her expression was absorbed, determined, her observation somehow both intimate and detached.

He had been right when he saw her in the ballroom last night. She was beautiful and rare, and he liked looking at her too much. She had pushed her hat off so that it hung by its ribbons at her back. Her hair was pinned up but contrived to look stylishly mussed. He realized there was no fashion involved. It was her natural look that he suspected her maid had made the most of when dressing her last night. It suited her so much that he wanted to smile.

There was intelligence in her high, delicate brow, humor and passion in her eyes, a vulnerability about her soft mouth, grace and determination in her posture. All these things drew him. But there was so much more to her than a particular combination of charms. He wished he were younger, more innocent, worthier. And yet would his younger self have appreciated her as he ought?

He knew she was kind and funny and brave. She had kissed him. He had tasted her mouth and the latent passion within her. He wanted her, and she was too young.

No, that was not quite true. Many women were married younger than Helen, and to men much older than Roderick. But he was too battered by life to be fit for marriage to any woman, let alone to one so innocent... And when in hell had marriage entered his stupid, fevered brain?

She stopped painting and drew herself back, gazing hard at her easel. Then, without warning, she lifted her eyes to his.

"What do you think?" she asked.

He walked across the ground between them, pleased that she wanted his opinion, relieved that she trusted him to come closer. Was it possible he really hadn't frightened her last night?

Her painting of the ruin was beautiful, in a dark, almost dreamlike way, enhanced by the sheer threat from the male figure who was little more than a shadow before it. Or a ghost. She had caught the movement of his last step, the direction of his gaze, but beyond that, his features were indistinct because of the distance and the gloom.

"You are right," he said. "The abbey does have an interesting face." All spiky, broken stone walls and tall, arched windows open to the elements. She had caught the tragedy of its former beauty, its lost grandeur.

"It has several," she agreed. "And I should probably apologize for using you as a mere aid to the impression I wanted. Do you think it works?"

"Oh, it works," he said without doubt, and the anxiety in her face relaxed. "You do know you have far more than a mere accomplishment? You have a talent. A gift."

She flushed. "Thank you. You are saying too much what I want to hear."

"I cannot be the first person to tell you so. Does Lord Tamar not agree?"

"He is kind. Most people are. But the art of an earl's sister will never be judged fairly. I might be flattered or scorned, but it will be nothing to do with painting. Oh drat, the rain is coming on again. You had better squash under here."

She spoke so naturally that he almost obeyed. But he knew better than to come any closer.

"I am already wet, and I would rather not drip on your painting. Should you not have a vast array of footmen and grooms in the vicinity?"

She wrinkled her nose. "According to Mama, yes. But Alice will cover for me. Alice is my next sister in age. Sometimes she comes with me and brings her guitar to help her compose, though the pianoforte is really her instrument of choice."

"Your sister composes?" he said.

"She is very good. More than good. *She* has a gift."

"You are a family of unexpected talents. Do your other sisters write poetry and plays and novels?"

"Do yours?" she countered.

He opened his mouth to give a flippant answer, then closed it again. "Actually, I don't know. They might. I should inquire."

"What of you?" she asked.

"I could not write or draw or paint to save my life," he said, then added, almost with surprise, "I used to enjoy music, though."

"Used to?"

"Well, I couldn't take a pianoforte on campaign." He smiled suddenly at the memory of some light and entertaining moments. "Though I occasionally came across one in billets and winter quarters."

"You have none at Black Hill House?"

"Actually, we do." He had almost forgotten. She must think him an idiot. All the same, his fingers flexed of their own volition, as though preparing to play. "I never took it seriously. I was only ever serious about war and soldiering."

"When do you return to the army?"

He shrugged. It was one of the many things he was trying not to think about. "I might sell out."

"To help your brother with the estate?"

"Lord, no. I know nothing of land or farming. Julius owns it; Cornelius stewards it. It is a home for them and my sisters. But I shall not stay."

"Where will you go?"

"I don't know."

She was silent for several moments, gazing critically at her beautiful painting. Then she said, "My sister Alice and I always meant to run away. To London or to Europe, depending on the state of the war. We planned to study music and art and make our own fortunes. The idea of giving in and making good marriages like Frances and Serena—and even Maria—seemed entirely wrong for us."

Women of their class did not really have any choice. His own sisters had considerably less than him, and they were only gentry. For aristocratic ladies, marriage was the only viable option. He didn't like the idea for Helen at all. On the other hand, there were worse fates.

"Don't run away," he said. "The world is a dangerous place."

"Maria was going to be our chaperone, but she married too, and Michael would miss her."

"Perhaps Michael could go with you. That would be safer."

She considered that. "No, he is a member of Parliament and too conscientious. He wants to change the whole world." She laughed. "I only want to change mine."

"Me too," he said. "Perhaps we should think on a larger scale."

She looked up, meeting his gaze at last. "Does it happen to you often?"

Lulled into a false sense of security, he still knew exactly what she meant and did not even think of lying. "Too often."

"Since when?"

"Waterloo."

She nodded, as though she had expected it.

Don't dare say you understand, he thought savagely. *You could not possibly!* No one who had not been there could grasp the sheer, horrific scale. Nor did he want her to, but he could not bear trite words of false empathy, not from her.

She said, "Even Wellington was appalled. According to my cousin, no one emerged unscathed. I suppose everyone carries wounds that no one sees. But battle wounds must be worst of all."

He curled his lip. "Are you trying to find excuses for me? There are none."

"I don't know what you need excuses for. I would help anyone in pain if I could."

"I am not in pain," he said impatiently. In fact, his only comfort was that neither were any of his dead comrades.

Her eyebrows rose. "Aren't you?"

He stared at her. *"The wounds no one sees?"* he quoted, deliberately mocking, because he was angry again for no reason. "For God's sake, what do you want of me?" he demanded between his teeth.

Her eyes widened. "Nothing."

Her very calmness was a reproach, and one he more than deserved. He drew in a ragged breath, fighting his temper, which she had done nothing to earn.

"On the contrary," he said with forced lightness. "I'm sure my absence would be appreciated. If I promise to be good—or at least civil—may I help you pack up your things?"

"Not yet. I want to wait until this is dry." She scowled at her painting, and, whether deliberately or not, her mind seemed to jump again. "I would paint it by moonlight, too. The moon is full just now, is it not?"

"Yes, but you don't want to come out here alone in the dark. The twins—my young brother and sister—have seen very suspicious goings-on. Horse thieves. And I hear a highwayman escaped from Blackhaven prison last night."

"Oh, something is always going on in Blackhaven," she said dismissively.

He frowned. "Seriously, my lady. The danger is real. Not just from horse thieves and highwaymen. Blundering about in the dark, any accident could befall you, and no one would find you for hours. If you must, take your brother, or at least a stout groom with you."

"I'd rather bring my sister." She smiled suddenly. "A moonlight concert by the abbey ruins! Only think of that! And I could paint it all."

"I suppose you want me to bring the pianoforte?"

She laughed. "Perhaps just a guitar or a violin. And when you're not playing, you can be our bodyguard. Against horse thieves, highwaymen, and other accidents."

An odd, speculative light came into her eyes, then vanished.

"What would you be if you were not a soldier?" she asked.

Nothing. I would be nothing. "It's all I know," he said with a shrug.

"If you were not an officer and a gentleman, you could be a doorman at the hotel or the assembly rooms. You would be excellent at throwing out the drunks and keeping the guests safe."

"Sadly, someone else would need to keep them safe from me," he said.

"Besides, I suppose there are already enough released soldiers desperate for work."

"True." But there was a germ of an idea in there, inspired by her words. He would think about it later. Just now, he was too distracted by Helen's presence and the fact that somehow his temper had eased, along with the anxiety.

She rummaged inside the bag at her feet. "Apple?" she said, holding one up to him. Since another had appeared in her other hand, he took the first with a murmur of thanks. They ate in a strangely untroubled silence, punctuated by crunching apples and the call of birds circling toward the sea.

She did not complain when he walked off and fetched her horse, and he could only admire the efficiency of her packing as the folding stool, easel, bags, and painting were loaded onto her mare.

"You would have made a good soldier," he observed.

"I'll take it as a compliment," she said lightly.

He bent to give her a step up into the saddle, then passed her the reins. It seemed quite natural to walk beside her, sometimes talking, sometimes not. They parted closer to the castle than to Black Hill, but his mind was so busy as he walked home that the time flew by.

Chapter Five

ALICE ADMIRED THE new painting with flattering enthusiasm. "Who is he?" she asked, pointing to the ominous figure.

"Just a passing walker," Helen replied, and then wondered why she kept Major Vale's identity secret. Perhaps because the relationship was too new and too precious to touch. Because it was hers. She began to understand Alice's new distance just a little better, even as they conspired to visit Whalen the following day.

Inevitably, they traveled in the old carriage, with the under-coachman and a footman, whom they dismissed at the market and instructed to meet them at the inn in two hours. From there they walked around to the theater, where flyers on the wall advertised a somewhat lurid play, jugglers, and European dancers. The front doors were open, and Helen was relieved to see the foyer was as large as she remembered it from a year ago, when she and Alice had first stuck their heads in and come up with the plan. Now, they approached the clerk in the ticket booth and asked for the manager.

In fact, Helen made it more of a command than a request. Alice regarded her with amusement, but Helen knew instinctively that such arrogance was the only way for two young ladies to be taken seriously. And, in fact, the clerk was back within a couple of minutes to conduct them to an office at the back of the theater.

Here, a slight, bespectacled man with thinning hair jumped up from his desk to greet them, and bowed low.

"Ladies, welcome. My name is Pritchard, and I manage this fine establishment. Please, sit down and tell me how I may serve you?"

"We are considering," Helen said grandly, "hiring your theater for a whole day and evening. We would exhibit artworks in the foyer, and hold a pianoforte recital in the evening. What facilities can you offer us?"

The manager's eyes gleamed behind his spectacles. He clasped his hands together with something approaching delight.

"What an honor it would be. May I know the name of the musician or musicians concerned, and the style of the art you wish to display?"

"I am the musician, and my sister is the artist," Alice said, as though daring him to laugh.

He didn't, although his clasped hands began to rub together as though of their own volition. "Charming. Quite charming. As it happens, we have a very fine pianoforte, which I can show you—although, of course, you would be welcome to use your own instrument. Obviously, we have staff to arrange the stage as you wish. We can supply and sell the tickets, arrange ushers, doormen, safety—"

"Safety?" Alice interrupted.

"Of yourselves," Mr. Pritchard said smoothly, "our patrons, and, of course, the art exhibits. We have our fair share of opportunistic thieves in Whalen, plus a few rough, unemployed sailors who are not welcome at genteel establishments. But you need never see such people. We can take care of all of that for you. Now, what dates were you considering?"

"What do you have available this month or next?" Helen asked.

Mr. Pritchard opened his desk drawer and removed a large book, which he opened. "Hmm," he said, riffling through the pages. "Naturally, we are busy for the summer season. There is nothing really before August, unless…" He glanced up over the spectacles that had slipped down his nose. "We have had a cancellation for one date that you could step into, but it is only ten days away. Would that be enough time for you? We can certainly set our printers to work at once to advertise with flyers and tickets, if you were interested?"

Helen and Alice exchanged glances. It was sooner than they had imagined.

"If it works well for you," Mr. Pritchard said, "we could always book a date in August, too."

"Ten days?" Alice said. "Is it enough?"

"Let's do it," Helen said. She was tired of waiting. "Providing we can agree on a price, Mr. Pritchard?"

Pritchard picked up his pen, scribbling down some figures while he murmured. "Hire…staff…printing costs…with discount for taking up a cancellation…" He looked up, beamed, and, like the bearer of unexpectedly excellent news, named a staggering sum of money.

Helen stood up. "I believe we have been wasting your time."

"And our own," Alice added.

"Ah, don't be hasty, ladies. Allow me to pare down some costs, and remember, *most* of the ticket sales would come to you."

"And without us, you would not fill this single date at all," Alice pointed out. "A considerably larger discount is only fair."

"And we shall print our own programs and see to our own safety," Helen said.

There followed a much more reasonable quote, which Alice beat down further before they agreed the deal and shook hands on it.

"I shall write you in the book for a week on Monday," Mr. Pritchard said, beaming once more. "What name is it?"

"Con—" Helen had begun to say Conway, their family name, but Whalen was quite close enough for people to associate that with Braithwaite Castle. "Connor," she said.

"Misses Connor," Pritchard murmured, scratching his pen

across the page. "Wonderful. Might I trouble you for the deposit to secure your date?"

MEG MAVEN CHOSE to walk home from what had turned out to be an unsatisfying shopping expedition. It did not matter how many jewels or how much embroidery or trim she ordered sewn into her gowns. They always looked what they were—provincial.

When they were married, she would make Roderick take her to London and introduce her to the best of Society. She was not foolish enough to go alone. She did not know the ways of the quality. The Blackhaven Assembly Rooms Ball had proved that if nothing else.

A clerk from the local bank hurried by, doffing his hat deferentially. Meg nodded graciously in return, but somehow it added to her restlessness.

She was tired of being a big, rich fish in this tiny pond. She had climbed from poverty to domestic service to marrying a rich old man who'd made a fortune in shipping. She had learned to modify her accent and lord it over the lesser ladies in the town who still gossiped that she was fast, *but then, my dear, what do you expect from the gutter? Her father was a docker!*

So he was, and a drunken one at that. But it was Meg who lived in the biggest house in town, who could buy and sell them all. They could all purse their prim lips in disapproval, but they were still obliged to acknowledge her and invite her.

It was not so with the local gentry, who invited none of them. That too would change when she married into the Vale family.

As she approached the theater, two young ladies emerged from the front door, so absorbed in their conversation that they paid no attention to passersby. Meg slowed, for she recognized them both.

Lady Helen Conway and her sister Lady Alice. That much, she had learned from the helpful Mr. Glover. They were sisters of the current Earl of Braithwaite, who lived in Blackhaven's magnificent castle, and everyone knew they were well dowered. No wonder Glover and Roderick were both interested. That did not surprise her. But what on earth were such aristocratic and youthful ladies doing alone in a theater? And at this time of the morning?

They hurried on in front of Meg, still talking, and turned right toward the inn. For a moment, she considered following. She would enjoy a cup of tea or even a meal at the inn. But her previous encounters with Lady Helen had hardly gone according to plan, and she knew she would have to be subtler.

She walked on toward her mansion house on the edge of the town. Reluctantly, she acknowledged that Roderick Vale was the cause of her bad mood, her restlessness, her dissatisfaction with life. She had been so sure he would be back, as soon as his itch needed to be scratched, and then she could proceed with her plans toward remarriage.

But it had been two weeks now, and she was both offended and afraid that her wiles really had not been enough to bind him. He, the brother of a landowning baronet, an officer and a gentleman, and a hero in his own right, was to have been her gateway to the gentry and the higher Society she sought. One day, she *would* be invited to the balls at Braithwaite Castle.

She had even imagined it might be this summer, except Roderick had suddenly ended their really rather enjoyable affair. Meg had not truly believed him. No one had ever dismissed her before. She was the one who decided when a connection had gone far enough. And she had the charm and the beauty, the wiles and the tricks, to keep any man she wanted. Except, apparently, Roderick Vale.

Which infuriated her, because of all the men she had ever known, he was the one who had pleased her most, both in bed and out of it. She had even been happy to overlook his madness and his violent nightmares. In fact, she had imagined they gave her some kind of hold over him. But he had walked away. He had to be the one man who would not dance to her tune.

And now, she supposed, she would have to begin again. Give up Roderick and look elsewhere.

Still, she thought, lengthening her step, perhaps she had already begun. Young Mr. Glover, who had begun by pursuing Lady Alice, now seemed at least half inclined to switch allegiance to Lady Helen. It would not take much for Meg to entangle such a fickle, impressionable creature, seduce him, and marry him. And he, God bless him, was heir to Lord Bow. She could be a viscountess one day...

Or, at the very least, she could use him to get back to Roderick.

She frowned. What *were* those Braithwaite girls doing at the theater?

RODERICK ACCOMPANIED SEVERAL siblings into Blackhaven, mainly because he had nothing better to do. The main purpose was to make Aubrey drink the famous Blackhaven waters in order to improve his delicate health, although he was happy to cede companionship in this task to Lucy.

Lucy was more restless than usual since the ball, which she had left secretly for at least half an hour with an unknown cavalier, and Roderick was worried about her. Trying to find a balance between her safety and the kind of heavy-handed nagging that would inevitably lead to open rebellion, he decided to leave Lucy and Aubrey to look after each other. He planned to walk on the beach and perhaps enjoy a pint of ale in the more disreputable of Blackhaven's hostelries.

As his siblings went into the pump room, a gentleman civilly held the door for them before sauntering out. Roderick, already turning away toward the beach, swung back again, frowning at the emerging gentleman, who blinked at him, equally startled.

"Skelly?" Roderick said.

The man grinned with obvious relief and sped up, thrusting out his hand. "Vale! I heard you were still alive!"

Roderick, who had heard no such thing about Captain Skelton, gripped the proffered hand hard. "Delighted to see that you are, too." Dear God, what an understatement. He had not even bothered to find out, so certain had he been.

"Came too close for comfort, old boy," Skelton admitted. "I sold out before I used up all my luck."

"What in the world brings you to Blackhaven?"

"Had to go somewhere before my family drove me mad with their care." Skelton grimaced and jerked his head toward the pump room behind him. "Agreed to drink the waters. And to be fair, they aren't doing me any harm. I have to confess I've been as weak as a kitten, but feeling better every day now."

Skelton had been badly wounded at Waterloo, one of the many not expected to survive. Roderick had accounted him lost along with all the rest and had to swallow the lump in his throat.

"Very glad to hear that," he said.

"You here for the same?" Skelton asked with obvious caution.

"Lord, no. I was born up here. Staying with my brother for a while—at Black Hill a few miles out of town. Where are you billeted?"

"The King's Head. Care to join me for some ale and a rake over old times?"

"I'll take the ale." And the inn was certainly more salubrious than the Blackhaven Tavern.

Skelton grinned and, as they walked, cast a glance over Roderick's civilian garb. "Sold out, too?"

"Not yet. Thinking about it."

Skelton nodded with sympathy. "The difficulty is finding something else to do instead. Don't want to live off the family forever. Could buy a little land with my prize money, perhaps, but I know nothing about farming."

"Me neither. But I've had a couple of ideas recently. We can tear them apart over that ale you promised me."

Seated in the inn's taproom, Roderick recognized another, less familiar face. The huge man jumped to his feet, rigidly at attention. "Major, sir!" he exclaimed, though he spoiled the effect by grinning. "Very glad to see you in health and strength."

"You too, sergeant," Roderick said, though he couldn't recall the man's name.

"Just North now, sir. Pat North. Disbanded."

"My father pays him to look after me," Skelton said with a grimace.

"Groom, valet, dogsbody," North said cheerfully. "Never been a servant before."

"You're not much of one now," Skelton informed him, flopping onto the seat. "Where's the ale for the major and me?"

The lines between officer and man, gentleman and servant, were obviously blurred, for North sat with them as if by right when he'd fetched the ale. It reminded Roderick of his childhood, here in Blackhaven, and at various capitals around the world where he had stayed with his diplomat father. He and Julius and Delilah had played with local children of all classes, accepting and accepted before rank and social position had interfered.

"So, what's your plan?" Skelton asked him.

Roderick lowered his ale. "A mere idea that hasn't quite got to the plan stage. All I've ever done, and all I've ever been any good at, was soldiering."

"Same here," Skelton said, and North nodded, sighing.

"I'd been wondering how such skills could be adapted to peacetime, and then I was talking to a young lady of my acquaintance about safety and this idea crept into my mind. A discreet service that can be hired for particular tasks—outriding on journeys, protecting cargo or people, buildings, or events. Something more discreet than large, liveried servants. Do you think there might be a call for such a service?"

Roderick regarded them, waiting to be shot down by friendly ridicule. It was almost obligatory. But to his surprise, both his companions were looking thoughtful rather than amused.

"With a choice of brute force or gentlemanly escort?" Skelton asked.

"Something like that. Prepared for both or either. And there are plenty of unemployed old soldiers and sailors looking for work they'd be good at."

"Lots of severely injured ones, too," Skelton said. "I don't see anyone employing one-legged men to protect their nearest and dearest."

"It depends on the kind of protection they want. Someone might be no good in a fight but can still spot an ambush from miles away. And every business needs organization and supplies—you and I are no strangers to those, whatever our health or strength."

North nodded slowly. "Got a lot of wealthy people passing through Blackhaven, seems to me. Not a bad place to start. But isn't it too small to make a decent living for all these people you mean to employ? To say nothing of your good self."

Roderick reached for his ale. "Yes, I think we'd have to include a city or two and be prepared to travel as far as London. Advertise in Carlisle and York and Newcastle, maybe to the north in Edinburgh and Glasgow."

"I thought you said you didn't have a plan," Skelton said wryly.

"You think it's worth a plan?" Roderick asked, both surprised and pleased.

"Not only that, I'm prepared to be your partner. And I expect North is prepared to be employed. What's first?"

Roderick laughed. The sound was unfamiliar, almost rusty. "I'll make that plan."

THE FOLLOWING DAY was Sunday. Helen's mother expected all the family present to go to church in Blackhaven, and no one demurred. The vicar, Mr. Grant, was both an inspiring preacher and a charming man. Besides which, the post-service gossip in the churchyard was always fun. And Helen held on to the hope of seeing Major Vale there.

She was almost afraid to look as she and Alice followed behind their mother, Gervaise, and Eleanor. Helen carried the baby, which presented a worthy distraction until they were all sitting in the family pew, which stood side-on to the rest of the congregation, and right at the front of the church.

A flash of red showed her Major Vale, in uniform—accompanied, it seemed, by most of his family. Mrs. Maitland caught her eye, and they exchanged smiles. Lucy and Delilah were also there, along with a set of obvious twins of around fourteen or fifteen, and a couple of other, handsome brothers.

Once or twice during the service, she imagined she felt the caress of Roderick's gaze, but when she risked a glance, he was always looking elsewhere. Her own wishful thinking, she thought ruefully. He could not possibly have the same obsessive interest in her as she had in him. In fact, if he thought of her at all, he probably regarded her much in much the same light as Lucy.

Well, it was up to Helen to change that. Her heart beat faster as she walked back down the aisle with her mother. It was not raining outside, for once, so there was considerable milling and chatting.

Helen hovered on the fringes of her family group, unwilling to be caught up in other conversations if there was a possibility of catching the major alone. Her chance came when he moved away through the gravestones. Discreetly, she wandered up the path, as though going to speak to Genevra Winslow and Alice's suitor, Mr. Glover, who smiled and bowed at her.

At the churchyard wall, Roderick paused, looking thoughtfully up at the sky. Helen halted then turned toward him with a smile. "Major Vale, how do you do? Bored with gossip?"

The lightening of his eyes was immediate. "I don't understand most of it," he said.

"Weren't you involved in the capture of the horse thief?" she asked, vaguely recalling a half-heard conversation about Black Hill between Mr. Winslow, Gervaise, and Eleanor.

"We only captured one of the horses, and that was down to Aubrey. Who knows what it was all about? Are you still happy with your painting?"

"For now. But I thought I would make a set of the abbey. I already have one from last summer in bright sunshine, and then the dark, rainy one you saw. I feel a moonlight one would complete the set."

He regarded her warily, and she smiled brightly. "Don't look at me like that. I have thought about what you said, and it would certainly be more comfortable to have an escort. On the other hand, my mother would forbid it, which means Gervaise would not let me do it either, let alone accompany me. And I could not, in honor, involve the servants, whom my mother is liable to dismiss in a fit of temper, should she ever find out."

"But you have a plan? Your sister playing the violin?"

"Oh, no, though I think we should definitely have the moonlight concert during the summer—perhaps when our guests come for the ball. Or later might be better. The weather *might* improve." She dared not pause for breath, so she charged on. "No, I thought you might escort me."

He blinked, though at least he didn't look angry. "Me?"

She smiled. "If you would be so good as to ride over at midnight—preferably bringing a horse for me—I could meet you by the eastern gate. I know I do not even need to add that the excursion is solely for the purposes of painting, preferably in congenial company."

"And I am the most congenial person you know?" he said.

"Well, I doubt you give tuppence for my mother's disfavor, and you wouldn't let Gervaise call you out, even if he was silly enough to try. And I believe in your discretion."

"If I were remotely discreet, I would have nothing whatever

to do with it."

"Thank you! Midnight tonight, then, at the eastern gate. You know where that is?"

She did not wait for an answer, though when she glanced back over her shoulder at him, the smile in his eyes made her stomach turn over.

Chapter Six

BEHIND HELEN'S EXCITEMENT as the day progressed was a faint sadness at keeping her assignation from Alice. Once, she would never have done so. They would have gone to the abbey together. But this was different. Although she had made sure the major understood this was not a romantic tryst, it felt so in her heart.

She had never imagined herself pursuing a man before. But what was she to do when he would not pursue her? There was an invisible bond, a deep attraction between them that she was sure he felt, too. She had only to look at her first sketch of him to see that. But more than that, more even than burgeoning friendship, she wanted to help him. Something had broken at Waterloo and was now mixed up with unreasonable shame and isolation, leaving him with a fragility no one seemed to see. Like a finely cracked glass about to shatter.

Instinctively, she knew he needed love to heal. And she wanted it to be hers.

The jeweled woman did not love him, or she would not have deliberately slammed that door, nor spoken of him like some animal who needed to be house trained.

Helen loved him.

She could tell herself it was infatuation, of the kind young women were subject to. It was what her mother would say, and

Gervaise, and her sisters. And who could blame them, considering her acquaintance with Roderick Vale was a mere three days old? Perhaps they would even prove to be right in the end. He might not be the man she thought him. But she *cared*, passionately, in a way that was entirely new, exciting, and even painful.

At a quarter to midnight, she rose from her bed, fully dressed. The castle had been quiet for hours. She pulled on her boots, donned her thick woolen cloak, and picked up the candle to light her way to the room that had become her studio more than the sitting room she had once shared with her sisters. Here she collected all the things she needed. It was not easy, carrying it all with one hand while the other held the candle. Nor was it a simple matter to stop everything clattering together or bouncing off walls and banisters as she crept along passages and down back stairs to the side door she suspected all her siblings had used for secret adventures.

Here, she abandoned her candle, after lighting one of the two waiting lanterns. Carrying both lanterns—she would need more than one to see anything at all, let alone paint it!—without clanking them together was another challenge. But eventually she managed to negotiate the door, slip around the side of the castle where she was less likely to be seen or heard by anyone wakeful, and hurry toward the east gate.

The familiar path was very different in the dark, alone, and her burden was undeniably awkward. She should have set off earlier. Now she was going to keep Roderick waiting. Panic that he would give up on her and go home forced her feet to move faster. At least she didn't have to worry so much about noise now.

Until the figure stepped out of the darkness and into the dim, shadowy lantern light. Her heart and stomach seemed to collide.

"What are you doing here?" she demanded.

"Waiting for you," said Major Vale dryly. "As commanded."

Relief and excitement swamped her. Her hands felt numb as he took the load from her, leaving her to manage the lanterns.

"Sorry," she said. "It took longer than I expected. I've never carried these things so far. Did you climb over the wall?"

"The gate is not locked."

That was odd. Someone must have forgotten. Or someone else from the castle was out and about, too.

Two horses were tied to the gateposts. The larger one seemed to be already loaded with something indistinct. Quickly and efficiently, the major divided Helen's things between the two animals, then boosted her into the saddle.

By the light of two lanterns and occasional blinks of moon, they set off along the track. She confided a few childhood stories about sneaking around in the dark with her sisters, especially Alice and Maria.

"In fact, Maria got into trouble once for being caught outside when she thought we had summoned her. We hadn't, but she couldn't explain without admitting that we often actually *did* throw stones at her window. Then we would all have been in the soup. Did you do the same and cover for each other?"

"Yes, I suppose we did… Though it was difficult when we lived in various embassies in foreign cities."

"It must have been fun," Helen said.

"We took it for granted at the time, but yes, I suppose it was."

As the conversation moved on, he told her a few amusing anecdotes about night marches in Spain, and she pointed out where Gervaise had been thrown from his horse and broken his leg during an expedition to the abbey a few years ago.

"Well, there is a warning for us," he murmured. "I'm doubly glad you didn't try this alone."

"Thank you for coming with me," she said. "It is much more fun with you."

He cast her a startled glance, then let out a breath of laughter. "Why, so it is!"

"You didn't think it would be," she accused. "In which case, why did you come?"

"To be there if you fall off your horse or are attacked by

highwaymen," he said.

"You have an overdeveloped sense of duty."

"It was never duty." As though appalled by his own words, he urged his horse on faster, and Helen smiled up at the moon.

The shape of the ruined abbey was both magnificent and ominous, looming blackly against the paler darkness. Wisps of misty cloud floated above it and even seemed to tangle with the tallest, broken arch. Helen could not wait to begin, which she did in double-quick time with Roderick lighting all four lanterns they had brought between them and then helping her to unload and set up her easel and stool and paints.

Although it was not raining, he planted the umbrella for her, and another for himself beside her. Then he took the unloaded horses to the same spot she had tied her mare the other day, where they could crop grass and leaves, and she worked with feverish intensity to portray the abbey in this new mood, in this new light.

Vaguely, she was aware of him beside her again, and was glad of it. Like a necessary background to everything. But she couldn't think of that while she worked. It was just there.

Gradually, as the picture took the shape and color she wanted, she began to relax, and spared her companion a quick glance. He lounged on the blanket beside her, watching her, a guitar resting against his thighs.

She laughed with sheer delight. "A moonlight concert after all!"

He strummed the guitar. "Apart from the moonlight."

The moon was indeed hidden again behind a bank of cloud. A little rain spat down on the umbrellas, but not enough to disturb them.

"Where did the guitar come from?" she asked, returning to her picture with a smile.

"From Spain, originally." He struck a dramatic couple of chords that made her think of Spanish dancers and warm, foreign hills. Then, softly, he began to play, and Helen's contentment intensified into happiness. The scene before her, the man beside her, his music, her painting, doing what she loved—all merged into new, profound beauty. She felt breathless, afraid, and euphoric all at once.

"My brain remembers, but my fingers are too stiff," he said. "I haven't played in a while." And almost immediately, he began to talk about music he had heard others play, about the great Beethoven and Mozart, and she found herself joining in. They talked about art and literature and politics, both seriously and in jest, and the time flew by.

"The sky is lightening," he said at last. "We had better go, or your discovery is certain."

By then her picture was dry, so it was easily packed away while he went to fetch the horses. They loaded everything up again, and as she turned to thank him, the smaller horse nudged her, and she stumbled into him.

At once, his hands came up to steady her. Her eyes flew up to his as she absorbed the hard warmth of his body against hers. Although he was probably too thin, he felt large and solid, at once safe and dangerous, though how that was even possible, she had no idea. Her breath vanished. Her body burned.

His gaze dipped to the region of her lips, and her heart turned over.

"What is it about you, Helen Conway?" he whispered, bringing up two bent fingers to caress her cheek. "The attraction of the forbidden?"

She swallowed. "I don't recall forbidding you."

"You are seventeen, with the wisdom of a mature woman. I am two and thirty and behave like a frightened child."

"You don't feel like a child to me." Without really meaning to, she turned her head so that his fingers touched her lips. She kissed them softly. "Neither of us are children."

His lips twitched at the corners, almost a smile, as he bent his head. Butterflies soared in her stomach, as though reaching for him. She sighed when his mouth finally sank on hers, and then all thought vanished in sweet sensuality. This time, he kissed her as a woman, a woman he made no secret of wanting. The hardness pressing against her stomach shocked and delighted her. The tenderness of his mouth melted her, arousing desires she understood instinctively.

She pressed closer, opening her mouth wider to kiss him back, to welcome his tongue with her own. When his hand brushed against her breast and softly closed, she gasped, shivering with pleasure. Desire spiked between her legs, causing her to wriggle against him.

He groaned and pushed her away by the shoulders. "This is why I should not come near you," he ground out. "Why *you* should most definitely not come near me. I'm no hero, Helen. I'm not even a good man. I use women selfishly, as a mere distraction, without love or even much affection—"

"Is that what the jeweled lady is to you?"

He broke off, blinking, and released her. Her whole body felt cold. But to her surprise, he took hold of her waist and lifted her gently into the saddle.

"She was," he said. "I told myself she understood the game, but I treated her ill."

"She has not given you up."

His lips twisted. "She will have to. You won't, because nothing will ever happen between us, Helen. Even if I were worthy in terms of birth and fortune and character, I am too…broken."

"I don't believe that," she said intensely. "I don't believe any of that." Something had already happened, and it was too wonderful to ignore. For the rest, she longed only to soothe his pain.

He swung into his own saddle and set off at a fast trot. She rode beside him as long as she could, but the ease of friendship had vanished. The air seemed to crackle with tension, with desire, and neither of them broke the silence.

OF COURSE, IT had been madness to go at all. Except that she would probably have made the journey without him, if not that night, then some other when she had managed the preparations herself.

So, if he hadn't been prepared to warn her family of her intention—which would have felt like betrayal—perhaps he had done the responsible thing. Only, what idiocy had prompted him to pick up the guitar like some damned courting minstrel? To let her under his skin and into this dangerous sense of intimacy? Most definitely of all, he should never have kissed her.

He had known that since the ball. She was too pretty, too unguarded, too…

He cut off that line of self-recrimination, aware that he was belittling the feeling, and so belittling her, which God knew she did not deserve. There was a clean sweetness about her that both soothed and disturbed him, but he could not dismiss her with trite or trivial words.

What did he do now? Leave her at the castle without a word? Say a firm goodbye? Warn her off and stay out of her way? It was probably the right thing to do, but he did not *want* to lose her friendship. And they were friends, whatever he tried to pretend to himself. He would always look out for her.

He glanced at her. He knew from the set of her mouth, the slight droop of her shoulders, that he had hurt her, which was astonishing in itself. And unforgivable. But as if sensing his scrutiny, she straightened in the saddle and turned to meet his gaze with a smile.

"You will be at the garden party, will you not? I believe your whole family is coming."

"Then I shall be there with them." Anything else would be discourteous, and besides, he was already looking forward to it, God help him. Once, he had enjoyed parties as well as the next man. When had he become such an old misery?

At Waterloo, of course. And now nothing could ever be the same.

But, damn it, he could do better than this!

They were almost at the castle gates. Dawn was breaking, in a muted, cloudy kind of way, but the birds were joyful. He dismounted and tied his horse to the gatepost once more. By the time he had turned, Lucy had slid out of the saddle on her own and was unfastening the straps around her easel and folding stool. He untied the rest of her things and took her burden from her.

"You shouldn't come any closer," she said. "The servants will be up and about any time now."

"I'll carry this part of the way for you. Can you sneak back in without being seen?"

A smile flickered across her face. "Yes."

"You are worse than my sister Lucy," he said, his sternness not entirely pretense.

"I like your sister Lucy."

"Lucy likes you."

Helen looked slightly surprised by the significance he accorded that.

"She has something of a gift," he explained. "Ever since she was a small child, she could sense people's character, knew whom to trust or not. When she expresses a view of someone, we all tend to listen."

"Clearly, I must talk more to Lucy."

For some reason, that pleased him. As though it actually mattered whether his sister and Lady Helen Conway became friends.

The castle was looming larger with every step. Every cracked twig, every flutter in the undergrowth, threatened discovery. And if she were seen with him at this time of the morning, she would be ruined.

As though she had come to the same conclusion, she halted and reached for the easel. He gave it up and admired how she managed to hold everything. It made him smile. Or at least want to. His mouth seemed to have forgotten how.

Hers hadn't. Her smile took his breath away. "We are still friends, Roderick Vale," she said, and marched off, veering slightly with the weight of her burden.

He turned away, feeling ridiculously happy.

AFTER TWO OR three hours of sleep in his bed, Roderick rose with a sense of purpose he had not experienced for months. Somehow, his foolish moonlight adventure with Helen had firmed vague ideas into plans.

As he rose, washed, shaved, and dressed, he thought back over his ale-fueled discussions with Captain Skelton and Pat North. They needed something, too, a cause or a career to get their teeth into. Skelton needed to stand on his own feet, and North needed to do more than nursemaid his old officer. And Roderick was in a position to help them while helping himself.

In the breakfast parlor, he encountered only Julius, gazing thoughtfully into his coffee. However, there was an air of vitality about him that had been lacking since Roderick's return. Julius, it seemed, was responding to Blackhaven too. He glanced up as Roderick went over to the sideboard to help himself to eggs and bacon and toast.

"Rod." He almost sounded surprised. "I'm riding over to the castle to talk to Braithwaite about our horse thieves. Want to come?"

Roderick was tempted. He wanted to see Helen again. But he refused to moon over her like a lovesick puppy when he should be doing something positive with his life. "Got a bit of business in Blackhaven," he said. "An idea I want to follow."

"Good," Julius said, setting down his cup and rising to his feet. "Good luck."

"Likewise," Roderick said.

Since he had no intention of making social calls, he rode into town and, leaving his horse at the livery stable, went in search of the printing shop he remembered very vaguely from his youth.

In the back streets of Blackhaven, the prosperity of the high street was sadly lacking. Wealthy visitors to the town did not need the services of printers or pawnbrokers, cobblers, washer-women, or cheap seamstresses. In his memory of accompanying his father here, there were more shops, and the printer's in particular had not looked so run-down. For a moment, Roderick wondered if it was still in business. But when he pushed the door, it opened easily, ringing a bell in the back office.

A slightly round-shouldered man in an ink-stained apron and rolled-up shirt sleeves came through at once and bowed. "Yes, sir?"

"I wish to have some flyers and business cards printed," Roderick said, taking the folded paper from his pocket.

The round shoulders straightened and the proprietor smiled. "Of course, sir. Let me take a note of your requirements…"

Five minutes later, they had agreed on sizes and price, and the printer, whose name was Nimmo, said he would have them completed by the following day.

"Business slow?" Roderick asked.

"Sadly so, sir. In times like these, only the pawnbrokers are busy. Even the wealthy, and the visitors to the town, have all their cards and invitations printed in London. To be frank, sir, I am surprised you found me."

"Well, I am a returned native. I live with my brother over at Black Hill, and I remembered your shop."

Mr. Nimmo's eyes widened. "Of course! I should have recognized the name! You are Mr. Vale's son! Sir George Vale's, I should say."

"I am."

"Very glad to have the family back."

"Well, there are nine of us," Roderick said. "They will be

happy to remind their friends of your shop."

Nimmo's smile was rueful. "Thank you, sir. I appreciate the thought, but I'm afraid it's too late for me. I shall have to close by the end of summer at the latest."

Roderick frowned. "I'm sorry to hear that."

"It's all too common a story just now, sir."

Roderick wanted to ask what he would do, what he *could* do. But he suspected that would be intrusive. Still, as he left the shop, the printer's bad luck annoyed him. Like everyone else, the man needed regular work, not just a few small orders, such as Roderick could pass his way.

He walked on to the inn, where he found Skelton enjoying a late breakfast, and joined him in a cup of coffee. He told his friend what he had done at the printers, and Skelton nodded with enthusiasm.

"So what now?"

"Well, I thought we could leave a few flyers around Black-haven and Whalen. And I'll take some to Carlisle. Then, I suppose, we see who will contact us. It will be my name, care of this inn, so you and North must look out for correspondence."

"I'll tell the innkeeper. He's a good sort. Was a soldier himself till he lost a hand."

"Damn," Roderick said. He hadn't known that. He had held himself too aloof from the community.

Leaning across to the next table, he picked up an abandoned newspaper. The *Carlisle Journal*. Julius read it, though Roderick had never troubled to. He read the London papers instead, even though they were usually days old before they were delivered.

He flipped through the paper's headlines and advertisements, then folded it up and tossed it back where he had found it.

"There is nothing in there about Blackhaven."

Skelton grinned. "Why would there be? Sleepy sort of place."

Full of wealthy, important, and aristocratic visitors, horse thieves, highwaymen, smugglers...a theater, an art gallery, businesses, charities. Opportunities were being missed because people did not know. Gossip was rife and inaccurate because they did not *know*. People *liked* to know about things that affected them.

Skelton said, "Should we advertise in the *Carlisle Journal?*"

"Yes, we should... As for staff, the vicar runs a charity for homeless old soldiers and sailors. We could do worse than talk to him. And my brother is involved in the hospital where they're still tending long-term wounded and helping them find work when they recover."

"Excellent plans," Skelton said. "Drink up and let's go!"

Chapter Seven

OVER THE NEXT few days, Helen concentrated on her paintings, on having the new ones framed and choosing which of the old to exhibit in Whalen. Alice practiced her pieces for the recital, and for a time, they lapsed into something close to their old relationship.

But there were times when Alice seemed distracted and stopped playing for too long to gaze out of the window. Helen was sure she was not thinking about musical techniques. But then, nor was Helen concentrating single-mindedly on her painting. Roderick intruded too often in her mind, and with every visitor to the castle, she found herself hoping it was *him*.

It never was, although his brother Sir Julius came once.

On Tuesday, their mother informed them she was "at home" for tea that afternoon, and that Alice's presence was required.

"You might as well be there, too," Mama said to Helen. "It is all practice for next Season."

"I was hoping the girls would come with me to Blackhaven tomorrow," Eleanor added. She nearly always gave her mother-in-law her place. As a result, Mama rarely opposed her. "Miss Talbot has invited us to tea in the afternoon."

"Who is Miss Talbot?" Helen asked.

"You met her at the assembly ball," Eleanor said. "Friendly lady with a wry wit. Her brother is Lord Linfield, the diplomat, who was at Vienna with Castlereagh and Wellington."

"Excellent idea," Alice said unexpectedly. "Perhaps we can go into Blackhaven a little early. We have one or two things to buy before the garden party."

"True." Helen nodded, deliberately not looking at Alice. They had to visit the printer and ask around about men to protect everything, although she had little idea where to begin. Perhaps with old friends from the barracks? Only, they were probably all afraid of the countess. Bernard Muir might have more ideas, and he was discreet by nature.

But first, they had to sacrifice their afternoon to her ladyship's "at home," which involved changing into more suitable attire and repairing to the drawing room with their mother, Gervaise, and Eleanor.

They were all rather protective of Eleanor in formal situations, for she had not been brought up to the position she had taken on by marrying Gervaise. Although born to a local gentry family, she had been abducted as a child and rescued by Romanies, among whom she had lived for most of her life. She was a lovable mixture of innocence and worldly cynicism, of fearlessness and vulnerability, but she learned quickly, and her devotion to Gervaise was absolute.

Although Eleanor no longer needed looking after on social occasions, the family still kept the habit of someone always remaining close to her. So, Helen was with her, having just ferried cups of tea to their several callers, when Mr. Glover, Alice's unwanted suitor, was announced.

However, he did not so much as glance at Alice as he greeted Mama, and then Eleanor. He smiled at Helen before choosing the place next to her and accepting a cup of tea.

It was only after all the guests had gone that she realized her mother was scowling at her.

"Are you trying to spoil your sister's chances?" she demanded.

Helen felt entirely at sea.

"Well, Mama," Alice said, rising to her feet, "if he transfers his affections as easily as that, even you must admit he is worthy of neither of us."

Appalled understanding flooded Helen. "But I did not… He did not… I never—"

"Of course you did not," Eleanor said. "You behaved with perfect propriety throughout. And so did he."

"If you ask me," Gervaise pronounced sternly, "all three of them are far too young to even be considering marriage."

"You see?" Alice pounced before their mother could speak. "That is why you are our favorite brother."

"Only brother," he said wryly. "You will excuse me? I have matters to attend to."

"So do we," Helen said. "The garden party, you know…"

She was being allowed to exhibit some of her paintings at the garden party, alongside Tamar's and those of a few amateur enthusiasts from the town. Alice would play the pianoforte, also. It was a good excuse for all their activity and rehearsals leading up to the event at Whalen.

However, they had no sooner repaired to discuss their plans for the morning than a vehicle clattered into the courtyard below. As one, they looked out of the window in time to see a familiar young lady all but tumble out of the carriage in her eagerness.

"Maria!" Helen exclaimed, jumping up and bolting for the door, Alice at her heels.

Everyone was delighted by this unexpectedly early arrival, and Maria was so happy to be home again that it put everyone in a holiday mood.

"We weren't expecting you until later in the week," Gervaise said, smiling and breaking free of Maria for long enough to shake hands with his brother-in-law.

"Oh, Michael is worrying about some constituent who is in trouble," Maria said, pretending to be offhand but clearly very proud of her husband's conscientiousness. "Eleanor, I love that new wallpaper! It brightens the room like sunshine."

It was only as they went up to change for dinner that Helen

and Alice had the chance to haul Maria into their sitting room. Once, she had shared it with them, joined in their fantasies of escaping to make their own fortunes. Then there was Michael. Maria had not married well by her mother's standards—Michael had once been merely Gervaise's secretary—but, like her older siblings, she had married for love. And Michael, now a member of Parliament, was proving to be a man of talent that even the dowager countess could not disrespect.

With some pride, Alice showed her Helen's newest paintings, and their sister looked gratifyingly impressed. "I would love some of those for our London house," Maria said. She turned to Helen eagerly. "Which gives me a thought! Have you considered having prints made to sell? That way, one painting is sold many times—although admittedly for less money—and it gets your work and your name seen."

"That is true," Helen said. And then, as she remembered their immediate tasks, she asked, "Do you or Michael know of a printer in Whalen?" After all, they needed flyers to advertise their event at the theater.

"There is one in Blackhaven," Maria informed her, still bending over the pictures.

Over her head, Helen and Alice exchanged conspiratorial smiles.

ONCE, THEY WOULD have included Maria in their plans, but she was *enceinte*, and they were wiser in the ways of the world and the respectability that always seemed to come upon their siblings with marriage.

Accordingly, the ladies split up outside the vicarage. Leaving Eleanor and Maria to call on Mrs. Grant, Helen and Alice went in search of the printing shop. Mr. Nimmo looked slightly dazzled at their entrance—they were dressed in elegant gowns for their morning call upon Miss Talbot—though he did not appear to know who they were. In fact, he seemed delighted to print their flyers for rather less than Mr. Pritchard had quoted.

Helen also showed him the picture she had brought and inquired as to the cost of printing a hundred copies.

"We would need a good engraver," he said, examining the piece closely. "Fortunately, I know one, although he is a little elderly now. Will you allow me to speak to him and then I can quote you a price? In the meantime, I can have the theater flyers ready tomorrow."

Thanking him, they left with some satisfaction.

"Now, who the devil do we approach about guards?" Alice asked.

"Bernard? Captain Green?" Helen suggested.

"They're likely to blab to Gervaise," Alice said. "But there are former soldiers in the town—the doormen at the assembly rooms?"

"Rather public." Helen jerked up her head suddenly. "Wait, though! Trent the innkeeper is an old soldier, and no one else is likely to know us at the inn."

"Good thinking," Alice said, and they set off in the direction of the King's Head.

They had chosen a quiet time of the day, and only one man lounged in the coffee room. He was very large, but nodded and tugged his forelock amiably. There was no sign of Trent or Mrs. Trent or any other member of staff.

"They're all round the back with the little'uns," the big man volunteered. "One fell over and sent up a terrible screech. Upset everyone, even though no harm's done. I'd stay out of the way for another five minutes."

Helen recalled that a creche was organized at the back of the inn, where mothers took turns to look after the small children while the others worked. She had no desire to try to hold discreet conversations with Trent in the midst of children's tears, so she sat down at a vacant table, and Alice joined her.

"I can get you something to drink if you like?" the large man offered. "I know where everything is. Though fresh cooking I'll leave to Mrs. T…"

"Oh, no thank you," Alice said. "We really wanted a word with Mr. Trent."

Helen nudged her, for she had just seen the man's overcoat flung over the chair beside him, and it looked distinctly military. "Are you by any chance a former soldier, too?"

The man straightened and smiled. "How'd you guess? Former Seargeant North, ma'am, at your service."

"Were you with the 44th?" Helen asked.

"No, ma'am," he said regretfully.

"Excellent," Alice said. "Would you mind if we asked what employment you have now?"

Sergeant North scratched his large head. "Actually, you might say it's all in the process of change. I work for my old officer, who was injured at Waterloo. Now we're looking to go into a new line of business. Guarding, private protection, outriding, that kind of thing. If you young ladies know of anyone—"

"We might," Alice interrupted. "Friends of ours have hired a theater, both the auditorium and the foyer, for a whole day and evening. There will be tickets for sale at the door, paintings displayed in the foyer—also for sale—and a pianoforte recital in the evening. Is that the sort of thing you mean?"

Sergeant North blinked and gazed from one to the other. "Yes," he said. "I reckon that's exactly the sort of thing."

"Could you quote us a price?" Helen asked.

North blinked again, and scratched his head. "Not sure it's decided yet. But if you can wait, Captain Skelton will be back any minute."

Before he did, Trent himself bustled in and, despite having only one hand, made two cups of coffee with quiet efficiency. Without fuss, North rose and picked up the tray with the cups and a plate of buttered scones and brought it over to Helen and Alice.

Helen's heart warmed at this casual goodness. She smiled at him, and as soon as he was out of earshot, she murmured to Alice, "Unless their fee is extortionate, we should go with them."

In fact, their fee was very reasonable, as Captain Skelton was delighted to point out to them. He proved to be civil young man in his late twenties, a little too thin, perhaps, with the pallor of recent illness or injury, but clearly recovering.

"My partner and I have only just begun the enterprise," he explained. "I don't even have a card to give you at this stage, though I believe my partner is collecting them today. Since you are our very first customers, we are delighted to give you a discount."

"We also require discretion," Alice said. "From you and your employees."

He looked at her more carefully, but agreed at once, and they agreed to meet again at the inn to make final arrangements the day before the event, if not earlier.

Feeling rather pleased with themselves and their stroke of good fortune, Helen and Alice left the inn and walked back to the high street to meet Eleanor and Maria at the hotel.

Here, they discovered they were also to have the pleasure of Michael's company.

"I hope Maria appreciates your sacrifice," Alice said as they all walked across the foyer together between deeply bowing footmen, clerks, and managers.

"Sacrifice?" Michael asked distractedly.

"An afternoon of gossip when you could be doing something much worthier."

"You make me sound very dull," he said. "But now you mention it, there is a concerning aspect of our foreign policy that I wish to discuss with Lord Linfield."

Maria laughed, apparently not remotely offended to have her husband's escort for such divided reasons. But then, this was their life. According to Alice, Maria—the gentlest of the siblings and the one who most hated confrontation and anger—was making a name for herself as a political hostess in London.

Miss Talbot's sitting room was already busy when the maid admitted them. The lady, no longer young, but somehow both attractive and comfortable, came forward to greet them herself.

"Lady Braithwaite, a pleasure to welcome you! You know my brother Linfield, of course. And my friend, Mrs. Macy."

Mrs. Macy, a quietly dressed but very good-looking young woman with smiling eyes, curtsied and stayed in the background.

"Do you know my sister-in-law, Lady Maria Hanson?" Eleanor said. "And her husband, Mr. Michael Hanson, who is our local member of Parliament?"

"How do you do?" Lord Linfield murmured, and shook hands with Michael. "Hanson and I are acquainted, but I am delighted to meet Lady Maria."

Linfield was a tall, handsome gentleman in his mid-thirties, with a friendly manner and highly perceptive eyes. He and his sister both knew Alice from the recent Season in London, but they made Helen equally welcome.

Presented with a cup of tea by Mrs. Macy, Helen at last felt able to glance around the other guests. She recognized a couple of neighbors, to whom she smiled and inclined her head, but to her disappointment there was no sign of Major Vale or any of his family.

Alice drew her over to sit beside a young girl who looked familiar, possibly because she was the most beautiful creature Helen had ever seen. She had glimpsed her at the assembly ball, but at close quarters, the girl was positively stunning—raven-dark hair and flawless, creamy skin over an exquisite bone structure. Her eyes were large and sparkling, her mouth full and soft like an unfurling rosebud. Helen could not put her finger on exactly what it was that changed this prettiness into extraordinary beauty, but it was undeniable.

"This is Miss Henrietta Gaunt," Alice told her. "Etta, my sister Helen. Etta was in Vienna and came home via Paris, so she has seen lots of art. Oh, and London for the Season, of course."

Helen blinked. "Goodness, after such travels, you must find it dull to be in Blackhaven."

"Not at all," Miss Gaunt said with surprising fervor. "I don't believe it is at all a dull place. Although it is pleasant to be less crowded."

"You did not care for the Season in London?" Helen asked with something like dread, since it was to be her fate next year, and while Alice had found unexpected entertainment there, Helen did not truly expect to be so lucky.

Miss Gaunt looked guilty. "I liked the dancing. And the music." She smiled. The effect probably had confirmed bachelors throwing themselves at her feet. Even Helen was dazzled. "And, yes, the art galleries and museums. And I met some very kind and interesting people." She lowered her voice. "Sadly, I am very unfashionable and prefer smaller parties where I know everyone."

"So do I," Helen said. "Blackhaven sounds just the place for you."

"Sadly, we are only visiting. Lizzie and Vanya have taken a house for the summer. She is *enceinte* again, and Vanya thought the waters might make her more comfortable."

"Lizzie is her sister, Lady Launceton," Alice explained. Her eyes gleamed. "They have a Dog."

Helen laughed. "Why do I feel that has a capital letter?"

"Because it's his name," Miss Gaunt said, her eyes laughing. "And once you have met him, there is really only one Dog!"

"I look forward to it," Helen said, intrigued, and then her heart turned over, for a flurry at the sitting room door resolved into three tall, imposing gentlemen: Captain Sir Julius Vale, Mr. Aubrey Vale, and Major Vale.

A flush of anticipation swept through Helen. But the brothers' entrance seemed to have a profound effect on the rest of the company too. They seemed to fill the room, and everyone noticed. Several faces brightened. One or two scowled. Henrietta Gaunt jerked suddenly away from the door, as if she were ashamed of looking. Alice, for some reason, seemed to droop with disappointment.

Their hosts appeared to be on very cordial terms with the Vales, who almost immediately split into three different directions. Sir Julius, surprisingly, chose to sit by Mrs. Macy, Miss Talbot's "friend"—who, Helen suspected, was more of a paid companion. Roderick and Aubrey kept coming in her direction, and she held her breath.

Roderick peeled off and went toward an unknown lady instead. It was Aubrey who sat beside them, and it was soon clear why. Whenever his gaze fixed on the extraordinarily beautiful Miss Gaunt, it was intensely predatory, reminding Helen unbearably of the first time Roderick had looked at her. Like his brother, however, Aubrey was perfectly courteous to all, and turned out to be charming and amusing company.

Since Henrietta did not appear to object to it, Helen rose and moved toward the vicar's wife, Kate Grant, of whom she had once been in considerable awe. Now, she couldn't remember why, for Kate was the kindest person in the world, as well as one of the funniest.

Helen wanted Roderick to come and speak to her there. He didn't, although he was now talking to a very dark man with gleaming eyes, and was apparently focused and entertained.

"Lord Launceton," Kate said, seeing the direction of her gaze. "Miss Henrietta Gaunt's brother-in-law. Wildly romantic character."

"How so?" Helen asked, intrigued in spite of herself.

"He's Russian, but with enough English blood to have inherited the title. Apparently his people were overenthusiastic in taking possession of the property and evicted the late baron's family—who ended up in Vienna with their diplomat uncle, which just happened to be where the new Lord Launceton was, guarding his tsar. And somehow the new baron ended up marrying the daughter of the old, so all the children are provided for once more. Though I do wonder how that came about."

"Very sensibly, by the sound of things," Helen observed.

Kate looked doubtful. "Not sure 'sensible' applies to any of them, but they are great fun. That is Lady Launceton with Eleanor. Go and be introduced."

Helen, who was having difficulty sitting still, all but jumped to her feet—and collided with Roderick.

Her face flamed with embarrassment—or she told herself it was embarrassment—as he steadied her with a firm grip on her elbow before he stepped back and bowed.

"My apologies, Lady Helen."

"It was my fault," she said, sounding like a breathless school-girl confronted with her first crush. Which was probably exactly how she appeared to him. *Is that all I am?*

Stricken, she glanced up at him, and could read nothing in his face but tolerant good nature. He might be a different man from the one she had sketched at the ball, the one whose expressions had so fascinated her then and later. After the night trip to the abbey, she had thought they were friends at the very least, yet now he was imposing upon her this huge distance, hiding.

Because I am a pest? Or because I do mean something, and that frightens him as charging French cavalry could not?

There was no time to find out. His attention had already moved on to Kate, whom he greeted by name, and there was nothing for Helen to do but continue her original path toward Eleanor.

Had she been blind not to see before this was how he regard-ed her? Had she wanted his attention so much that she had imagined his interest, however reluctant? He had come to the abbey to see her—twice—but both occasions could be attributed to some kind of duty, to his sense of responsibility. Looking after her as though she were the child he had once accused her of being.

She cringed inside at the very thought.

Or was he hiding *now*? Because he did not know what to do? Because she was not the kind of woman who could "handle him"? Should she have spoken to the jeweled lady after all?

Either way, she felt doubly glad she had not given in to her instinct to tell him about the Whalen theater project, nor ask his advice about guarding it.

The rest of her afternoon was miserable, and it took a huge amount of effort to conceal the fact. She was relieved when Eleanor declared it time to depart. And then, after they bade farewell to their likeable host and hostess, she found Roderick holding the door for them.

She felt all of a wounded animal's instinct to strike first, and so she sailed through the door with a mere, distant nod of thanks. Her aim was to seize Alice by the arm and use her as protection. But Alice had already dashed ahead with Eleanor, and Maria was holding Michael's arm, leaning into him as though tired, which caused Helen a flicker of worry. Childbirth was a matter for great celebration, but also considerable danger for both mother and child.

Helen drew in breath and fresh perspective, while Roderick paced silently beside her along the passage toward the staircase.

"Am I to gather that I am out of favor once more?" she asked with light mockery.

His glance was still careful. "No. That I was trying to look after your reputation. We have no excuse to regard each other as more than mere acquaintances."

"You mean we *are* more than that?"

He held her gaze and slowed his pace. "We will never be more than that, Lady Helen. A kiss does not make you in love. Neither does bodily hunger."

Her face flamed. Shame and fury flooded her, depriving her of words and even the breath to speak to them. By some miracle, she forced her chin up and sailed ahead of him after her family. Somewhere, she was aware of him keeping pace beside her, but in any way that mattered, he was miles away.

He even conducted them to the waiting carriage, handing the ladies inside. Helen pretended not to see his hand. "Goodbye," she said, following Alice.

Immediately she addressed her family with her best, sparkling smile. "Oh, I do so want to meet Henrietta Gaunt's Dog! We must call on them one day soon."

And then the steps were up, the door closed, and the horses in motion. She did not look out of the window.

No one had ever struck Helen. But if they had, she thought it would have felt like this.

Chapter Eight

DEAFENED BY THE guns and the screaming of men and horses, Roderick still shouted his men on. Some fell, but soldiers always fell in battle. Mourning came later. In the present, they charged on, hacking their way through the enemy to the wall that afforded their defense.

But no one could climb the wall. Shots seemed to rain down from nowhere, and they tumbled into the mud in droves. Then the cavalry charge came out of nowhere, trampling the fallen, cutting down the fighters like wheat in the field.

Roderick was used to hard fights. He knew only to keep going, and keep going, cut and thrust and boot and fist, using his body like a battering ram, ignoring the wounds and the pain. And then came the moment he realized he was alone. His men were all gone. His fellow officers were all gone, along with their men. No one was left but him.

The horror deluged him like a tide. They could not all be dead, not *all*…

More men were dying, the enemy this time as comrades came to the rescue, too late, too late. Over the screams of the dying, the shouts of battle, and the incessant crashing of the guns, he heard his own cry of unbearable loss, of shame and grief, of rage and pain. Utter, all-consuming pain that would never leave him. He could not breathe for the dying falling on him, the enemy falling on him. He could not move, only scream his agony…

"Roderick," said a brisk voice. "Wake up, Rod. That's enough dreaming. Roderick!"

He opened his eyes and could see nothing but darkness. Still, he could not breathe, but at least he could move, flailing and rolling until he saw the candle illuminating his sister Felicia standing by his bed in her nightgown.

There was no real relief in being awake. Everyone was still dead. All that remained was to avoid distressing the living more than he already had.

He swallowed. "What is it? Was I shouting?"

"Yes. Quite a nightmare, I gather."

The nightmare hurt no one. It was the reality he could not live with. He rubbed his face with one shaking hand. "Sorry. Did I wake you?"

"No, the twins woke me. It was they who heard."

He had deliberately chosen this room at the top of the house to avoid just such calamities. "Tell me they didn't come in."

"They were too careful of your dignity. I am not."

He tried to laugh, but it was a poor effort. The fringes of nightmare and memory hung about him, oppressive and blurring. He shook his head as though to clear it.

"I'm fine now." He struggled into a sitting position before he remembered he was naked. He preferred to sleep without any restriction on his limbs. "You can go back to bed. Tell the twins not to worry."

"The twins will worry whatever I tell them," Felicia said, lighting his bedside lamp from her candle. "It's what the twins do, or hadn't you noticed?"

"I noticed they were interfering with Julius. I had my orders along with everyone else."

Felicia sat on the edge of the bed. "It seems to be working out quite well for Julius. I think he is still in love with Antonia Macy. I like her."

Roderick dragged his mind back over the recent dinner party with Lord Linfield, his sister, and Mrs. Macy. And then to the gathering this afternoon at the hotel, forcing himself to acknowledge the observations lurking behind his own problems. "I think she is good for him. He has been more like himself in the last few days. But I don't think we put that at the twins' door."

"Oh, I don't know. They made us all go to the ball for one reason or another. And they are always up to more than we think."

He twitched his lips into an almost genuine smile. "Is that a warning?"

"They are a force of nature. Warnings will do none of us any good. You have a lot of nightmares, Rod."

There was no point in denying it. "Does everyone know?"

"We have all heard, from time to time. This seemed to be particularly bad. Did something happen today?"

I was deliberately vile to a sweet and lovely girl who liked me, who might have saved me. I destroyed any possible future we might have had. I hurt her.

He shook his head violently. "I thought they were getting better. Less frequent. They will stop in the end."

"Talk to Julius," she said. "He too has seen battle. You might help each other."

Julius, a hero of Trafalgar and many sea battles since. Roderick scowled. "I won't burden him with anything else, and neither will you. He is already carrying all of us—with the possible exception of Cornelius. Besides, I don't need help. I just need peace."

Felicia rose to her feet, reaching for her candle, and abruptly, shame swamped him. He had to stop behaving like this.

Without looking at her, he snatched up her free hand. "Sorry, Fliss. I know I'm impossible."

She ruffled his hair. "No, you're not. Difficult, but not impossible. Sleep well, Rod."

"Good night, Fliss."

He had no intention of going back to sleep. When she had gone, he listened to the distant voices of his sisters and brother, speaking low. Then there were the clicks of several closing doors on the floor below, and silence.

Roderick threw off the bedclothes and went to the window. The first pale light was in the sky. He would watch the sun come up, if it was visible through the clouds. Later, he had several old soldiers to see and perhaps put on a small retainer to hold themselves in readiness for any business that came their way. Skelton and North already had an accidental client, a task in Whalen which he would leave them to take care of while he sought more business further afield.

It was time to leave the army and look to his future.

THE DAY OF the castle garden party dawned dry but cloudy.

By then, the castle was full of family and a few of the honored guests who had been invited to stay for ten days or so around the summer ball to be held next week. For Helen, it felt rather wonderful to have all her family around her again, like a cocoon of childhood safety. Only, the restless discontent would not quite leave her. She thought far too often of Roderick Vale, sometimes with hurt or anger, sometimes with grief for him as well as for herself.

I could have made him happy, she thought wistfully, more than once. But she couldn't. Just at the moment, she doubted anyone could. Trying to keep her own unhappiness in the background, she threw herself into preparations for the party and the exhibition. There were flyers at the theater itself, and they had scattered more around the town of Whalen, in places the more prosperous citizens were likely to see them.

"What about Blackhaven?" Alice asked as they returned in the carriage. "I can't help thinking we need Blackhaven visitors to make this a success."

Helen nodded. "I suspect you are right. Only…you would be much more easily recognized by Blackhaven people. Not so much me. I can hide in the background most of the time. But you will be in plain sight in front of an audience, and surely someone from home will recognize you." She caught her breath. "Is that what you want, Alice? To force their hands so that the let us go to Europe in order to get us out of the way?"

Alice opened her mouth to deny it, then closed it again while she considered. "They would never send us alone or disown us. Besides, I'm not sure I do want that just yet. Do you?"

Part of Helen did. To escape the Season looming over her next spring, to see new places and new art, to just paint and paint until the pain niggling at her heart went away.

She shook her head slowly. "No. We are not quite ready, are we?"

Alice smiled crookedly. "No. But at least we are now mature enough to recognize the fact. Perhaps in a year or two, if this goes well and we manage to do it elsewhere too…"

Helen nodded. They would do it gradually. Was that relief she felt at not being forced into a decision?

"Which brings us back to the same question," Alice said. "Do we advertise the event in Blackhaven? And I'm not sure you will be any safer than me from recognition. The theater staff know nothing about art. Nor does Captain Skelton, if he is even there himself. You might well have to answer questions, although of course you do not need to admit to being the artist."

"It is still an odd thing for Braithwaite's sister to be doing," Helen agreed. "I…" She broke off, blinking rapidly. "Oh, Alice, the solution is staring us in the face!"

Alice followed her gaze to the pile of masks she and her sisters had been inspecting for the masquerade ball next week. "Disguise!" She laughed. "The masked pianist! Oh, I wish we had put it on the flyers now."

"No, this way is best. They will take you more seriously than if we advertised with such a charade. But the mask will help spread the word later, perhaps. For myself…during the day, I shall wear some kind of cap that makes me look like a governess, and in the evening, the mask and… I suppose you would not consider wearing a wig?"

Alice shuddered. "I would not. When we used to dress up, they made my head itch, and I can't interrupt my playing to scratch my head."

"Not the most refined behavior, perhaps," Helen agreed. "Let me look at those masks again…"

With such important matters decided, Alice's main concern seemed to be the absence of the poet Simon Sacheverill, who had originally promised to read some of his poetry at the garden party. Since the guests had been very excited by the prospect of meeting the great man, everyone was annoyed to have been let down.

"Well, he is something of a recluse," Eleanor said. "I don't know anyone who has actually met him."

"Neither do I," said Maria, who lived in London. "I suppose it mutes the excitement a little. But for true poetry lovers, it is the words that matter, not gushing over the man who wrote them. Why doesn't Helen read them instead? She was always best at it."

"I haven't practiced!" Helen protested with some alarm. "Alice would be much better before an audience, and she *likes* poetry."

"No, you have the better voice," Alice said just a little too quickly. "And you read with more feeling. I always sound sarcastic, which doesn't work well with such verses."

Helen objected no more. She would not be the only one to read their favorite poems during the afternoon, and in truth it gave her something to think about other than the possible presence of Roderick Vale.

Apparently, the whole family was expected, complete with the fifteen-year-old twins, who were too young to be regarded as adults, but were certainly much older than Helen's nieces and nephews staying at the castle. Apparently, Henrietta Gaunt had siblings closer in age, and there was Colonel Benedict's daughter, too.

Helen fully expected Roderick to send his apologies.

In the half-hour before the formal opening of the garden party, Helen looked over some of the new work that her brother-in-law, Lord Tamar, was exhibiting. There was a new portrait of Gervaise and Eleanor that made her smile, because he had caught Eleanor's sense of fun and, somehow, its sneaking effect on Gervaise's inclination to seriousness. They were good for each other, like two sides of the same coin.

Hastily, she banished an intrusive vision of Roderick Vale.

"These are *good*," Tamar said behind her. He was examining her new abbey paintings. He sounded so impressed that she flushed with pleasure.

"Do you think so? I was quite pleased with them, but I was afraid they were too…storybook."

"All paintings tell a story, if you look. No, you have made something new and rather wonderful out of an overdone subject. This one, under the stormy clouds, is particularly good. Who is he?" He waved one hand in the direction of the blurred, shadowy figure in front of the ruin.

She didn't even think of lying. Tamar was the only one of her family who truly understood this part of her life. "Major Vale. He was so obliging as to stand still for a few minutes."

"Helen!" Frances called from the hall below the gallery. "Guests arriving!"

"Battle stations," Tamar murmured.

RODERICK HAD NO intention of going to the garden party, but Felicia talked him into showing his face.

"We have to go for Julius's sake," she said. "Something is

wrong between him and Antonia, and he needs our support—if not a soldierly boot."

Roderick cared a great deal for his brother's happiness. On top of which, he realized that in a place the size of Blackhaven, he and Helen would have to get used to running into each other occasionally. So he gave in with good grace, resolving to show his face and leave shortly afterward.

He chose, however, to make his own way there, and found an unexpectedly relaxed atmosphere. Children were running wild between a large marquee on the lawn and somewhere else on the far side of the castle. He was fairly sure he recognized the twins organizing the game.

The countess herself welcomed him cordially in the garden. "So glad you could join us, major! Your brothers and sisters are all around somewhere. There is wine and refreshment in the marquee and inside the hall. We have art and poetry inside, with music to follow. You know Lord Launceton, of course?"

Roderick shook hands with the English baron known as "the mad Russian," who seemed to have been detached from his sword for the occasion, and the countess fluttered off to greet her next guests.

"You look like a man longing to return to the army," Launceton remarked as they strolled toward the castle."

Roderick twisted his lips. "The uniform? It's the only decent garb that fits me. Somehow, I forgot to go to the tailor. I've decided to sell out." As things stood, he would be absolutely no use to the army in any case. "Do you miss it?"

"I was only ever playing at soldiers. Only there was the French invasion and patriotism, so I stayed. Now, when I wear my old uniform, it is largely to annoy the proud and prejudiced among your English. We plan to divide our time between Russia and England, since I appear to have land in both. What of you?"

"Land in neither," Roderick said lightly. "But I am looking into a few things. If you're the Colonel Zuvarin I've heard of, I'm surprised you have settled down so easily."

"That has been my discovery since I met Lizzie. I've never known a moment of boredom, and there is always fun to be had with a houseful of Gaunts. I expect it is the same with Vales."

Roderick opened his mouth to deny it, but in fact he *did* feel a certain happiness living in Black Hill with all his siblings for the first time ever. But it was a stopgap. It would not be right forever.

Helen would be right forever.

No, she damn well wouldn't.

As they wandered across the great hall together, he picked up a glass of wine and saw there were pictures exhibited in the gallery. Since there was no sign of Helen there, he made toward it, leaving Launceton to his own devices.

The gallery was hung with a mixture of oil and watercolor paintings, some of them excellent in his opinion, others second-rate daubings that he suspected were perpetrated by neighbors and friends of the family.

Head and shoulders above them all, of course, were Lord Tamar's works, technically brilliant, eye-catching, and powerful. And yet, according to Helen, he was largely self-taught.

Roderick recognized Helen's paintings easily, not just the two abbey pictures that he had already seen. There were portraits of her mother and sisters, another lady he was sure he had met, a seascape, and a view of the castle at dawn. There was also an amusing sketch of Hyde Park at the fashionable hour when everyone who was anyone walked, rode, or drove during the Season. Somehow it gave the impression of everyone jostling to be seen, and some of their expressions were ridiculous. One of the horses actually looked embarrassed, while another seemed to be commiserating with it.

Roderick couldn't help smiling.

"Clever, is it not?" said a voice behind him.

He turned and beheld a carelessly dressed man with wild black hair and an amiable expression. "Very."

"Tamar," the man said, offering his hand.

Roderick took it. "Vale. Roderick Vale." Though he looked

quite carefully, he saw no sign of recognition at the name. He should have been grateful, but what he actually felt was pique. Stupidly.

"The same artist painted these," Tamar said, indicating Helen's other works.

"I know," Roderick said, nodding. "She has talent."

Tamar smiled, perhaps with more interest. "She does."

"I understand you are teaching her?"

Tamar shrugged. "A little, here and there, the way I learned. Mostly, her gift shines. Which is both a blessing and a curse to someone in her position."

"But obviously her family does not forbid her to paint."

"Not to paint. It would be another matter to exhibit outside her home."

Of course, there would be no sales, no income, no independence, no choice but marriage and children. "And yet this is her passion," he murmured without meaning to.

Tamar's gaze intensified. "You seem to know my little sister very well."

"No." With difficulty, Roderick kept the regret from his voice.

"And yet I know you."

Roderick frowned. "I know your work, but I have never met you."

"I *have* met you. In Helen's sketchbook."

Roderick's lips twisted of their own accord. "Apparently, I have an interesting face." He gestured with one hand toward the paintings. "Like the abbey."

Tamar laughed. "I hope you see her too," he said cryptically, and wandered off to speak to a couple clearly waiting for his attention.

Unbalanced by the encounter, Roderick left the gallery and blindly followed some other people toward a salon. Too late, he recognized the beautiful voice drifting out of the door. He told himself it would be disrespectful to turn back and fight his way toward more wine, but in reality, he didn't even want to. Her voice drew him as it always had.

She was reciting poetry. At first, he did not even hear the words, just her voice as he drank in her stance before the mantelpiece at the front of the room, a leather-bound volume in her hands.

Moving inside the room, to let others in behind him, he leaned one shoulder against the wood-paneled wall and, along with everyone else present, gazed his fill at Helen.

The emotion in her voice was reflected on her face. She *felt* the words as she felt her pictures, with her whole being, and that fascinated him. The poem began to infiltrate his brain, a lament to lost love, self-deprecating, clever, and yet not quite funny, for the poet's pain came through it all.

So did Helen's. Tears stood out in her eyes, unshed but unmistakable. The poem moved her to tears because she understood it only too well.

Me? I did that to her?

The thought, even the remotest possibility, was unbearable. Tearing his gaze from her face, he straightened and moved toward the door—slipping away, he hoped, without any of the absorbed poetry lovers being any the wiser. His emotions, and his mind, were in complete turmoil.

Chapter Nine

HELEN HADN'T SEEN him enter the room, but she saw him leave. Already vulnerable from the searing poetry, she thought her heart would break.

Somehow, she got to the end of her reading, graciously accepting the applause while smiling and reminding everyone the genius was Simon Sacheverill's. She surrendered her place to the next reader, a willowy London gentleman who was to read his own work.

She escaped, and instead of turning right back to the great hall and the music already drifting pleasantly toward her, she went left and hurried upstairs and along the familiar passages until she came to the haven of her own bedchamber.

She had not the luxury of wallowing in this ridiculous emotion. A shower of rain blew against the windowpane, but she could still hear the voices in the garden and the music in the hall below. She had duties, not the least of them to her own sense of pride and dignity. So she did not give in, merely used her moments of quiet and privacy to draw breath and wash her face. Then, at least mostly in control of herself, she left and walked back toward the main staircase.

There was some sort of game going on in the long gallery amongst the small children. As well as at least one nursemaid, Serena had once been with them but had clearly handed over responsibility to Rosa Benedict and two other almost-adults who were clearly siblings, if not twins.

Twins.

Rosa greeted her with pleasure, and indeed Helen's heart warmed to see her old friend. Rosa was a quiet, shy girl with a mischievous soul. When Helen had first met her, she had not spoken at all. Until Caroline Benedict had worked her own magic on both Rosa and her reclusively inclined father—who had become Caroline's husband.

"You drew the short straw?" Helen said, smiling and waving beyond Rosa to the gaggle of tiny children thundering up and down the gallery. Some were her nieces and nephews, others the children of friends. One was Rosa's half-brother, Caroline's son.

"Only for a few minutes. We let the nursemaids have a break. This many children is hard work when they are excited. They're like scurrying ants, but it will be teatime soon. Oh, these are the Vale twins, Leona and Lawrence. Lady Helen Conway. We—Oh, rats!" Rosa broke off to rush away and rescue an unknown child who had tripped and fallen on the carpet. It was notable that the wailing shut off as soon as Rosa picked him up.

Helen smiled and became aware of two pairs of eyes regarding her with intense interest.

"We think you know our brother Roderick?" the girl said amiably enough, although the name was enough to tighten the nerves in Helen's stomach. "Major Vale? Didn't you dance with him at the ball?"

"I did," Helen said, holding out her hand. "And I am very pleased to meet you."

They both shook hands with her, amidst polite bowing and curtsying.

"We're pleased to meet you, too," Lawrence said. Although most things about him were still very boyish, his eyes looked somehow old, despite their sharpness. "We think you are good for Roderick."

Helen tried to sound amused. "I cannot imagine why you

would think so."

"He is happier," Leona said. She wrinkled her nose. "Some of the time."

"What makes you think he was ever unhappy?"

The nursemaids had come back, and an older boy was arguing with Rosa. They went down the main staircase to the great hall. The twins walked more slowly toward the stairs, on either side of Helen.

"He was different when he came home," Leona said. "After Waterloo. He has nightmares."

"That isn't uncommon," Lawrence said quickly, almost as though defending his brother. "Rosa says her father had nightmares for years. He was a colonel, invalided out. But Roderick is like a burning fuse. We are worried about him."

Helen opened her mouth to speak, though in truth she did not know what to say, and it didn't actually matter, for Leona spoke first. "He was…lighter for a few days. After the ball."

Helen swallowed. "I'm sure being with people is good for everyone who has troubles."

They both smiled at her, which was dazzling, because on one level their smiles were exactly the same. On another, Leona's was utterly feminine and Lawrence's almost manly. They would break hearts in a year or two, if anyone could ever separate them for long enough.

"That's what we think," Lawrence agreed. They had arrived at the staircase, but instead of walking down, he dropped to sit on to the first step. "So we were glad he came today. Only he's *skulking*. He went outside."

"In the rain," Leona added. "He does that a lot."

Helen decided to be equally blunt. "Are you asking me to go after him?" she asked. "In the rain?"

"Are you afraid to?" Leona returned.

"Of course not!"

"Good, because he is a gentle man." She pronounced the words separately, so there could be no doubt that she was not referring to his birth. "But he does frighten some people. So does Julius, though in a different way. They are sort of…*imposing*?"

Lawrence nodded. "And Rod's temper is worse. Erratic. Uncertain. It never used to be. He was fun, actually."

"Why are you telling me this?" Helen demanded, brushing past Lawrence and sinking down on the step two below his. "To see if I'm afraid? Do you want me to go after him or not?"

"It depends," Lawrence said, "on whether or not you like him."

Helen looked from one to the other. "You have already decided I like him, or you would not have told me all this. You would have left me after *We think you are good for Roderick*."

They grinned, clearly more flattered than offended.

"Well, we might have introduced you to our sister Lucy," Leona said. "She is the best judge of character. Roderick went left toward the stables."

"Then he is probably gone."

"Oh, he didn't ride here. He would not insult his hostess by smelling of horse. We'll come with you, if you like."

Helen regarded her with some amusement. "You two are quite relentless, are you not?"

"It has been said," Lawrence said seriously. He stood up and offered her his hand to rise.

She gave in to the inevitable, mostly because she wanted to. And in truth, something cowardly in her was glad of the twins' covering presence—should they actually find him. Not because she was afraid of Roderick but because she wanted to *look* as if she was only going along with them.

The Scottish pianist was playing something very fine that Roderick would surely have loved. But Helen was given little time to enjoy it. The twins glanced once toward their youngest sister Lucy, who appeared to be flirting with Dax—otherwise Lord Daxton. Once, he had been considered a dangerous young man. Now he flirted from habit without really meaning it. Everyone knew he was devoted to his young wife. They visited

Blackhaven often, and even Mama had grown fond of them.

Helen left the great hall with the twins and turned left toward the front entrance to the castle. They crossed the gravel drive in a slight mist of rain. Helen tried not to peer ahead in search of Roderick.

"Roderick likes horses," Leona said. "Of course, he was a dragoon, so he saw a good deal of them there."

"We found him sitting in our stables once," Lawrence added. "As if he preferred their company."

"I suppose it's less demanding," Helen said. "And yet one doesn't feel alone."

They both glanced at her, and she held her tongue.

The stable yard was empty. Judging by the voices and occasional low laughs coming from the tack room, the grooms were enjoying a break there.

Helen led the way into the main stable building. Her own old mare whinnied, and a couple of the other horses copied her greeting. Then Helen's stomach lurched, for Roderick sat on a stool in the corner, his back against the wall, a flask in one hand.

He did not look pleased to see her, but at least he rose to his feet. Almost immediately, his gaze went beyond her. "Ah. You've been twinned," he said sardonically.

"We met Lady Helen upstairs," Leona said. "She is a friend of yours."

"Of course," Roderick said, "but is this the best place for you to play?"

Helen knew what he was doing—casting her back to the realms of childhood, too young for his manly attentions. Although even the twins were too old to "play" in the way he implied, so she laughed.

Roderick blinked, as though taken by surprise, then took another swig from his flask and screwed the top back on. "They are, of course, your stables."

"Lucy is flirting with Lord Daxton," Leona informed him. Perhaps, like Helen, she was sure he was about to leave the castle premises.

"Then Julius is just the man to sort it out."

"Julius has his own problems," Lawrence said severely. "So does Lucy."

A frown of irritation pulled at Roderick's brow. For an instant, he seemed about to blister them all verbally, then, with a mutter, he strode to the stable door. Unfortunately, Helen had moved at the same time, although she didn't quite know why— an instinctive gesture to stay him, perhaps. Whatever, he almost walked into her, and she refused to scurry out of his way like an overawed child. So they both halted, too close together, and glared at each other.

There was a challenge in his hard, mocking eyes. She could feel his warmth, sense the invisible, very physical tug of attraction and need. She remembered him in her arms, his mouth on hers... And he knew it. He was remembering, too. But she would not step aside, and he knew that too. The civility had always been required of him, but deliberately, he took his time. Perhaps he thought it would frighten her, or at least awe her.

He stepped aside, bowed ironically, and walked away.

RODERICK KNEW HE was behaving badly, and just when he had decided to be courteous. But the interruption had unbalanced him again. He cursed the twins' interference, for although Helen was the only person he wanted near him, she was the last he could tolerate in present circumstances.

The sooner he got out of the castle, the better. In fact, he was already walking toward the gate, running away.

From what, for God's sake? He stopped abruptly in his tracks. There was no enemy, no battle, no one to hurt or even offend him. It was Roderick who had been offensive, several times, to that sweet lady. And what the devil had he just taught Lawrence about the respect due to women?

I am making a mess of this. Again.

So make it right. Make it all right.

He kept walking, all the way around the castle to the entrance to the great hall and went to sort Lucy out.

In this, he was only partially successful, but at least he discerned that there was something wrong. And, with a jolt, he worked out what. The man to whom she had been infamously betrothed in babyhood—Lord Eddleston—had appeared out of the blue, here at the garden party, just as Lucy, Roderick suspected, had fallen in love with someone else.

He could not solve that, but he could and did look after Lucy. And since the company was now dancing informally, he walked up to Helen and asked her to dance too.

She was far too well brought up to refuse him, even though it was a waltz. Even as he took her in his arms, the sweetness of affection and desire seeped through him, distracting him. How blissful just to drift with the music, with her softness and beauty in his hold, her grace, warmth, and perfume teasing his senses.

But that wasn't why he had asked her to dance. "I have been unforgivably boorish," he said. "I apologize."

He saw the surprise in her eyes, though she said at once, "I accept your apology."

She had such a large heart, this girl he kept trying to dismiss. He drew in his breath and said the rest. "You know I am a mess of a man. I am not good to be around for very long. But I hope—I will try—to be better. I am trying to sort things out. While I do, I will not inflict myself upon you. If I do fix myself—and I have no idea how long it will take—I will call upon you. I don't expect you to wait for that day. But I will come anyway. May we part as friends?"

He felt the relaxing of her body as though it were his own. Her eyes, her whole face, were lit by an inner glow that almost undid him. *Affection? Mere affection? Who am I trying to fool? God help me, I love her. I love her.*

He almost blurted it out, but that would not have been fair. He had soothed her pain. Now was not the time to cause more, and he knew he would. He was in no state to do anything else.

"This is Blackhaven," she said. "Friends have no need to part. But I shall not press you. I shall accept your conditions of our friendship. Under one condition."

"Name it."

Her fingers tightened on his. "That you call on me when you need me. That you accept, or even ask for, help when you need it. You have family and friends who want that."

He swallowed. "I know."

And then, at last, he could dance in silence and just feel her peace, her beauty, and his own love. Pain and tenderness. And the stirrings of joy.

THE DAY AFTER the garden party at the castle—to which, of course, she had not been invited—Meg Maven finally contrived to run into young Mr. Glover. He was hurrying across the foyer of the Blackhaven Hotel as she strolled in alone to enjoy a luxurious tea.

It was a pleasure she had discovered a few days ago, when, frustrated at never catching sight of either Roderick Vale or Glover, she had sat in the tearoom and soaked up the admiring male stares like a sponge.

Spying Glover was another unexpected pleasure, and he made no effort to avoid her, as Roderick undoubtedly would. Instead, he halted, bowing and smiling, just as though she were a gently born lady.

"Mrs. Maven, what a pleasant surprise."

Graciously, she gave him her hand. "I have been shopping and am in dire need of a cup of tea!"

"But you are alone. Allow me to escort you?"

"I would not trouble you, sir."

"I assure you there is no trouble, only pleasure. I would love a cup of tea more than anything. I have been packing."

"Oh dear," she said with genuine dismay. "You are not leaving us, are you?"

"Oh, no," he said, conducting her into the tearoom, where a waiter at once showed them to a discreet table. "I am only removing to the castle. I chose to come early to look around the area and am now taking up my invitation. But the countess does not expect me before five."

"To the castle?" Meg gushed. "How wonderful. I should love to see it, although I am not acquainted with her ladyship." She allowed a hint of regret into her voice. "I suppose you will go to the ball, also."

He shifted uncomfortably. "I will."

"And dance with Lady Helen? Or was it Alice?"

Glover flushed. "I would be honored to dance with either, but I am realistic about my poor chances!"

She lifted her eyebrows and gave her best tinkling laugh. "My dear! Are they so swamped with princes and dukes that they will not even dance with the dashing son of an earl?"

"Oh, it is not like that. Lady Alice is a very independent young lady."

Something in his voice caught her attention. Oh yes, she had been right. "And Lady Helen?" she asked innocently.

"She is younger, gentler…"

"Less shrewish?" Meg guessed.

It surprised a laugh out of him before he tried to deny that either of them were remotely ill-tempered. Then he broke off, exclaiming, "But why am I here with you talking about other ladies?"

They were presented with tea, dainty little sandwiches, and cakes. Meg waved the waiter away and poured the tea herself.

"Why?" she repeated. "Because I am too old for you in years and experience. Lady Helen would make the perfect bride for you. However," she added, passing him a cup of steaming tea, "perhaps you are acquainted with Major Vale?"

"I know who he is. His brother Aubrey is a good fellow."

"The major is very different, though equally attractive in his own way. For a man like him, it is very easy to fascinate a naïve young lady. The rumor is, she favors him."

Glover looked crushed.

Meg smiled and patted his hand. "Don't look like that. All is not lost. I believe we are in a position to do each other a favor."

His eyes widened. "How so?"

Meg took a scone, halved it, and spread butter on one piece. "Until Lady Helen came on the scene, Major Vale and I were all but engaged to be married."

"I'm sorry," Glover said with sincerity.

Meg smiled. "Don't be. It is all part of the game. My major and your lady are clearly wrong for each other, so we must find a way to swap things around to the correct partners. You and her. Him and me."

"How?"

Meg rummaged inside her reticule and passed him the folded flyer from the theater in Whalen. It had been easy to discover what the earl's daughters had been up to the day she had seen them. Although of course they were calling themselves Connor, not Conway.

"If you would be so obliging as to escort me to that event, I think you will find a way to be a hero to Lady Helen."

"Really? How?"

"You will know the right moment, believe me. And you will be happy ever after."

He smiled wistfully. Then his eyes refocused on her. "And in return? What might I do for you? Or if I am engaged to Helen, will he come naturally back to you?"

"Probably," she said. "However, I don't believe I could accept him back...without at least playing a trick on him for his faithlessness."

"How can I help?" he asked eagerly.

Meg took a delicate bite of her scone, swallowed, and picked up her teacup before she answered. "Get me into the castle ball," she said. "It's a masquerade, after all."

Chapter Ten

A LTHOUGH HELEN'S TALK and her waltz with Roderick might not have been entirely satisfactory, she hugged to herself his implicit admission of caring, and his promise to come to her when he no longer considered himself a mess. She understood that he needed time to recover, but she could not rid herself of the belief that he would do so better and quicker with her by his side. The twins had told her as much when they said he had been lighter after the ball where they met.

She had promised not to force any further intimacy, but she had no intention of avoiding him. On the other hand, the growing numbers of guests in the castle required her attention, particularly because she and Alice planned to spend an entire day away. In the days between the garden party and the Whalen exhibition, she did not see him at all.

She did, however, hear plenty about his family's doings. Gervaise had been helping Sir Julius in his pursuit of horse thieves, who turned out to be much more dangerous arms smugglers, and there had been a bit of a scare involving Mrs. Antonia Macy, who, however, became engaged to Sir Julius the following day.

Helen was glad for them, though she wondered what Roderick thought of it. He had seemed to like Antonia, but that was different from living with her as his sister-in-law and mistress of his childhood home.

"Do you think the other siblings will like this marriage?" Helen asked Alice once.

"They do."

It crossed her mind to wonder how Alice could be so certain, but since Lord and Lady Wickenden were announced just then, they had to end their private conversation.

The Whalen exhibition took a great deal of planning. She met once more with Captain Skelton at the inn to finalize matters.

"There will be two of us during the day, four for the evening recital," he informed her. "I shall be there myself, as will North, whom you've met already, and two chosen men with references, also former soldiers hired by my partner.

"We'll collect you in the coach at first light by the castle gates, load up all your gear, and escort you to Whalen. When your display is set up and the doors opened, one man will remain there, while the other will patrol the room." He smiled. "That will be me. Oh, and here is our card, because we hope you will recommend us to the castle people for any future needs."

Helen took the card, and would have placed it in her reticule at once, except a printed name leapt out at her.

Major Vale.

Her stomach lurched. "Major Vale is your partner?" she said, lifting her gaze to Skelton's.

"You know him?" Skelton sounded surprised. After all, Helen had allowed him to believe that she and Alice were merely attached to one of the castle guests. "Best of good fellows, and an excellent officer."

Helen ignored the question in favor of another. "Does *he* know we have engaged your services?"

"Of course. But he also knows North and I can manage without him. It is more important that he looks for more business further afield."

She didn't know whether she was disappointed or relieved that Roderick would not be there himself. She was certainly surprised he'd accepted the scheme without at least interrogating her. It seemed she had been wrong to fear his disapproval. It was foolish even to try to keep it from him, for he knew already.

"Of course," she murmured with a bright smile. She dropped the card into her reticule and could not help wondering if he had chosen deliberately to stay away to avoid her. Well, after the exhibition, she would speak to him about that…

The morning of the exhibition worked like clockwork. Leaving a note for Maria in their sitting room—*Away for a day of rest, back late, so please divert Mama. A&H*—they carried everything out in the dark from the sitting room to the castle gates. It took three trips, each, but it was all there before the carriage appeared, driven by the large Sergeant Pat North. Captain Skelton rode beside the coach, but dismounted to help load everything into the carriage. There was barely room for Helen and Alice.

It was all accomplished with silent good nature, and then they were on their way. Unexpectedly, Alice curled her fingers around Helen's and squeezed. It was a huge moment. The beginning, perhaps, of the dream they had harbored since childhood. And they were doing it together.

WHILE HELEN HUNG her pictures to the best advantage she could create—helped by the amiable Captain Skelton—North maneuvered the pianoforte across the stage to Alice's bidding. Mr. Pritchard took a friendly interest and even advised on lighting, according to Alice when she rejoined Helen in the foyer in time for the theater opening.

For this part of the day, they both wore simple morning dresses and old-fashioned caps that covered their hair and made them look older and lower in rank, just in case anyone who knew them wandered in. Alice effaced herself whenever anyone new entered.

Captain Skelton, in a smart blue coat over buff pantaloons,

strolled about the foyer while North stood by the open door in his military tunic, inviting people to step inside and enjoy the beautiful paintings.

A prosperous-looking middle-aged couple stepped over the door, and the great day began.

Although the event was hardly crowded, Helen was so delighted to have sold two paintings before luncheon that she ran through to the auditorium where Alice was rehearsing and danced with her across the stage.

After midday, there were more visitors, one of whom almost sent Helen scurrying back to Alice. A beautiful, ostentatiously dressed young woman who seemed vaguely familiar. Helen almost smiled at her before she remembered she was incognita. Almost at the same time, she recognized her as the jeweled lady from the ball. Mrs. Maven. The woman who had once been Roderick's mistress, and who had deliberately slammed the door to upset him.

Captain Greene had said she lived in Whalen.

She was with a group of other women, all richly dressed, too. From their speech, she took them to be the wives of prosperous tradesmen of some kind.

"They're pretty," Mrs. Maven said dismissively after glancing at a couple of them.

The other women clearly modeled their opinions on hers. "Wretchedly expensive for what they are."

Several other visitors clearly overheard her, glancing from her to the paintings before them. Helen panicked. She had agonized over the pricing. She knew from Tamar that it shouldn't be so low that her work was perceived as tat. At the same time, she was an unknown artist. She bit back the hasty defense springing to her lips. After all, she was hardly part of the conversation, and she certainly didn't want to draw Mrs. Maven's attention. But then, she wasn't sure that Mrs. Maven even knew who Helen was.

Captain Skelton had no such scruples.

"Expensive?" he repeated, pausing his perambulations beside

the women. "Do you think so? I find them exceptionally reasonable for such beauty. We have two of this artist's paintings, and they really do add grace to my wife's drawing room, and to her boudoir." He smiled and leaned forward conspiratorially to confide, "But between ourselves, I was influenced by more than aesthetics. I believe this artist will become the rage, and the value of her pictures will only rise."

Helen, who knew perfectly well that Captain Skelton had neither wife nor drawing room, had to turn away to hide her smile.

"You are saying they are a sound investment, sir?" Mrs. Maven said.

"I would not be so impudent as to give such advice. I merely give you my own reasons for purchasing." He bowed slightly and moved on. Catching Helen's awed gaze, he winked.

Mrs. Maven bought a large seascape. Her friend bought a smaller study of the Braithwaite orchard in full blossom. Only once, while she spoke to a gentleman about the abbey pictures, did Helen catch Mrs. Maven's gaze. She could read nothing there, and their mutual glance slid away almost at once.

Although some visitors came clearly out of curiosity only and had no intention of buying—particularly the poorer among them—Helen was heartened to overhear only compliments about her work. She couldn't help wishing Roderick were there to witness her small triumph.

At five o'clock, they closed the theater for an hour. North went and bought them some dinner from the nearest tavern, and they all sat companionably in the empty theater lounge to consume it. But Alice, whose big moment was still to come, could not settle. She barely ate anything before she left again to dress for the evening.

Helen knew she should follow, but when the evening guards, Harper and Black, arrived via the stage door and North went to show them their duties, she could not resist the opportunity for a brief, private conversation with Captain Skelton.

"Did you and Major Vale meet in the army?" she asked. "Were you in the same regiment?"

"Not the same regiment, but the same brigade most of the time. Known him for years."

"Were you at Waterloo?"

"I was."

She drew in a breath. "I count Major Vale a friend, but he will not talk to me about Waterloo."

"Not a fit subject for the ladies," Skelton said uncomfortably.

She held his gaze. "It has to be a fit subject for friends. I know everyone who survived the battle suffers in some way. I need to know what happened to him."

Skelton carried his own scars. She knew that and regretted asking him to return there, even in his mind. But perhaps he knew, or suspected, Roderick's deeper trouble. At any rate, after a brief pause, he drew in his breath and spoke in a rush.

"We had orders to capture one of the French positions that was slowing our advance. But the intelligence was poor. Enemy reserves were hidden close by. When we attacked, Vale's men took the worst of it. Even so, the enemy were surrendering when the reserves attacked from nowhere. We were decimated. Officers *and* men. But again, Vale took the brunt. I thought no one of his unit had been left at all until I saw him the other day in Blackhaven. I think we both imagined we were looking at ghosts. I was wounded, not supposed to survive, but I did. Many of my company survived. Vale was not so fortunate."

Helen almost wished she had not asked. She rose and touched his shoulder. "I'm sorry," she murmured, and went to join Alice, trying to adjust from Skelton's appalling story—and the horrors she could not help imagining from his bare words.

This daring adventure of theirs, Alice's increasing anxieties, seemed so trivial by comparison. And yet this was real, too, part of the peaceful life men had suffered and died to ensure.

Alice looked magnificent in white and gold, her skin pale from nerves, her hair piled high in a style that was deliberately too old for her. Helen added a few extra pins to maintain it through the evening. She tied the gold mask in place for her. It covered most of her face, but did not impede her sight of the music or the keys. Helen added a delicate brush of paint across her lips and stood back.

The result was a spectacularly beautiful woman of indeterminate age, but probably somewhere between five and twenty and five and thirty.

Helen smiled. "I would like to paint you like that."

"Hmm. Mama would have hysterics. Hurry and change into your own evening gown, Helen. You want to catch the early arrivals on their way to the concert."

For evening, they had agreed that Helen should abandon the cap, which made her look like a particularly well-dressed parlor maid, and wear a mask instead. But her style was the opposite of Alice's. She wore an old gray evening gown, some past concession to mourning for a distant relation, and a silver-gray mask.

"Understated," Alice approved. "And just a little mysterious. Perfect."

Satisfied, Helen moved away. "I'll be back before you go on stage."

"What is the purpose of the mask, if I'm asked?" Captain Skelton inquired.

Helen considered. "To emphasize that art, whether music or paintings, looks deeper than the naked eye."

"Oh, very good!"

Helen grinned back. "I thought so."

The tickets for the concert had not sold out, but they were still expecting a sizeable audience, many of whom came early specifically to look at the paintings.

"Insipid," pronounced one brash man not yet in his forties.

Helen cringed and pretended not to hear.

"My dear, how can you say so?" the lady with him exclaimed. "Because they are watercolors and not oils? Look at these of the ruined abbey and think again. They are not insipid—they are delicate."

Helen tried not to preen.

At the door, North sent away a parcel of ruffians. The disparaging gentleman bought the whole abbey set. Helen felt her cheeks burn pink with pleasure as she took his card and wrote down his name and addresses for Skelton's men to deliver the pictures tomorrow. This would cover a good deal of their expenses.

"Why the mask?" the lady with her customer asked.

"Publicity trick," her husband said with a hint of a sneer.

"Something like that," Helen replied. "I'm sure you will understand once the pianist appears on stage. I know you will enjoy the concert. Thank you for your custom, sir, ma...dam."

She almost forgot to speak the final syllable, for Mrs. Maven was sweeping through the foyer, resplendent in gold, diamonds, and lace. And by her side was Alice's admirer, Mr. Glover.

Somehow, Helen managed to smile and bid goodbye to her customers, but her mind was racing with speculation and dread. Why had the woman come back here? Why had she brought Glover? Had she just given up on Roderick and found her next favorite? Yes, that must be it. There were not so many entertainments in Whalen with pretensions to gentility. This event would be perfect for their embarking on a courtship...

Only, could one really go straight from Roderick to this callow, fickle youth? Of course, love was unpredictable and uncontrollable. And considering what Mrs. Maven had done to Roderick at the ball, she could not possibly be in love with him.

But she could still be angry.

"Oh, come and see the pictures," Mrs. Maven said, her voice sounding clearly over the general babble. "I'll show you the one I have bought..." She almost dragged poor Mr. Glover in Helen's direction.

Oh yes, the woman *had* recognized her earlier, and now she was set on mischief. And Helen could not rely on her mask to keep her identity from Mr. Glover. Surely he would recognize her as soon as she spoke. Could she swear him to secrecy? Perhaps, but it might still cause a scene, and in any case, she could not discount some deeper malice on the part of Mrs. Maven.

There was only one solution.

Pretending she was summoned by another customer, she walked swiftly away and swerved toward Captain Skelton, who stood by the auditorium door looking suave and watchful.

"I need to see my sister," she said. "Will you take the cards of anyone interested? I'll only be a moment or two."

Although he frowned, Skelton nodded. He could hardly be as watchful as he wished if he was dealing with her customers. But perhaps there would be none.

She fled down the passage to the dressing room, knowing she had only a few moments before Alice went on stage, and every instinct told her to warn her sister against Mrs. Maven and the presence of Glover.

But even as she burst through the door, she realized the unkindness of saying anything at all about it. Alice was about to go on stage, alone, the center of all these people's attention. Her nerves were already in pieces. She was terrified by this, her first public performance. Helen could not possibly distract her with this new trouble now.

Besides, she remembered with relief as she almost did not recognize her own sister, Alice was in disguise. Mrs. Maven could point to all the similarities she liked. The very idea would be preposterous to Mr. Glover.

"I almost missed the time," Helen blurted instead, seizing her sister's shaking hands. "You will hold all eyes and then all ears. I know it. They are desperate here for music like yours, and you are especially good!"

"I feel sick," Alice said. "I wish we had never begun this idiocy."

"Oh, no, it's going wonderfully. I sold my abbey pictures. Now it's your turn."

A knock at the door sounded. Mr. Pritchard called, "It's time,

Mrs. Connor."

Although he knew perfectly well that they were both unmarried, he had taken to stage custom of addressing Alice as "Mrs."

"Thank you," Alice croaked, staring desperately at Helen.

"Come. I'll wait in the wings, cheering you on." Only until her sister started to play, of course. After that, Alice would be aware of nothing but the music.

At the edge of the stage, Alice let go of her with extreme reluctance, her frightened eyes taking in the huge number of people, more than she had ever played to before. And none of them knew she was an earl's sister.

Except Mrs. Maven, presumably.

Squashing her own fears, Helen smiled. "Go. Be brilliant. Be yourself."

Very slowly, Alice began to walk on stage into the glow of the light. The noise in the auditorium quietened as everyone stared at her in eager curiosity. She was still trembling, for the skirts of her gown shivered minutely.

She sat. She laid her shaking fingers across the keys. And played.

With a sigh of relief, Helen bolted back to the foyer, releasing Captain Skelton to patrol the auditorium if necessary. The foyer was empty, except for North, whose head was cocked as though he were listening to the music. It was faint, muffled by the doors, but still superb. Helen smiled and wanted to weep with pride.

RODERICK RETURNED TO Blackhaven exhausted but triumphant, with several commissions to write in the book. Although Skelton and North would still be away on their first booking at the theater, he wanted to leave the news for them coming back.

Trent the innkeeper let him in to Skelton's room, where the book was kept, and left him to sit and write in the work he had obtained. When he had finished, he left the book open on the wobbly desk and swung away. A theater flyer drifted down to the floor, and he bent to pick it up.

He had never inquired as to the nature of the exhibition or the evening performance they were protecting... An exhibition of drawings and paintings, mostly watercolors, and a piano recital by a Mrs. Connor.

No. It couldn't be...

He closed his eyes. *It could.* She had hidden it from him. There was pain in that, but mostly there was fear. For her safety in a crowd, in a theater full of louts. The protection of Skelton and North and two little-known employees was not nearly enough against desperate townsmen who had rioted only last month.

Why had he not seen that before?

Because then, Helen had not been involved. Because she and Alice were earl's daughters, and God knew what havoc recognition would cause. Dear God, they were in massive danger, and Skelton... Did Skelton even know? Skelton was not up to this idiocy, this menace!

Roderick was being unreasonable, and he knew it. But he was anxious and furious, and God help him, he wanted to share her triumph. Why had she not told him? Had she not trusted him to be in command? Did she consider the still-recovering Skelton more protection than him?

He stormed out of Skelton's room, stuffing the flyer in his pocket, and clattered downstairs. "Trent! Will you stable my horse and lend me another?"

Chapter Eleven

DESPITE HIS EFFORTS to reason with himself, Roderick's feelings of dread only increased on his ride through the dark. He prayed he would have no worse to deal with than Skelton's affronted glare at his unnecessary interference.

He trusted Skelton and North. But they did not know all the facts, that the clients had unknown enemies merely by their birth, that they were prime targets for blackmail, theft, and ransom of all types.

Whalen was not quiet. The local watch were breaking up a drunken brawl at the docks. And as Roderick rode on toward the town center and the theater, he became aware of another, noisy disturbance. A fast-moving riot that made his blood run cold.

He urged his horse on faster until, ahead, he could make out a large group of mostly young men, running behind a torch-bearing leader. Such angry protests against lack of work, poor wages, and hunger were not uncommon these days. Roderick had seen them before—rampages of destruction and helpless fury that ended, generally, in the arrest of the chief perpetrators and no change whatever, unless for the worse.

He had some sympathy, but not with *this* demonstration. Not when they were surging down the street toward the theater, and as far as he knew Helen and her sister were still there. Skelton had not the men to deal with this.

They'll shelter in the theater, Roderick realized with some relief. *Barricade themselves in, if necessary.* The worst danger would be the damned torch, but so far at least that seemed to be merely to light the way, not to set fires.

He almost dismounted to appear less threatening, but some instinct, perhaps the one that had always saved himself and the bulk of his men right up until Waterloo, warned him something about the whole scene was *wrong.* The apparent riot was rowdy enough, loud enough to be terrifying, but it moved too fast. They did not pause to destroy, to shout; they carried no placards, called no chants to make their demands or declare their cause.

He glanced hastily up the side street that led to the more affluent part of town—why had they not gone that way, toward those who had power and wealth?—and saw a carriage pulled by two smart horses that looked vaguely familiar.

In front of it, watching the riot proceed, was the anxious figure of a young man. Roderick was sure he had seen him before too, though he wasted no time on remembering from where, for the woman beside him was intimately known. Meg Maven in flowing silk and lace, sparkling with jewels.

Now Roderick's nerves screamed. The rioters increased their pace as they approached the theater, and over their heads he made out the shape of another carriage. There was no coachman on the box. If North had been there, he could just have whipped up the horses and charged through, but as it was, the rioters could push the carriage over, set it on fire, attack whoever was inside and tried to escape… *Please, God, don't let it be her. Let it be empty…*

He did not wait to find out, spurring his horse into a gallop, as though on a cavalry charge. His hand even automatically went to his side for his sword. Vaguely aware of human footsteps pounding after him with no hope of catching up, he kept his gaze on the carriage and the theater front.

Someone exploded from the front doors and leapt for the carriage box. From the size of him alone, it had to be Pat North. *Drive, for God's sake—why don't you go?* The rioters were almost upon him—but Roderick saw why he waited.

Lady Helen Conway emerged from the theater and halted as though stunned by the scene before her. His own two employees, Harper and Black, followed hastily as though arguing with her.

"Back inside!" Roderick yelled, but even if they had heard him, it was too late. Helen started instinctively toward the carriage.

If Roderick knew anything, it was how to deal with terror in battle. He ignored it, planned through it, even as a small group of men barged past the carriage to Helen, surrounding her, trying to separate her from her escort. Harper and Black struggled valiantly, trying to keep with her, but they were unarmed and too few to protect her in this melee. However, Roderick was mounted, and that had to be advantage enough.

The bulk of the rioters were banging the side of the carriage, yelling at North, who was standing up on the box, laying about him with his whip. As Roderick charged his horse straight at the rioters, he glimpsed Lady Alice's pale face at the carriage window. And behind her, Skelton, his pistol drawn, though he knew better than to use it in such a situation.

"Sir!" North yelled. "The other—"

"I know!" Roderick shouted back, scattering men to right and left. "Drive! Now!" He kicked the man wrenching at the carriage door, sending him sprawling, and the already-furious horses bolted into action, flying up the road.

Roderick didn't waste time watching. His poor, confused horse whinnied wildly as he forced it to continue the charge at the men who not only surrounded Helen but were dragging her away. A couple of others seemed to be doing no more than distracting Harper and Black, engaging them in a fight so their fellows could abduct Helen.

Roderick had never missed his sword—or any weapon—so much. He barged the abductors, reaching down from the saddle to haul one man by his collar and hurl him into his fellows who were fighting Harper and Black. It gave his men a chance while he battered another rioter in the head with his elbow and his fist slammed into someone else's face.

Something glinted in the torchlight, a slashing silver blade, hacking at his arm. He ignored it, for Helen, bless her, stamped on her most persistent captor's foot and lunged toward him. He reached down for her, their hands clasped, and he hauled her up into the saddle behind him.

"Yah!" he yelled at his horse, who needed no second urging to flee. With a last buffet of his fist at the armed man, they were free, galloping down the road. Other images tried to take over— galloping down other streets in captured Spanish towns, fleeing from indefensible attacks from within, the horror of Badajoz... But he would not recall battles here, not *any* battles.

Helen clung to his waist, holding him in the present, anchoring him. They were not safe yet. He twisted around. peering beyond her in the direction of the theater. No one was in pursuit. He slowed the horse. The carriage was clear away, although the rioters, oddly fewer in number now, pursued it, and more melted into the shadows as they went.

Harper and Black picked themselves off the road and dusted themselves down. They were safe too, apart, presumably, from a few painful bruises. Another man stood beside them, hatless, and Roderick remembered someone on foot behind him when he'd galloped toward the fray. Trying to help? Perhaps.

With the action complete, memory swamped him. He fought it with anger.

"What were you thinking of?" he demanded between his teeth. "What *idiocy* compelled you do such a thing—in *Whalen*, of all places!—without telling a soul?"

The words exploded without permission. He knew they were unfair, and that added to his rage. At least he could not see the hurt on her face as he urged the horse on.

"Not a soul?" she repeated coldly. "Apart from the company we hired to protect us. Your company, major, I believe?"

"You didn't give Skelton the facts, did you? He has no idea

who you are."

"You mean Braithwaite's sisters deserve more protection than the poor Misses Connor?"

"Yes," he shouted, and glared up at the sky, fighting the deluge of images that threatened to drag him away.

Helen reached past him, seizing his arm. "Roderick, your arm," she said in fright. "You're dripping... Is that blood?"

He glanced at it impatiently, and it immediately began to hurt. The knife had slashed right through his coat, making a long cut in his forearm. He couldn't see the wound, just the blood. It didn't help with the battle images crowding his mind.

"It's minor." He didn't know whether it was or not, and he barked out the words with unintended anger.

Behind him, her voice came cold and polite, an unspoken and well-deserved reprimand. "Where are we going? Should we not be catching up with the carriage?"

"Not like this. There used to be a decent inn on the edge of town. We'll hire a carriage there."

"And summon a doctor."

"I don't need a doctor. Others do..."

"Who?" she demanded, and he shook his head to clear it.

He was sweating with the effort to keep back the memories, and he was sure the dreams were waiting.

"The George Inn," he said, because she had to know. But he could not leave her alone. He straightened in the saddle, concentrating on the feel of her arms, her scent, her closeness, the sound of her voice, even if the words seemed unimportant.

Don't lose her, don't lose her, don't lose her... The command repeated in his mind, and somehow, he held on.

HELEN'S FRIGHT AT the riot awaiting her outside the theater, her fear for Alice and for herself, vanished in the heat of her much greater fear for Roderick.

He had been magnificent, like a knight of old on his white charger, swooping down from nowhere to rescue them all. It had been easy to fight her way to him, bliss to hold him in the saddle, her secret tears of relief and wonder soaking into his coat.

Until he had verbally attacked her.

Although she would not let him away with it, she understood the attack was all part of his anger, the uncertain temper that had haunted him since Waterloo. Part of the same condition that had him leaping for cover at loud noises and fed nightmares, both asleep and awake.

What terrified her more was the bleeding wound in his arm and the increasing rigidity of his body, interspersed by sudden twitches. And he was not answering her. Nevertheless, it was he who guided them to the George Inn.

An ostler hurried to meet them.

She dismounted hastily without help, preserving what dignity she could.

"Stable the horse, if you please—feed and water him," Helen said. She almost expected Roderick to be still in the saddle, staring straight ahead, but he slid down beside her, relinquishing the reins to the ostler without a word. In the light of the stable lanterns, beads of sweat stood out on his forehead. Trickles ran down his face.

She took his arm, guiding him into the house, where they were greeted by the innkeeper's wife.

"There has been an accident," Helen said briskly and quite inventively. "My horse has bolted and my husband is injured." It was a respectable inn. If they were not married, they might be refused. "Some hot water and bandages are required, and if you would send for the nearest doctor—"

"No doctor," Roderick said distinctly.

By the inn's cheerful lights, he looked white and ill. She made another decision.

"No doctor until I look at it myself. We had better have a

bedchamber," she said to the innkeeper's wife. "You can bring the bandages there."

The woman issued instructions to a maid and led the way upstairs to a decent bedchamber, which she showed off with some pride, lighting the lamps as she went.

"Thank you," Helen said. "Could you send up something to eat? Some broth, perhaps? And brandy."

"Of course, Mrs....?"

"Connor," Helen said, instinctively avoiding the names of Conway and Vale, and the woman hurried off.

Roderick still stood, rigid, in the middle of the room. Helen led him by the hand to the bed, much as she'd led him to the meeting room after the slamming door at the ball. Except this time, his eyes were not glazed. He knew where he was.

"Sit," she said, tugging gently, and he sank onto the bed.

Helen lit a branch of candles on the table and brought them over. "Can you take off the coat?" she asked. "Or will I find scissors to cut it away?"

For answer, he bent his head, took the fabric between his teeth, and, with a clearly practiced gesture, tore with his good hand. It ruined his coat and shirt, and sleeve buttons rolled across the floor, but it was quick.

A maid came in with a bowl of water, clean rags, a bottle of brandy, and two glasses. Helen thanked her and set about cleaning the wound. He wiped his sleeve across his face and watched her face rather than his own wound.

"It does not disgust you," he observed.

"We were all brought up to be ladies of large houses and estates. Caring for illness and injury is part of that. Or should be. You must have been moving, spoiling his aim for a deep wound. I don't think it needs stitches, but we should ask a physician."

He glanced carelessly at the still sluggishly bleeding wound. "It's minor. I can bandage it myself." He even reached for the bandages, but Helen batted his hand away.

"I need to be sure it is clean."

He lifted up the brandy bottle instead, unstoppered it, and splashed the contents liberally over his arm. A hissing sound came from between his clenched teeth, but he showed no other sign of pain. Helen placed a makeshift dressing over the wound and began to bind it. Again, he watched her face.

"Alice will make them come back for me," she said, thinking aloud. "They won't know where to find us."

"Skelton will follow my orders. He'll take her back to the castle. He knows you are safe with me."

"How can he possibly know that?"

"Because Black and Harper from the theater will report it to him. They're probably all together again by now."

"What if the rioters catch them again?"

"The riot disintegrated as soon as I got you away."

She paused, frowning up at him. "What do you mean?"

"I mean it surged out of nowhere, to very little audience. Everything happened really quickly and then faded away. That's not a riot, it's a distraction."

"With what purpose?"

"You, of course. And Skelton was not expecting it because he had no idea who you were."

"What difference would that have made?"

He did not answer, just rubbed his forehead until she finished tying the bandage and poured a glass of brandy, which she thrust at him.

He took it absently, then after a moment remembered to thank her.

By then, the oddities of the day and the evening were crowding her mind. She said, "Your jeweled lady, Mrs. Maven, came to the exhibition this morning. She even bought a painting. And she came back for the recital with Mr. Glover."

"Who is Mr. Glover?"

"He is a guest at the castle. Alice's rejected suitor, although she insists he has switched allegiance to me."

Roderick nodded as if this made sense.

"The funny thing is," Helen said, frowning, "there was a moment outside the theater tonight when I thought I saw him charging toward us, as though to help."

"Don't trust him," Roderick said.

She blinked.

His eyes refocused on her. "I would not be surprised if he and Meg cooked this whole thing up between them."

"But that's ridiculous! Who would start a riot just to frighten Alice and me?"

"Someone with a grudge and too much money. The grudge is my fault; the opportunity is yours."

Combative once more, he sprang to his feet and staggered. She reached for him at once, but he had already sat hurriedly back down.

"Damn it, I feel weak as a kitten," he growled.

"You fought off the dreams, didn't you?" she said softly. "You're exhausted. We shall stay here tonight."

"We most certainly shall not. When you don't come home, your sister will raise the alarm, and when we are found—as we will be—your reputation will be ruined."

"Alice will know what Captain Skelton knows. She will hide my absence at least until tomorrow morning."

A knock on the door interrupted whatever reply he was about to make, and the maid brought in two bowls of steaming broth and half a loaf of bread with cheese and fruit. When she had gone, Helen brought him a bowl and placed it on the bedside table with a slice of bread.

He ate it without standing up. Helen ate hers beside him. But his eyes kept closing and then flying open as he forced himself to stay awake. Eventually, he set down the spoon, and she took the bowl from him.

"Let me help you with your coat," she said.

Almost like a child, he allowed it. Then he rolled himself in the coverlet on top of the bed and lay down. He seemed to be asleep as soon as his head touched the pillow.

She hesitated, wondering whether to send for a doctor after all. He had been so set against it, and was it really her place to insist? He was not about to die. If anything, he looked better, less pale. And he was no longer sweating or twitching. She would wait until morning at least, though it would have to be an early start…

Refusing to crumple her dress, she managed to unfasten and remove it before splashing water over her hands and face. She doused all the lamps and padded back toward the bed.

Her heart drummed because it felt so daring to climb into bed beside him. He might have been on top of the blankets and she beneath, but she could hear his deep, even breathing. She could smell the scent of his body. If she reached out, she could touch him.

She turned, moving as close as she dared. She felt all warm and excited to have him so close in this strange intimacy. It made her imagine him under the covers with her, touching, kissing her good night.

Roderick's kisses…

She imagined herself holding him, kissing him back, and her whole world drowned in sweetness as she drifted into slumber.

Chapter Twelve

MEG WAS FURIOUS as she watched Roderick charge down the road and spoil all her plans. Although it would hardly ruin her, she had paid a fair bit of money to hire all these men, and she liked to get her money's worth. And here was damned Roderick, exploding out of nowhere to ruin everything.

Poor Glover would be superfluous. And Roderick, not Glover, would be the hero to the girl. Exactly what Meg did not want. It took Roderick mere moments to extract Helen, and not because Meg's men gave in. They knew he was the wrong rescuer because he was not on foot. But he set about them from his horse, snatched the girl from their clutches, and rode off with her behind him in the saddle.

Unwillingly, Meg admired his audacity and efficiency. He had freed the carriage and Helen in one charge and left the man who should have been the savior of the day running uselessly late.

She got back in her carriage. "Drive to the theater," she instructed the coachman.

"But ma'am, all that disturbance—"

"What disturbance?" she said wryly, for shadows were already running past her and melting into the opposite side streets. "We must rescue Mr. Glover." Since there was no one else left to save.

Glover was discovered talking to two strangers outside the

theater, with no other threat in sight. Roderick, his charger, and his maiden were nowhere to be seen.

"Thanks for your help, sir," one of the strangers was saying as Meg stepped down from the carriage unaided. Glover did not even appear to be aware of her. "But don't you worry about the young lady. The major has her safe now."

Meg intervened. "Are we to take it, then, that you *know* the man who rode off with the young lady?"

"Yes, ma'am. Our employer."

Well. The little girls had hired guards. She had never imagined they would be so sensible. At least it meant there was a reason Roderick had been hanging about.

The guard who had spoken bowed and presented her with a business card. "If you ever have need of us, ma'am. Excuse us. Got to get back to the others."

They strode back inside the theater, where the nervous manager awaited them.

"Come," Meg said to Glover. "The carriage will take me home and then return you to Braithwaite Castle."

"But what of Lady Helen?"

She had already climbed inside, so he was forced to join her to talk. "Presumably Major Vale will take her safely home."

He glowered at her. "I did not know you were arranging anything so dangerous."

"My dear sir," she drawled, "there is no point in rescuing her from a situation that is *not* dangerous. Rest assured, our rioters were well paid to drop her in terror as soon as you appeared."

"So we frightened the wits out of the poor girl for nothing."

Meg did not like to have failure cast in her face. "Oh, cheer up, Mr. Glover. All is not yet lost. You saw both young ladies at the theater. You saw one of them alone in a closed carriage with one man, and Lady Helen rode off into the distance on the same horse as a gentleman of very dubious reputation. If you cannot make something of that with her brother, then you do not deserve her."

He stared at her. "Are you suggesting I blackmail Lord Braithwaite into letting me marry his sister?"

Meg shrugged. "How much do you want her? But I did not mention blackmail. Be creative, Mr. Glover. She is not home yet."

DESPITE THE LUMPY mattress and the strangeness of the room, Helen slept heavily. She half woke once during the night as the mattress moved and dipped, as though, behind her, Roderick was turning over. It made her smile. Whatever happened, she would never regret sharing this night with him. But she was far too sleepy to turn over and look. Instead, she drifted off once more, his distinctive scent at once closer, cleaner, and earthier than before...

She woke again, still in darkness, with a warm body plastered to her back. Awareness was gradual and ultimately stunning.

At some point in the night, Roderick had climbed under the covers. More than that, he was naked save for the bandage around his arm. She knew that was there because it rested on her waist, warm and heavy through her shift. For a little, she just lay and absorbed the sensation. No one save Alice or one of her other sisters had ever shared a bed with her, and those few occasions had been for warmth in some drafty inn during one of the family's many journeys between Blackhaven and London.

This was very, very different. This was a *man*, the hardness of his arousal pressed to her thigh. Her heart beat, and beat so loudly it should have wakened him. For he did appear to be asleep, his breathing deep and even. Her stomach tingled with unfamiliar desires.

Well, they were not *entirely* unfamiliar, but they were more intense and more deeply understood. It was all to do with this man, and his nakedness, and the hot, delightful way it made her feel...

In wonder, she shifted just a little closer. With a sound of satisfaction, somewhere between a sigh and a growl, he tightened his arm around her, and that astonishing shaft of hardness slid forward between her legs, causing her to gasp with wonder. His hand splayed across her stomach, his thumb touching her breast, his little finger almost at the heated juncture of her thighs.

Oh my… Should she move? Part of her was enjoying the present position too much. The other was curious, restless, wanting more of this closeness. His hand slid upward, over her breast, and relaxed.

I should not allow this.

I want this.

But he is asleep… Isn't he?

Very gently, she shifted, turning on to her back to peer at him in the darkness. Another little grunt of pleasure and he hauled her beneath him, his mouth hot and desperately sensual on hers, his weight a new, exciting pleasure.

He moved against her as though absorbing her shape, her skin, into his own. The effect was devastating. So was the feel of his naked back beneath her trembling fingers, warm and smooth save for the bump of a jagged scar across his left shoulder.

His hand swept downward over her hip in a slow, caressing dance that moved inward over her thigh to the center of her suddenly raging need. She gasped into his mouth. He made an articulate sound of pleasure, and then it was not his hand that slid between her thighs…

She moaned, for she knew what this meant, and she loved and wanted him. It was a marriage, private and beautiful and *necessary.*

He broke the amazing kiss at last. Some hint of pale daylight must have seeped through a crack in the shutters, for she could see his eyes were open and staring down at her.

He rolled off her with lightning speed. "Dear God, I'm sorry," he said hoarsely. "Forgive me."

"Th-there is nothing to forgive," she managed, stunned all

over again by the swiftness of rejection.

He sat on the edge of the bed, reaching for something on the floor. Judging by his subsequent movements, it must have been his breeches.

She shook now from quite different feelings, but somehow, she managed to light the bedside lamp.

"There is no need to panic," she said, more coldly than she had intended, probably an instinctive covering for her hurt.

"There is every reason," he replied in similar tones. "Even you, Helen, must be aware of the dangers of climbing into the same bed as a naked man."

She stared at him. He stood at the side of the bed, shirtless, glaring down at her. There was a pattern of scars across his right arm, and a few more on his chest.

"*I* did not remove your clothes," she retorted.

His gaze fell. He might have blushed. He dragged his fingers through his hair. "No, I did that, didn't I? I was half-asleep. I forgot you were there."

Hardly flattering. "I'll try not to let it go to my head."

Ignoring her, he strode to the washing bowl and splashed water over his face and neck. His back rippled, making her shiver.

"Don't get the bandage wet," she warned, trying to be practical. "I should change the dressing before we leave."

"It's fine," he said distantly, rubbing himself dry and then pulling on his shirt. "Let's just get this nightmare over with."

Her blood froze. *Nightmare?* This precious night was merely a nightmare to him?

"Yes, do let us get on with it," she said, her voice curiously small and hard. She slid out of bed and threw her gown over her head.

She used her fingers, viciously, to comb her hair, then shoved it into a rough bun behind her head, jabbing in the pins with unnecessary force. She did not look at him.

At last, he said, "Do you want help with the hooks?"

"No, it's fine," she said, swinging the cloak around her and looking for her bonnet. He was fully dressed in cravat and coat, holding his gloves.

"We should have breakfast first," he said more gently, "and inquire about hiring a carriage."

"I have no time or money for breakfast," she snapped. "After all, I shall have to pay you more for the extra time as it is."

She was being deliberately insulting, and they both knew it. Perhaps he even knew why. But he chose to play the only adult in the room.

"Then perhaps you will think twice before committing any other such folly."

Helen had had enough. "What on earth makes you imagine you have any say in how I conduct my life?"

"The right of friendship and—"

She laughed. "Friendship? Sir, you have insulted me in every way I can imagine. I am not your friend. More to the point, you are not mine. You blow hot and cold so often that I am dizzy and will tolerate no more of it. You can't have it both ways. You cannot ask me to stay away from you and choose someone else if opportunity offers, and then try to interfere in my life. I know which of us needs to grow up, Roderick, and it is not me."

His face had whitened again, an odd, stricken look in his eyes. But she would not give in, not again. Understanding did not work for him, and in any case, she was far too angry.

She swept out of the room, leaving the door wide open, and sailed downstairs.

OF COURSE, HER stomach rumbled all the way back to Blackhaven. She felt guilty about giving Roderick no time to eat more than a hunk of bread and cheese. She bit her lip when his horse was brought out to him, saddled and ready.

"You intend to ride?" she blurted. "With your injured arm?"

"I won't use it," he said indifferently, opening the carriage door for her. He lowered his voice. "I don't want this horse sent back to Trent at the King's Head, where he came from, with tales of how he arrived here at the George. Nor do I want you seen in a closed carriage with me."

His gloved hand took hers to hand her inside, and a moment later, she was shut away from him.

There would be no chance of apology from either of them on the journey, let alone reconciliation. Only more misery. He had saved her last night. But on the other hand, he'd implied it was all her fault anyway. Resentment still burned, but so did anxiety for him.

The journey was not long, though it felt like an age. She saw him frequently from the window, always upright and alert, but with no hint of the rigidity of last night, when he had seemed held together by a very fine thread. Now he was watchful, as Captain Skelton had been yesterday, frequently riding a little ahead and then dropping back. He held the reins in one hand with casual strength, controlling his mount easily while his injured arm lay mostly still. She wondered how much it hurt and wished she had changed the dressing.

Instead of taking the quicker coastal route, they traveled by the back roads that skirted Blackhaven. To her surprise, the carriage came to a halt in a bare stretch of road some distance from the castle's east gate. A few moments later, Roderick, on foot, opened the door.

"We'll walk from here," he announced.

He was right. Letting her out at the castle gates had lots of potential for unwanted gossip. Here, there were scattered cottages and even a substantial farmhouse visible on the hill. So she stepped down without complaint.

Leading the horse, he instructed the coachman on the quickest route down to the town and the coastal road back to Whalen. He paid the man, who touched his whip to his forehead in gratitude and drove his horses onward.

"Will you be able to slip into the castle unnoticed?" he asked as they began to walk.

She nodded. "No one will be surprised to see me out and about so early. My gown may be a trifle unsuitable, but the cloak covers it up. You will let Dr. Lampton look at your arm?"

"Yes," he said, and Helen, expecting resistance, glanced at him in surprise. His lips twitched. "I am not an actual idiot, contrary to most evidence. Thank you for taking care of it last night."

Tears tightened her throat. "Thank you for rescuing me. And Alice."

He hesitated, then seemed to come to a decision. "I saw her watching the so-called riot. Meg Maven. With Glover. He might be a mere catspaw, appalled into doing his best to rescue you, but until you find out which, you should not trust either of them. Go nowhere alone with them."

"I doubt I could if I wanted to, cocooned once more in the bosom of my family."

His eyebrows tugged together. "You have not planned any more escapes?"

She stared back defiantly, then surprised both of them with a bitter little laugh. "You are just like them after all, aren't you? Keep her wrapped in safety, allow her to dabble in her little hobby so long as she does not step outside the silken box of convention in which she is trapped."

"That is unfair," he said quietly.

"Is it? You have rescued me, berated me, lectured me, warned me, and blamed me, but never once have you asked if we were successful in our event. Or even if we enjoyed it." She turned down the short track that led to the east gate and was fiercely glad that it took him a moment to catch up.

And then two people emerged from the forest, stopping dead to gawp at them.

"Oh dear," she said shakily, unsure whether to laugh or cry. For it was Gervaise and Mr. Glover.

"Thank God," Gervaise said, striding forward and seizing her in a crushing hug.

Helen hugged him back briefly, forcing a laugh as she stepped away. "What a fuss, Gervaise. It is not like you to miss me so much." A genuine fear pierced her guilt. "Nothing is wrong, is it?"

Gervaise's demeanor changed. His gaze lashed Roderick and came back to her. "You tell me," he said coldly. "You vanish for a day and a night, then return in the morning escorted by this…gentleman. Perhaps you will tell me what is *not* wrong?"

Of course, Gervaise's reaction, and Glover's silent presence, said all that was needed. She was rumbled.

Presumably Alice was, too, but Helen would keep the explanation to her own doings, just in case.

"What about the fact that I am here, safe and well?" she said breezily. "For which you may thank Major Vale, when you have recovered your manners."

Gervaise's mouth fell open in shock. She had never been rude to him before—he was too much older, and the kindest of brothers besides.

She turned to Roderick, holding out her hand. "My thanks for your help and your escort, sir."

Roderick did not look as if he would be quite as easily dismissed, and in any case, Gervaise was clearly not having it.

"I am afraid I require an explanation first," he said steadily.

Helen looked from one to the other. Both were imposing in their own way, and neither looked remotely intimidated. Thoughts of fights and duels whirled in her brain, making her wish she and Alice had simply stayed at home. The triumph of the great recital and exhibition crumbled to guilt and fear.

She opened her mouth to say something, anything that might distract Gervaise from Roderick and put the blame at *her* door, where it belonged.

But Roderick spoke first. "I had occasion to do Lady Helen a small service."

"What sort of service?" Gervaise asked.

"A small contretemps from which her ladyship needed to be removed quickly. Her ladyship—and indeed Mr. Glover—will confirm that."

"I can confirm the riot in Whalen," Glover said, flushing, so that Helen knew he had made no mention of it to Gervaise. Why not?

"Riot!" her brother exclaimed, paling. "Dear God, Helen—"

"But not," Glover interrupted, glaring at Roderick, "where she has been since."

Yanked back from natural worry to haughty guardian, Gervaise also stared at Roderick. "Or in whose company."

Alice's? Helen wondered wildly. Could she and her sister save each other here?

"Not Alice's, for she is safe in her bed," Gervaise continued, ending that last faint hope.

Only the truth, or part of it, would serve now. She crossed her fingers behind her back in a gesture reminiscent of Maria, who could never bear confrontations.

"Major Vale was injured," Alice said in a rush. "I would not let him travel in such a condition, and so we stayed the night at an inn in Whalen. Where, before you dare suggest otherwise, he behaved like a perfect gentleman." *Most of the time...* But she could not allow herself to remember those wild, glorious moments, not right now.

Gervaise was completely white now. Worse, desperate disappointment stood out in his eyes. "You expect me to believe that? When I find you strolling through the countryside together like—"

"Don't say what you will regret," Roderick barked. "The fact that you find us on foot proves only that we sent the carriage away before the driver could know who Lady Helen is or where she lives. You will see my own horse only a step down the road. In difficult circumstances, we have done everything possible to preserve the appearance as well as the reality of her ladyship's reputation."

Gervaise stared. "Including staying at a public inn? Where I suppose they will not remember you?"

"They might the remember the major's blood," Helen retort-ed, since her brother seemed to have forgotten this important factor, "but we used a false name."

Too late, she realized she should have used the plural. Names. Definitely not Mr. and Mrs. Connor. She prayed Gervaise wouldn't notice. Color flooded suddenly into his face, implying that he did.

But he said only, "It will not do."

"It will have to," she said. "Truly, Gervaise, there is no harm done."

It was another mistake. The ruin of his youngest sister's repu-tation *was* harm, to her and to the rest of her family, and for her to suggest otherwise to Gervaise put her firmly back into the role of erring child who must be punished and taught the correct path.

Besides, his hurt made him furious.

"Tell that to your mother," he snapped.

It was her turn to pale. "Oh, Gervaise you have not—"

"Of course I haven't!"

Sibling honor held true, but now she knew she would pay.

"But this cannot go on!" he fumed. "I have granted you too much leniency, too much freedom. I cannot trust you to keep within the bounds of propriety. Whatever did or did not happen last night, you will be married within the month and answer to a husband's discipline instead."

Helen's jaw dropped. But there was a way out here. An un-expected path to happiness after all…

"I would be honored to give Lady Helen my name and my heart," Mr. Glover said, so quickly that he might have been expecting it.

She blinked at him. *Not you!*

The silence was deafening. She could not look at Roderick. *Speak, damn you!*

"Since I would appear to be the cause of the ultimatum, Lady Helen may count of my protection if she prefers."

If she prefers? Whatever happened to *Don't trust Glover?*

She cast a withering glance around all three of them. "If I needed protection—which I don't—I would not look to *any* of you for it."

With that, she walked away and did not look back.

Chapter Thirteen

I F RODERICK COULD have given her his own calm as she stormed away from them, he would. She was angry and disgusted with all of them, including her beloved brother, and he didn't blame her in the least. They all deserved her contempt.

Particularly Roderick, and that was clear in her eyes when she glanced so briefly his way. He knew why, of course. He had let Glover make the first offer. But he was damned if he would marry her for such a false reason. She would marry him for love—hers and his—or not at all.

The thought, the sudden, raging desire to be her husband, made him giddy. Everything spun suddenly into place. She was not some distant future to be won when he was "better." She was *now*. She loved him *now*, as he was, broken and damaged, and she helped him feel better, *be* better. And he…

He had always known the gift of her care, her love, was precious, but how could he have been so blind to his own feelings? He had always loved her. Ever since he had seen her across that crowded ballroom, so pure, so vital, so utterly desirable. So terrifying to a man afraid to commit himself to more than a roll in the hay.

I love Helen. With all my heart, I love her. And he had to let her walk away. For now. But it was not over. He would win her, find a way to make her understand that his offer was nothing to do with Braithwaite or reputations. It was all *her*.

The crowded realizations passed through his brain with what he thought of as battle speed. His eyes refocused on her angry brother, who was still glaring at him. So was Glover.

"My offer stands," Roderick said curtly. "And not because of the present situation."

If that surprised Lord Braithwaite, he hid the fact. He could be a haughty bastard. But then, so could Roderick.

"As does mine," Glover said.

"Then unless I discover anything further against either of you, I will allow her to choose between you. The announcement will be made at the ball. Good day." With the curtest, slightest of nods, Gervaise stalked through the gate to the castle after his sister.

Roderick turned in the opposite direction, but not before he had seen the smirk on Glover's face. Helen was unlikely to be allowed out of the castle before the ball now. Glover was staying there and had access to her every day. Besides which, Roderick remembered, Helen's mother favored Glover, though for Alice, not Helen.

When was the damned ball, anyway? Surely at the end of this week?

Roderick remounted his borrowed horse and rode into Blackhaven, where he was fortunate enough to find Dr. Lampton free and willing to look at his injured arm. The last thing he needed now was infection from the wound. But Lampton pronounced it clean, smeared some disgusting-looking potion on it, and put on a clean dressing.

"You'll live," the doctor said, handing him a small jar of what looked like the same ointment. "Re-dress it each day and use a little of this on the wound."

"What does it do?" Roderick asked, eyeing the jar with disfavor.

"Reduces infection and speeds up healing."

"What's in it?"

"No idea," Lampton said. "And I don't have an inexhaustible supply, so do not waste it. Good day."

Roderick liked him, so he shook Lampton's hand and departed. Having returned the borrowed horse to the King's Head, he retrieved his own and rode home to Black Hill. It took him a long time, because he kept stopping to admire the view and then staring at it, lost in thought.

He had not gone to pieces in the crisis of the riot and Helen's attempted abduction. Even afterward, though it was hard, he had been able to force himself to stave off the nightmares—well, at least to think through them. He had not lost himself completely, though it was probably fortunate that no one had fired a gun in his vicinity. But this proved he could do it. He *was* recovering.

He rode on, stopping again to appreciate the view of the sea crashing against the rocks. This was a beautiful place. Should he stay here, continue with the promising business he had begun with Skelton? Or leave that to his comrade and return to the army?

He would likely be sent overseas, to Canada or the West Indies or Gambia... He had never been to any of these places. It would be fun, and Helen would like to see the world, he was sure. And he would see things through fresh eyes if she were with him. He would not like her to stay at home while he went without her, perhaps for years at a time...

He would ask her when he managed to see her. It was a decision for both, but at least he felt he had a choice now. He *could* return to the army.

Realizing that he was damp, that rain was not just pattering but deluging to the extent he could no longer make out the sea, he pulled up his collar and rode home.

Here there was great rejoicing, and Lucy glowed with happiness because apparently she really was betrothed to the same Lord Eddleston she had been reviling forever. Julius appeared to like the man, and Lucy herself was the best judge of character they knew, so Roderick, suspending final judgment, resolved to be friendly in the meantime.

In fact, young Eddleston was immensely likeable, and quite up to the challenge of the Vales *en masse*, even the twins. He bantered with Lucy, and they made each other and everyone else laugh. It came to Roderick that Lucy would never be able to twist Eddleston around her little finger, as she did with most people. Instead, he had the feeling Eddleston would merely join in her mischief. Was that a good thing?

"Will he do?" Roderick asked Felicia in a low murmur as dinner came to a close.

Felicia smiled. "He is everything I ever wanted for her."

A ringing endorsement. And so both Lucy and Julius would soon be married. Eddleston would take Lucy away, and Antonia Macy would become mistress of Black Hill—and rightly so, for she made Julius happy and accepted all the oddities of the Vale household. Everything was changing. Roderick, too, would leave soon, sooner than he had meant to, although perhaps he should stay longer to make sure the others were contented in the new arrangement. Delilah and Felicia, the twins, Aubrey... Cornelius would stay as steward. He enjoyed it, though it must be hard and lonely work.

"When is the Braithwaite ball?" he asked into the general hubbub.

"Friday," Lucy said. "Are you actually going to attend without a fuss?"

"Of course. I am too terrified of old Lady Braithwaite to offend her in the slightest."

Three days. Three days to make everything right.

IT WAS THE evening after the recital before Meg realized she had not received her painting. She had been promised delivery that morning. Perhaps the Braithwaite girl was spiteful. More likely she was too terrified by the later events of the evening to organize delivery to her patrons.

What on earth was an earl's sister doing selling her own paintings, anyway? Admittedly, they were pretty, and some people had appeared to consider them good, but heavens above, did the girl not have money enough?

The next morning, Meg wore one of her favorite walking dresses in a bright shade of lilac and strolled into the breakfast parlor.

She could not hide her gasp of sudden fear.

"Good morning, Meg," Roderick said, turning from the window to face her.

He was stunning, her Roderick. All hard lines and lean muscle. Handsome, desirable, heroic. She almost regretted his imperfection, although it was the only hold she had over him. Why the devil had her butler not told her the man was here? No doubt because the servants were used to seeing him at all hours of the day and night. She had never rescinded the order that he was always welcome. She had just stopped expecting him.

"Roderick," she drawled. "What a pleasant surprise. Have you come to join me for breakfast? Ring for Harrison."

"I sent him away, and I have not come for breakfast."

"No?" She sat down and poured herself tea from the pot before reaching for the toast, over which she regarded him with mocking invitation. "Then why have you come, after so long an absence?"

He indicated the parcel propped against the empty fireplace. "To deliver your painting, of course."

"Ah, yes. *Miss Connor's* pretty daubing. You are her messenger boy now?"

"No. I bring my own message."

"You miss me?" She kept it light, but she wished with surprising strength for it to be true.

"I always meant there to be honesty between us, so I will tell you in all truth that no, I don't miss you."

She couldn't deny to herself that it hurt, but she would never show that pain to him.

"I will further tell you," said that relentless voice, "that your ridiculous charade yesterday put far too many lives in danger, and if I ever even catch a whiff of your doing anything similar, I will have you charged. Furthermore, you will leave that lady and her entire family out of your vendetta against me."

She smiled with genuine amusement. "Roderick," she chided, "I have no vendetta against you. Of course I don't. On the contrary, I intend to marry you."

For the first time ever, she had the pleasure of surprising him. It did not make her feel good. She hadn't expected him to look quite so…appalled.

"Oh, stop sulking, Roddy," she said. "You know how good we are together. I may not have a title or family who can be traced back to the Conqueror—whoever he was. But I am strong and passionate, as you are. Together we can light up the whole world, not just this dismal little neighborhood. Cards on the table, my dear—I want you, and I am prepared to fight for you."

He did not look angry, but there was some emotion in his harsh face as he walked across and stood looking down at her, a faint frown on his brow, quite at odds with the unexpected gentleness in his eyes.

"Very well, Meg. Cards on the table. Some things cannot be won by money, gaming, schemes, or threats. I am one of them. We both know I am no catch. And we both know you don't love me in the slightest. I have not treated you well, and for that I apologize unreservedly. But for the rest, we will never be married, and I meant everything I said this morning."

Meg laughed. It sounded just a little too strident for genuine amusement. "What, you mean to marry the milk-and-water aristo? You'll be bored before your wedding night is half over. Good grief, one word from me and she'll—"

He did not touch her, but quite suddenly her blood chilled in her veins and the words dried up in her tightened throat. She had never seen his eyes so hard, like winter ice that could crack at any moment and drown her. She shivered.

"She will what, Meg?" His voice was so soft and cold that she forgot to breathe. "You will stay away from her and from her family and from me. Is that understood?"

"Oh, don't be so melo—"

"*Is it understood?*"

"Yes," she whispered.

He turned on his heel and walked out.

Meg stared after him, contemplating the ruin of her plans, all her wasted time... With one swift sweep of her arm, she sent tea, crockery, and toast flying off the table and crashing to the floor.

If only he had still been there to hear it, he would have been gibbering on the floor.

She frowned suddenly. Was that how the girl had done it? Fed him sympathy and motherly care? He wanted that more than the bed sport she provided?

I could give him both.

That thought needed further exploration. As the servants buzzed in, clearing up the mess she had made, she sat back from the table, deep in contemplation. Another demonstration, perhaps, where it would be Meg who took him to safety and soothed him... Yes, it could be done, if only she could get near him.

But of course she could! That was why she'd had Glover give her his card for the Braithwaite ball. It would be perfect. She would take Roderick from under her ladyship's youthful nose, and be perfectly gracious while she did so, for after all, the Braithwaites were important in every part of the country.

She sprang to her feet, walking around her busy servants as though they did not exist. Once she had been in their lowly position, but no longer. She had been delighted to be the wealthy Mrs. Maven, but to be Mrs. Roderick Vale would be a step up socially.

An instant of self-awareness troubled her, slowing her step.

There were other men with more than him, men more easily manipulated. Like Glover, for example. She could be a countess if she exerted herself to even half this extent, and yet here she was, plotting this hard to become the wife of a mere second son. Roderick might, at a pinch, inherit the baronetcy, but his elder brother showed no signs of croaking. On the contrary, Sir Julius was engaged to be married, and there were likely to be children. Meg was very unlikely ever to be Lady Vale.

I don't care.

Titles were not everything. Roderick could provide the heroic cachet she wanted, and entry to the best of Society. That was all she had ever wanted.

Relieved to have this slight anomaly understood in her own mind, she carried on to her boudoir and summoned her maid. It was time to plan her costume, as well as her final, victorious campaign.

She liked that idea so much, she actually smiled at her maid.

FOR HELEN, THE only redeeming feature of her return to the castle was that so far, at least, Alice was not implicated in her disgrace.

Of course they exchanged news as soon as Helen was sent sternly to her room. She went without fuss because she needed to be alone—after she had ensured Alice was unhurt and they decided the best way forward.

Only seconds after she closed her door, a scratch on the outside heralded the arrival of a bleary-eyed but determined Alice flying across the room.

"Thank God you're back! Where have you *been?*" Alice clutched her by both elbows, glaring at her with a familiar mixture of relief and annoyance.

"Major Vale got me away from the rioters—it turns out *he* is

Captain's Skelton's elusive partner. But he was injured in the fight, and we had to stay the night at an inn in Whalen."

"Succinct," Alice said, still staring. "Now the details."

"After yours."

"The coach was attacked. Your major charged the rioters—"

"He is not *my* major," Helen said in a hard voice.

Alice looked skeptical but otherwise ignored the interruption. "The horses took off at the gallop, which bounced us all over the place, and I could not make Captain Skelton go back for you. For such an amiable fellow, he was unexpectedly firm, even when I probably sounded hysterical and ordered him like a servant, and threatened him with no pay. He just said calmly that the major had it in hand and would bring you to catch up with us before we reached Blackhaven."

"He didn't."

"No, he didn't. Were you *hurt?*"

Helen shook her head. "No, they pulled me a bit, separating me from Mr. Harper and Mr. Black. I admit I was getting genuinely frightened when I saw the major riding to save me." Her voice wobbled.

"It must have been quite magnificent."

"It was quick," Helen said, refusing to admit the magnificence. "I stamped on the most impudent fellow's toe and managed to get close enough to grab the major's hand. He pulled me up into the saddle and we rode off. That was when I realized he was bleeding and that our riot had dispersed. He told me the other fellows would catch up with Captain Skelton and explain we were safe and on our way."

Alice nodded. "That happened. Only you did not. The men helped me unload all the stuff, and even carried it to the side door for me. I was terrified we would be seen, but we got away with it. It took me ages to cart everything back to our room, but I was glad to be occupied until you came back. Only you didn't. I fell asleep sitting up. Why are you looking so…like Maria when she's been scolded?"

Helen tried to smile, sinking down onto the bed. "I have been scolded. Gervaise saw Major Vale escorting me to the castle gate and thought the worst. Apparently, I am no longer allowed out of the castle grounds for any purpose without him, Frances, Eleanor, or Mama. What's more, I am to marry, though I have kindly been given the choice between Glover—who was there listening to everything—and Major Vale."

"Oh, Helen." Alice sat beside her, blinking rapidly. "Oh dear... He'll calm down, of course, providing he has not told Mama."

"He hasn't, but he will."

"Leave him to us. And Eleanor." Alice frowned. "What does he actually know?"

"That I was in Whalen—he does not seem to know about you, and we should keep it that way, lest you find yourself married too."

Alice giggled, which at least relieved the tension in Helen's aching body. "Well, he's bound to ask for more details. Only..." She frowned. "Why is he so angry when he does not even know you were selling pictures? Because you were with Major Vale? You could have met him on a morning stroll."

"Because he was already looking for me. Glover was with him. I did not tell you before the recital because I didn't want you worrying while you played, but he was there at the theater. He obviously told Gervaise he had seen me there."

"Just you? Not me?"

"Apparently not. Glover asked one of the servants for me this morning and was told I was not in my room. So Glover spilled his worries to Gervaise, who obviously saw my bed had not been slept in, and that you were sound asleep in yours. They must have begun a discreet search when I walked into them."

"With Major Vale."

"He accused me of being ruined."

"Are you?"

Helen wasn't even angry. She licked her dry lips. "We stayed in the same room at the inn, under the name of Connor. As though we were married. There is no reason it should ever come out. No one saw me except the innkeeper's wife and a maid. And an ostler. Two ostlers," she added, remembering the morning.

"It *might* come out," Alice said. "But who would believe it? Unless…" Her eyes widened.

"Exactly," Helen said. "Someone could make the connection between the Connors at the inn and the Connors at the theater, whom Glover and Mrs. Maven both know to be us."

"Is that Gervaise's fear? And who the devil is Mrs. Maven?"

Helen ignored the second question. "He never even mentioned the pictures. He seemed more concerned with Major Vale being an evil seducer, which he must have got from Glover."

Alice regarded her. "Is he?"

"What?"

"Major Vale. Is he an evil seducer?"

"Of course not," Helen said crossly. She made to get up, to hide from her sister's unbearable questioning, but Alice caught her arm.

"But he is…special to you, is he not? I've seen you with him several times. And I saw your sketchbook when Tamar was looking through it."

Heat burned up her cheeks. "He has an interesting face."

Alice was silent for a long moment. Then she said, "Choose Major Vale. And a long engagement. Then you can marry him or jilt him as you choose."

"Depending on gossip or Gervaise's caprice?"

Alice blinked. "Gervaise is not capricious."

Helen slumped. "I know. But I will not marry Major Vale. There would not even be a long engagement. Gervaise wants it done within the month."

"A month?" Alice repeated, clearly startled. "Do you believe he will really insist on that? Helen, did the major… Did he seduce you? Or try?"

Helen flapped an impatient hand. "Of course not. He never

touched me." *Not consciously, at any rate.* "He has no interest in me whatsoever, though honor has compelled him to offer marriage."

"Will you take it?"

"Under no circumstances. If it comes to it, I will face them all down, even Mama, and refuse to make my vows at the altar. That should scare both unwanted suitors off. And if Gervaise throws me out for it, well, I can finally be the artist I want to be."

"The prospect is not making you happy," Alice observed.

"I am tired. The bed at the George was lumpy."

Alice rose to her feet. "Then I'll leave you to catch up on sleep. It won't be as bad as you think, though, Helen. Gervaise will come around."

Chapter Fourteen

G ERVAISE DID NOT come around.

Inevitably, at a meeting of all the siblings that did not include spouses or the dowager countess, the story of the theater exhibition and recital came out, along with the riot and Major Vale's injury.

"So that is why he was there," Gervaise said, after a long silence.

"We didn't know at the time," Alice said quickly, "that he was Captain Skelton's partner, and the captain had no idea who we really were."

"Maybe," Gervaise muttered.

"At any rate," Frances said, "it seems we owe the major a debt of gratitude. Had he not been there, mounted, at the right time, God alone knows what would have happened to Alice *or* Helen. He is obviously no stage villain, Gervaise."

Gervaise waved a dismissive hand. "I never truly thought he was. I just expected him to have more care for Helen's reputation."

"We are on the edge of the known world up here, as far as Society is concerned," Serena said. "I really doubt her reputation is in jeopardy. There was nothing in the *Carlisle Journal* even about the riot, and the servants have heard no whispers. No one who matters saw her…"

"Don't be so ridiculous," Gervaise snapped. "We have a castle full of the *ton*! An earl's son saw her at the theater, and we have no idea who else was there, or who saw her return with Major Vale at nine o'clock in the morning looking as if you had both slept in your clothes!"

"I thought you would be grateful for that," Serena said humorously, and won only a scowl in return.

"Why are none of you taking this seriously?" he demanded. "Do you not realize the damage that could be done? Not just to Helen and her chances. Ruin of this kind spreads! Alice's chances will be spoiled, too. You could all be ostracized. Perhaps you and Tamar are independent enough not to care. Perhaps Frances and Torridon are safe in their Highland fastness. But what of Maria and Michael? He is a member of Parliament, and scandal could most certainly ruin them both."

That wiped the smiles off everyone's faces.

Maria said quietly, "That is not fair. I will not be an excuse— and neither will Michael—for forcing Helen into a distasteful marriage."

Though warmed somewhere by Maria's defense, Helen whitened at Gervaise's words. Foolishly, it had never entered her head that Maria and Michael could be hurt by this. And Alice... Alice was no longer a known quantity. Helen had no idea what she wanted from life anymore.

But Gervaise's anger had vanished. "No, it is not fair," he agreed. "But it is a fact of life that cannot be changed in a month. I'm sorry, Helen. This is not about blame anymore. But you must marry to nip this in the bud. Major Vale does not seem to be distasteful to you."

"On the other hand, marrying Glover would keep his mouth shut," Alice said, glowering around her siblings. "Are those the kind of reasons that led to *your* marriages?"

"None of us have been angels," Frances said ruefully. "But none of us stayed overnight at an inn pretending to be married to the man who shared our room. Serena was the worst of us, and her crime was merely dancing three times on the same evening with Dax. This is a different level of scandal. Gervaise is right that we need a solution. And I am sure we all agree it should be one that does not make Helen unhappy."

Helen rose to her feet. "Do let me know what would make me happy," she said defiantly as she walked out of the room.

She was already crying by the time she threw herself on her bed and wept, because Gervaise was right—she *had* to marry one of them.

IN THE THREE days leading up to the castle ball, Helen felt curiously isolated from everyone else's excitement. Her eighteenth birthday passed in a numb haze of congratulation and celebration that seemed to have little to do with her. It was just something to be marked before the ball.

Even the jaded London guests seemed to feel that the masquerade element to the festivities made it something a little different, and all the talk was of costumes and dances. Although Alice said little, Helen had the feeling she too was excited.

Only Helen seemed to dread it. Because she had made up her mind, and her heart hurt. Coming across Roderick's twin siblings on the far side of the orchard did not help.

"Good morning," Leona said brightly. Her brother bowed with mature grace.

"Good morning," Helen responded. "Have you come to call? Have you brought brothers and sisters?"

"No and no," Lawrence said, and though it should have been a relief, Helen's heart dropped further still. "We were looking for you. Roderick wants to know if everything is well."

Did he? Or had the twins made that up? No, he was a good man. He would care that much. "Of course," she said brightly. "How is he? His arm?"

"His arm?" Leona repeated. Clearly, they knew nothing of his injury, which perhaps meant that it was healing well. She went on almost immediately, "He is well but anxious to see you. He was hoping that you would meet him at the abbey ruin tomorrow morning."

"I can't," Helen said, though the pain intensified.

"He said to tell you that he would wait there anyway."

"There is no point," she said, aiming for lightness. "I am in disgrace and confined to barracks."

"Then what about here?" Lawrence suggested. "At dawn? He is always up early, and apparently you are too."

"No," she said, and for some reason felt guilty when their faces fell. She tried to smile. "I know you are trying to be kind, to your brother as well as to me. Tell him I am well, that I shall be at the ball, and that he is safe."

"Safe," Lawrence repeated with a frown.

"Safe," she said firmly. "And I shan't be here tomorrow, so there is no point in his coming."

"He will come anyway," Leona said.

Helen doubted it, not if they passed on her message accurately. "I'm going back to the castle for breakfast. You are welcome to join me."

The twins exchanged glances, then in perfect unison shook their heads.

"We should get back," Lawrence said.

Unexpectedly, Leona touched her hand. "He loves you, you know," she said softly, and they departed, leaving Helen to weep afresh for the innocence of youth.

HELEN LONGED TO sleep late the following morning, but she sprang into full wakefulness at dawn. The birds were singing outside, welcoming the new day. She wished they would be silent, and determinedly closed her eyes.

Was Roderick waiting behind the orchard? Could he really be so close and she not running to meet him?

I told him not to come. If he is not there…

Of course he is not there.

Maybe I should warn him that I shall choose Glover?

He already knew that. She had told him via the twins that he was safe. He would understand what she meant. Safe from her, from a marriage he offered out of honor and no love.

She turned over, her back to the window, but already knew she would not go back to sleep. The tug toward the orchard was too strong. She was afraid that if she rose and dressed, she would go. So she stayed in bed, eyes open, staring at the new ball gown and silken domino cloak that she would wear for this evening's misery. But after tonight, everything would begin to get better. She would be out of this restless limbo and into a new life.

All she had to do was hold on.

She waited until nine o'clock before she rose and dressed for breakfast. Just as Jinny, the maid she shared with Alice, was leaving, Alice herself came in.

Helen did not rise from the stool before the glass, though she swiveled around to regard her sister when Alice threw herself onto the bed.

"I have never seen anyone look so miserable at the prospect of a ball," Alice said.

"It is not the ball that appalls me."

"I know," Alice said. "And that is not right."

"Tell Gervaise. Though, actually, he *is* right. The risk to you, to Maria and the others, is too great. Marriage to Glover will shut his mouth."

"If you marry Major Vale," Alice suggested, "*he* will shut Glover's mouth."

"I cannot marry Major Vale."

"Because you love him?" Alice said softly.

Helen dropped her gaze to her lap, watching her own fingers

twist together.

"You won't marry him because you love him," Alice repeated. "Have you any idea how foolish that sounds? How foolish it *is*?"

"He does not love me," Helen said, a tinge of harshness in her voice. "And that would be worse than anything."

"How do you know? You haven't even seen him since Gervaise issued his ultimatum. On top of which, if we do not trust Glover to keep his mouth shut, how can you trust him as your husband? Will he even let you paint?"

Helen blinked. "I-I don't know. I would always find a way."

"And you do know you will have to share a bed with him? Whenever *he* chooses?"

Helen flinched.

"Of course, he might be the best of good fellows," Alice said with false encouragement. "In which case, is it fair to marry him when you love Major Vale?"

"Stop it, Alice," Helen whispered.

But Alice didn't. "Does Glover love you?"

"Don't be silly. I suspect he is too shallow ever to love anyone." Whether or not he had been involved in the riot and the attempted abduction.

"*Devil* take it, Helen," Alice said furiously, "we don't need your martyrdom! We need you to fight."

"How?"

"Agree to this foolish betrothal if you must. For now. We'll enlist Mama to make sure the wedding is not too soon, and then we'll find Glover a charming, *disgustingly* wealthy heiress to jilt you for. Blackhaven is full of 'em."

An unexpected surge of laughter threatened to turn into tears. Helen swallowed, but realized her spirits had still lifted.

She frowned at Alice. "Actually, that is not such a bad idea. Mama will have nothing indecently hasty or hole-in-the-corner. And Glover does fancy himself in love with remarkable speed. Who do we know who is filthy rich?"

"I thought of Miss Poole, but she got married the other day. I'm sure we can find out. In fact, I'll set the Vale twins on it. They will be quickest."

Helen glanced up. "You know the Vale twins?"

"Doesn't everyone?"

Helen supposed that was true. In any case, there was a little more lightness in her step and in her heart as she rose and accompanied her sister to breakfast.

RODERICK HAD WAITED by the orchard for three hours, his back resting against the stone wall, his seat feeling increasingly damp. He tried to distract himself by working out a schedule and the number of men necessary to fulfill their business commitments in the following week. He limited Skelton's involvement to the shorter, nearer tasks, and marked himself for the longer journeys.

That done, he found it hard to do more than listen for Helen's footsteps. But the twins' report had not been encouraging. He had come on the off chance that she might change her mind, but he was not truly surprised when she didn't appear. He thought he knew, to some degree at least, what was going on in her head, and somehow he had to convince her she was wrong. And since she did not come this morning, that would have to wait for the ball, when there would be far too many people and the damage might already have been done.

He thought about her, so close and yet so far away. Was she lying in bed, thinking of him? God, he hoped so... He could almost imagine her thoughts, hurt and confused, glancing off his own. He wished he could see her mind, show her his. And his heart. He willed her to see them, intensely, as though such communication were truly possible.

But, of course, she did not come.

He rose stiffly, tugged at the seat of his riding breeches, and walked smartly back to where he had left his horse.

Black Hill House was surprisingly quiet when he got home. At least the twins were not waiting for him on the stairs with disappointment in their eyes for his failure.

"Where is everyone?" he asked Julius, encountering him in the library, where he was writing letters.

"Oh, around," Julius said vaguely. "Lucy and Felicia are up to something. I believe we are to be amazed at their costumes, since they are refusing even to travel with the rest of us to the castle."

"And the twins?"

"Out looking for heiresses, apparently."

Roderick blinked. "What?"

"That's what I said. They received a note and scampered off."

Roderick sat down, frowning. "Do you suppose we should let them run quite so wild?"

"When they are together, yes. They will grow up soon enough. And according to Delilah and Felicia, they are never foolish or rude. They are also a mine of information. I doubt much happens in the environs of Blackhaven that escapes them. If it does, Aubrey will know it from pump room gossip."

Something tugged at Roderick's mind, the memory of a conversation with Skelton about communication in the town being only by gossip. There was an important, intriguing idea there that he must not lose.

"How is the guarding business?" Julius inquired. He had set down his pen and seemed inclined to talk.

"Showing promise. I'm not sure whether to run with it and sell out, or go back to the army."

"You do know you don't have to rush into either?" Julius said, a shade awkwardly. "My marriage makes no difference to that."

Roderick nodded, touched, in spite of himself, that his brother took the trouble to say it. "I have not been an easy companion," he said in a rush. "I would not blame Antonia for throwing me out."

Julius smiled with genuine amusement. "She wouldn't, even

if I let her."

Roderick swallowed. "It takes time." Further words eluded him, but Julius seemed to understand anyway, for he nodded.

"Especially the nightmares," Julius said.

Roderick stared. "You too?"

"They do get better, but as you said, it takes a little while. I think we are both getting there."

Without warning, tears tightened Roderick's throat. He didn't doubt his brother's nightmares, but it was the kindness of saying the words, of making the equivalence with Roderick's own, deeper problem, that undid him.

He rose too fast. "Thank you," he managed in a hoarse, strangled voice, and somehow got himself out and to his own room. He wanted to cry away the pain just once before he took up the reins of responsible life. He wanted Helen.

THE CASTLE WAS unusually quiet and peaceful that afternoon. Everyone was resting in order to be fresh for the evening's festivities.

Helen was not resting but pacing up and down her bedchamber like one of the caged beasts outside the Exchange in London.

When the knock came, she assumed it was Alice and called, "Come in."

But it was Gervaise who thrust his head around the door. "I thought you might be in bed."

"No, I am not tired. I just don't want to be with people."

"Including me?" he said ruefully, coming in and closing the door. "Sorry, Nell."

The use of his old childhood name for her melted her hardened heart. More than that, it gave her hope.

"I am not the monster you think me," he said. "Please believe I am trying to do the best for you and for the whole family."

"I know that. And you must know I never meant things to come to this. We thought we were prepared for everything, but we did not plan on being separated by an armed riot. Alice and I are sorry, too."

"You are so young, you and Alice, so independent in spirit. I was angry—partly from relief at finding you safe—but in truth, the more I think about it, the more I blame Major Vale rather than you."

"That is not fair," Helen said. "He did not know we were his clients. As soon as he discovered it, he rode to the theater, and it was as well for us that he did."

"We shan't quarrel over it," Gervaise said. "I know you are an innocent. Have…have you made up your mind which of them you will take?"

So there was to be no reprieve after all. Not from the engagement, at least.

"I believe so," she said steadily. "Is that what you came to ask?"

He shook his head. "No. Eleanor tells me I should give you as much time as possible, time at least to speak to Major Vale again before I announce anything. I believe she is right. We can do it at the unmasking, if you like, or before the last dance?"

She shrugged. "It does not matter."

At that, shame and misery flickered in his eyes, quickly followed by a strange, sad determination. "I wish it could be different. I wanted better for you."

"So did I," she whispered. She swallowed and straightened. "But don't worry. I brought us to this and will play my part in making it right." *I just hope the twins can find us an heiress in time…*

But even that solution would have to be dependent on no whisper of scandal coming out in the meantime.

Chapter Fifteen

For Roderick, the first part of the ball was dominated by Lucy. First by her appearance in a jaw-dropping costume, part of which was a massive headdress from which leapt a small, vaguely familiar puppy. Although this caused a great deal of hilarity, it seemed to have been performed solely for the benefit of her betrothed, Lord Eddleston, who was all but crying with laughter.

"Bless her," Delilah murmured in Roderick's ear. "She believes no one recognizes her."

"To be fair, apart from us and Eddleston, I doubt anyone does. The chit is quite mad, and Eddleston clearly eggs her on."

Delilah surprised him with a dazzling smile. "Wonderful, isn't it?"

He found himself grinning back, but since the present dance had just ended, he went quickly in pursuit of Helen as she was escorted back to her sisters. He had not had the chance to speak to her since arriving. Only the older and younger countesses and Braithwaite himself had welcomed their guests, and since then, Helen had never seemed to stand still. He had spotted her easily in the crowd, though, in a pale primrose gown and mask with a golden yellow domino. She looked like a bright butterfly flitting from flower to flower.

This time, as luck would have it, he caught up with her at the same time as Glover. She had her back to Roderick, but Glover sent him a smug, triumphant smile.

"My lady," Glover said. "May I hope for this next dance?"

Perhaps she had seen the direction of his gaze, or simply sensed Roderick's presence, for she glanced back over her shoulder.

Roderick bowed. "I come upon the same errand."

"And are soundly beaten," Glover said, offering Helen his arm.

Roderick itched to hit him. But for just an instant, he held her gaze, read her trouble and doubts and misery, and then she smiled gaily and took Glover's arm.

"Perhaps later, major," she said, already walking away.

It did not bode well for his chances. It did not bode well at all. She was making sure he never got near her, and there could only be one reason for that. In spite of everything, she had chosen Glover. Roderick's own idiocy—followed by Braithwaite's—had brought her to this pass.

Somebody stopped beside him. Lord Braithwaite himself, gazing after his sister and Glover.

"She has not yet made her choice," Braithwaite murmured. "At least, not to me. It will be before the last dance."

"Are you urging me to my press my suit?" Roderick asked wryly.

"No," Braithwaite snapped. "I am still furious with you, and I trust neither your judgment nor your morals." He seemed to bite back the rest of his words and continued more calmly. "But I was not entirely fair the last time we met. This situation is far from perfect, but clearly you rescued her from one far worse, and for that, I thank you. However…"

"How did I know there was a *however*?"

"She would not have faced such danger had you not allowed her to retain your services. She tells me you did not know. I say you should have known, and that you did not is gross negligence. It speaks ill for your new venture."

Roderick narrowed his eyes. "I cannot stop you speaking ill of the business. But be aware that when you do, you will be hurting innocent men, not me. I fully intend to return to the army, married or not."

Until that moment, he hadn't even known his decision. In fact, he wasn't even sure he meant it. It was said solely to spike Braithwaite's guns before he strolled away with deliberate insolence. He might want to marry the man's sister, but he refused to be talked down to like a thoughtless child.

THE SECOND OF Lucy's affairs to distract Roderick in the first part of the ball came via the squire. Winslow was also the local magistrate, and while seizing a breath of fresh air on the terrace, Roderick came across him instructing a couple of constables in a low voice. The constables quickly melted into the darkness.

"Trouble?" Roderick asked.

"No, there shouldn't be," Winslow said. "One of other guests believes we might have an unwanted visitor at the ball. Masks are a mixed blessing."

Roderick, with his own stuffed in his pocket, said, "Not mixed, just irritating. Who are you looking for?"

"Fellow called Irving. A gentleman by birth, apparently, now an accused murderer evading arrest."

Startled, Roderick uttered a rather military oath. Then, as vague memory intruded, he frowned. "Wait. Is this anything to do with young Eddleston?"

"I'm afraid so. His sister was the victim. Allegedly, of course, and some years ago. But evading arrest is not in Irving's favor."

"No," Roderick allowed. "By why the devil would he come here?"

"Probably to extract some kind of revenge on Eddleston."

Roderick needed something to do while Helen danced with

yet another man. Besides which, Eddleston seemed to make Lucy happy. "Want me to look around?"

"If you would not mind," Winslow said gratefully. "Don't want to cause a fuss by calling on the 44th. I suspect our man is on the grounds somewhere. Eddleston thinks he's headed for the terrace here, but I would rather catch him before he gets so far."

"Then you don't mind if I hit him?" asked Roderick, who really wanted to punch something. Hard.

"Be my guest. Though you may have to fight Eddleston for the privilege."

Roderick nodded and strolled down from the terrace. Methodically, he began to quarter the darker grounds around the castle.

He was blessed with excellent night vision, which had saved his hide on more than one occasion during the war, and he listened for every tiny sound that might betray another presence. At first he saw no one, except the two constables on the same mission as himself. The constables were heading back to guard the area in front of the terrace, since that was where, for whatever reason, any attack was expected.

Roderick moved silently further back, and then his ears picked up a *swish*. He jerked his head toward the sound, and something moved in the shadows near the terrace. The figure of a man removing a cloak in the shelter of a tree. It was not either of the constables, whom he could just make out standing stock-still on either side of the terrace.

The terrace itself was empty as Roderick changed direction and prowled silently toward the unknown man. Then Eddleston appeared on the terrace and skulked sensibly in the shadows. But the watcher had seen him, for he moved, lifting something in one hand to rest it on a tree branch. In the darkness, from this angle, Roderick could not make out what it was, but he kept moving forward, silent and steady.

Then two things happened at once. Lucy stepped out onto the terrace, and Roderick heard the chillingly familiar click of a cocked gun. That was what the unknown man had in his hand, pointing straight to the terrace. He could see it now—a wicked, double-barreled pistol.

Eddleston spoke low and urgently to Lucy, but, being Lucy, she argued and kept coming toward him.

Roderick, terrified for both of them, sped up.

Perhaps Eddleston heard the click too, or perhaps he simply sensed danger. Either way, he hurled himself from the shadows, straight at Lucy, yelling, "Now, damn you!" just as a shot cracked through the air.

There was no time for fear or dreams of the past. In the present, this attacker still had a shot to fire, and if he hadn't killed Lucy or Eddleston with the first, he could try again with the second.

Yelling to scare off the horrors of memory, Roderick hurled himself at the attacker, who was moving jauntily toward the terrace. Roderick wrenched one arm up his back and seized the pistol. The constables got there a moment later.

"Let me go, you fools!" their captive yelled. "A man is dying up there! A lady!"

"They had better not be," Roderick said. It was a promise, ice cold and grim as death itself. "Or you will suffer before you hang."

And then came Lucy's pitiful cry. "No! Tyler, no, you can't die!"

The relief of hearing her voice eased Roderick's terror. Leaving the captive to the constables, he ran up to the terrace, vaulting over the low wall to where his sister bent over her betrothed, clutching his hand, tears coursing down her cheeks.

"Let me in, Lucy," he said briskly, feeling for a pulse. "Fetch Dr. Lampton. I'll bring him inside."

"Not that way," Braithwaite said, unexpectedly by his elbow. "The blue bedchamber, Miss Vale. Lampton will know the way."

A strong pulse beat in Eddleston's neck, although the man was out cold, and there was, lamentably, blood. As Roderick began to lift him, away from the shocked guests who were spilling onto the terrace, Braithwaite made to help him.

But Roderick, suddenly possessive and protective of the man his little sister loved, snapped, "I can manage. Lead the way, if you please."

To give the earl his due, he made no fuss, merely walked down the steps and around the path to a side door. And Roderick bore all Lucy's hopes inside.

THE GUNSHOT PENETRATED the music and chatter of the ballroom, overriding all Helen's other, suddenly trivial, troubles.

By then she had taken to avoiding not only Roderick, but all her sisters and brothers-in-law too. Since she was the "baby" of the family, everyone else seemed to imagine they had a duty to give her the benefit of their advice and instruction. On the whole, they were evenly between Glover—"immature but charming enough to amuse you, and he will not be a heavy-handed husband"—and Roderick—"a much more attractive man, of course and of strong personality, but I cannot like the sneaking way he kept you in Whalen all night and caused all this farce."

Unexpectedly, Serena's husband Tamar was the worst. And Helen could not escape him, for they were dancing at the time. Because he had understood her compulsion to paint, had encouraged and taught her, there had always been a special bond between them. Foolishly, she had assumed this would mean he alone would not try to interfere.

But almost as soon as the waltz began, he said, "You can't take Glover unless you mean to be miserable for the rest of your life."

She said nothing, hoping he would stop. Instead, he said more urgently, "Helen, I've seen your sketchbooks. One unpleasant caricature of Glover from weeks ago, and pages and pages full of

Vale. You cannot feel like that about a man and marry another."

"Tell Gervaise," she said tiredly. "But then, neither of you have to marry either of them."

"Trust me, Helen. Trust Serena. She will tell you the same thing if she hasn't already."

She might have done. Helen had lost track of who had favored whom. "Serena knows no more than—"

The gunshot interrupted her, and she stopped dead on the dance floor, staring up at Tamar in sudden fright. It might have been thunder, but somehow she knew...

Roderick!

Another couple bumped into them and apologized. As one, Helen and Tamar began to hurry toward the French doors. A few others had stopped dancing too. Others were already spilling out onto the terrace, and a growing surge of voices and squeals made it clear something untoward had occurred.

Fear for Roderick filled her mind with a hundred unlikely scenarios. A duel? Glover had shot him. Roderick had shot Glover. Or Mrs. Maven had shot Roderick for interfering with the riot. Someone else had been shot and sent Roderick into one of his terrifying nightmares. Or perhaps in the throes of one of those nightmares, he had shot a complete stranger...

Lucy Vale, tears pouring unchecked down her cheeks, had hold of Dr. Lampton's hand and was tugging him in the opposite direction.

Oh, God, not Roderick, please not Roderick...

Eleanor's voice rose over the top. "There has been a bit of an accident, but no need to worry. There is no danger, and all will be well again very shortly. Back to the waltz! My lord?"

Lord Wickenden, resplendent in a satyr's costume that suited him only too well, obediently swept Eleanor back onto the dance floor. Helen spotted Maria quietly detaching Lucy from Dr. Lampton and walking briskly with them to the staircase.

Abandoning Tamar to his own devices, Helen darted after them. Some remnant of her social training kept a smile pinned to her face as she went and grasped Maria by the arm.

"Who?" she demanded, hurrying along beside her sister. "Not—"

"Lord Eddleston," Maria said quickly. Which also explained Lucy's tears. "Major Vale carried him upstairs, and Mr. Winslow has the perpetrator in custody. Go back, Helen—there's nothing you can do except keep the party dancing. He is not dead."

It was hardly fair to poor Lord Eddleston, but Helen almost fainted with relief that it was he who had been shot. And an instant later, pride swelled, because the sound of the shot had clearly not incapacitated Roderick. He was carrying the injured man for treatment...

Breathing evenly once more, she returned to the ballroom, where the faltering waltz was once more in full swing. After this would be the supper dance, and then the unmasking. She prayed silently for Lord Eddleston, whom she knew slightly and liked instinctively. There was a sense of mischief about him that must suit Lucy very well, and yet behind the lightheartedness there must be a serious side, a strength of character that made him Gervaise's friend and ally. And Michael's.

There was always more to people than met the eye. Even Mrs. Maven. It would be so bad for Roderick to go back to her, and Helen was fairly sure he would not...

Why did she keep thinking of the wretched woman? That was the second time this evening. She hauled her wayward thoughts back to her surroundings and found she had been gazing in the direction of a handsome lady dressed as Cleopatra. The costume, the mask, and even the lining of her flung-back domino cloak sparkled with jewels.

A jolt shot through her. It *was* Mrs. Maven, waltzing with Bernard Muir—who, fortuitously, was dressed as Caesar. Any last doubts Helen might have harbored vanished when the lady glanced beyond her partner and met Helen's gaze. She smiled, a mischievous, dazzling smile of triumph.

Helen pretended not to see, and moved on in search of

Tamar, but her thoughts were an indignant riot. That smile told her she was here legitimately. Mama would never have invited a woman of lesser birth, so she must have come on someone's coattails.

The blood sang in Helen's ears. No wonder the woman was so pleased with herself. She had come with Roderick.

Helen's heart froze into a hard, painful stone in her chest.

But at least she knew she had made the right decision. There was no further point in dragging things out. As soon as he returned to the ballroom, she would tell Gervaise she had decided on Glover.

EDDLESTON HAD NOT the look of a dying man, and Dr. Lampton seemed to agree with that verdict. When Roderick left his little sister alone with her betrothed, he found his feelings toward his future brother-in-law rather warmer. Eddleston had almost certainly saved Lucy's life, taking the bullet that could easily have killed her. That made him worthy, in Roderick's book. In fact, it made Roderick immensely grateful—and not just for Eddleston, but for his whole family. The siblings might have been scattered and parted for years, but they had always been there when it counted.

Unfortunately, the first person he encountered on returning to the ballroom was Glover.

At least he was not dancing with Helen, and this must be the supper dance. She was whirling around the floor with one of the Winslow boys, who must have been an old friend.

Roderick's heart ached. But it was not over yet. He wanted to stand alone and watch her, but Glover appeared at his side, buzzing like an importunate fly. With an effort, Roderick made out the words.

"…beautiful. Hope there are no hard feelings."

Roderick focused his gaze on the speaker, saw his bravado and the attempt to intimidate a man he probably saw as old and past it. But no, Roderick had learned to read young men well, and Glover did not see him like that at all. He was only pretending to because he felt threatened by Roderick's greater experience and, no doubt, the fact that it was Roderick who had saved Helen in the riot.

He lifted his eyebrows. "I have none. But you should know that whichever of us wins the lady's hand, I shall be watching you."

Glover smiled, deliberately provoking. "You would marry her knowing she has a *tendre* for me?"

"Coxcomb," Roderick said with contempt. "The lady has spirit and intelligence. She already knows it was you who betrayed her to her family to cause just such a situation as this. If you imagine she will not realize that you and Meg Maven paid for a riot so that you could rescue her—or as it turned out, could *not* rescue her—you are an even bigger fool than you look now."

The blood rushed into Glover's face, along with something like horror and desperate shame. He looked like a guilty schoolboy whose irresponsible prank had garnered unforeseen consequences.

"Sir, I did not know!" Glover stepped closer, speaking low and urgently. "I was only supposed to—"

"Save her?" Roderick cut in. "From what, did you imagine? A threatening kitten? An amorous elderly gentleman who had imbibed a little too freely?"

"You mock me, sir," Glover said.

"Yes, I do. And you deserve that and so much more." Roderick walked away to chat to Miss Talbot and Antonia.

He supposed he should finally put his mask on, if only to remove it at the imminent unmasking.

Chapter Sixteen

AS THE FINAL notes of the supper dance faded away, Eleanor called out, "My lords, ladies, and gentlemen, it is past midnight! Before we go into supper, please form a circle for the unmasking!"

A buzz of excited laughter echoed around the room. Grinning at Helen, Geoffrey Winslow murmured, "I wonder who you could be?"

"Then you cannot be the man I know you to be!" Helen retorted, taking his arm and walking with him into the large circle. She glanced hastily around and found Roderick beside Antonia Macy, his soon-to-be sister-in-law. Not with Meg, then. Where was she?

"Who are you looking for?" Alice whispered in her ear. She was with Cornelius Vale.

"Meg Maven is here. I saw her."

Alice's eyes widened, for Helen had finally explained the woman's role in the Whalen riot. "Seriously? How? She would never have been invited, and the staff are strict now about collecting the cards of all the guests. Someone must have brought her. Or let her in. You know, I don't like the way she is always behind trouble…"

"There she is," Helen murmured, nodding a few places to the left of Alice. "Cleopatra. Next to Bernard Muir."

But not for long. While Eleanor was congratulating her guests on their marvelous costumes and general mysteriousness, Meg's gaze found Roderick. Making the most of Bernard's distraction, she slipped back out of the circle and around the outside, making straight for Roderick's side.

Alice must have guessed the same thing, for she muttered, "Oh no, you don't." An instant later she whirled, caught Meg by her elegant, braceleted arm, and whisked her back into the circle between herself and Cornelius.

His attention caught by the flurry of movement, Roderick glanced in their direction. Helen dragged her gaze free.

Geoffrey Winslow untied the strings of Helen's mask and fell back in mock amazement. "Never! It's Lady Helen! Let me reveal myself!"

While she smiled at his clowning, Cornelius untied Alice's mask. Meg tried to step back and slip away again, but she was too slow. Alice ripped the mask off her face and gazed her fill.

Helen could not smile anymore. Alice's expression changed from surprise to haughty disapproval. Both were very well acted, but a feeling of dread settled in Helen's stomach.

"Madam," Alice said icily, but so quietly that no one beyond their little group should have heard. "I do not believe you were invited."

If she had hoped to embarrass Meg, it had the opposite effect. Mrs. Maven's smile was dazzling, and her voice loud enough to reach anyone who cared to listen.

"Allow me to say that your ladyship is mistaken," Meg said clearly, with a humility as false as Alice's previous surprise. "I entered on the invitation of my betrothed, to the gracious welcome of Lady Braithwaite herself."

A pulse throbbed in Helen's head. Could this be true? Eleanor was kind by nature and would certainly never send away any companion of a friend...

"Your betrothed?" Bernard asked, glancing at Cornelius, who, apart from a faint frown, did not appear to be remotely interested.

"My betrothed," Meg stated with even greater clarity. Her gaze flickered to Helen, and then she swung her whole body toward Roderick. "Major Vale."

Helen's heart shattered into a thousand pieces. Why had he done such a thing? Surely not to make Helen jealous! To teach her a lesson? Or did he just miss Meg? Meg and the physical intimacy he could never bring himself to indulge with Helen? Or was there more, much more to Meg, as there was to everyone? Something that would outweigh her cruelty, her scheming…

Oh, please don't marry her. She will make you so unhappy!

For a horrible moment, she thought she had said the words aloud, for under the gaze of most of the castle guests, Roderick left Antonia's side and walked toward Meg. And suddenly Helen realized that it was not true. There was no betrothal, but Meg had come to make it so, relying on Roderick's honor and gentlemanly conduct to save an old friend, a woman, from being branded a liar, and in such company as this.

How dare you? Helen raged in silence, even though she herself was prepared to marry someone for considerably less honorable reasons.

"Major Vale is your betrothed?" Alice said with blatant disbelief.

Helen wanted the floor to swallow her up in darkness and make everything go away.

Meg laughed and opened her mouth to reply. Helen half turned away because escape was the only solution now.

"Of course not," Roderick said. He did not raise his voice, but suddenly you could hear a pin drop in the ballroom. "Mrs. Maven jests. She knows perfectly well that I cannot be betrothed to her, charming as she is. For I am already betrothed to Lady Helen."

MEG WAS PLAYING more than a cruel, silly joke. She thought she was compelling him, and Roderick never gave in to such pressure. He certainly would not let her win after her dangerous tricks against Helen. He could no more marry her than a snake, whether he lost his so-called honor or not.

Claiming betrothal to Helen was his best counterattack, even if it seemed to pull the same trick as Meg had just attempted. He gazed only at Helen.

She had half turned away from him, poised for escape, but at his words she paused and turned slowly back to face him.

"Oh, thank God," Alice muttered.

Roderick locked his gaze to Helen's, trying to convey all he felt, and at the same time warning her to go along with it for now. He would hold her to nothing she did not want. But she seemed too confused to understand. Emotion raged in her eyes—anger, outrage, pity…

Pity, because if she refused him, she imagined she would humiliate him.

Braithwaite strode across to them. "Is this true, Helen? Do you wish to marry Major Vale?"

She wouldn't do it. She was too angry, and perhaps rightly so. She thought him no better than Meg. And now she would marry Glover, who was not just a lightweight, but an untrustworthy lightweight.

A painful smile stretched her lovely lips, lips that had kissed him with such passion, such sweetness. Already he ached for the unhappiness her marriage to Glover would inevitably bring her.

"Of course I still wish to marry Major Vale," Helen said in a rush. "We are indeed engaged—with your approval?"

Roderick closed his eyes, unable to bear the wash of relief and joy.

"Of course with my approval," Braithwaite said with quite unexpected warmth.

Opening his eyes again, Roderick found the earl offering him his hand. Roderick grasped it, and then Braithwaite placed Helen's hand in his instead.

Cornelius thumped him on the back. "You old dog! Kept that very quiet! Congratulations, big brother! Lady Helen, welcome to the Vales."

The congratulations became something of a nightmare, for through it all, Roderick was chiefly aware of Helen's rigid form beside him, a smile plastered to her face while she clearly wanted to be anywhere else in the world.

He did not even see Meg's expression, although he heard Bernard Muir saying, "Mrs. Maven had you worried for a moment, though! Excellent jest, ma'am, and I definitely win the wager!" He swept her away, thus rather cleverly removing any further awkwardness and proving the whole thing to be a joke.

At last, everyone was heading into the supper room, delighted with the evening and the new gossip, although he was sure many whispered that Lady Helen could have done better for herself than the second son of a minor landowner, an old soldier.

Her hand had slid free of his some time ago, but now he took it and placed it on his arm. Even through her gloves it somehow felt cold. "Shall we go into supper? Or shall we go somewhere quieter to talk?"

Again, her hand slid free. "I am promised to Mr. Winslow for supper. Excuse me."

And she flitted away, catching up with the rather surprised Winslow youth.

"Have you made a mess of this, Rod?" Cornelius asked, gazing after her.

"A huge mess," Roderick agreed, once more bleak after his dizzying moment of happiness. Around him remained only Cornelius, Lady Alice, and Antonia, although Julius was striding to meet them.

Alice said bluntly, "She thinks you don't love her. She thinks you are doing this merely for honor. And, by the way, how *did* that woman get in here?"

Roderick stared at her. Was that what they both thought? That he had brought Meg and then publicly rejected her, perhaps only to force Helen's hand? "What in God's name do you take me for?"

For an instant, Alice searched his eyes, reminding him of Lucy and her clear, perceptive gaze. Then, unexpectedly, she smiled. "Ah. Glover. Of course. I'll tell her. Don't give up, major."

With that, she took off with Cornelius. Antonia took Roderick's arm, warm and sisterly, but they had only taken a step before his actual sisters all but fell on him in a welter of congratulations, surprise, and demand for details.

WHEN SHE COULD no longer avoid it, after supper and before the next dance, Helen found herself in a moment of privacy in the anteroom, with Gervaise and her mother.

"Then it's true," Mama said furiously. "You have engaged yourself to that man without even consulting me, let alone asking my permission. What kind of commoner is he that he dared not even approach me first?"

"He approached *me*, Mother," Gervaise said. "I am, after all, her guardian. I did not tell you because Helen was...unsure."

"And that ridiculous charade at the unmasking? That made her sure?"

"It was the best way out of the awkwardness," Helen said.

"Otherwise, she would obviously have asked you first," Gervaise said smoothly, with an almost imperceptible wink over his mother's head at Helen.

She wished she could laugh.

Mama said, "So whose betrothed is that woman?"

"No one's," Helen said, and suddenly wanted to cry for Meg and for herself. What on earth had she done? "It was all a jest of Bernard's that went too far."

Mama sniffed. "Well, at least you are not marrying *him*."

"There's nothing wrong with Bernard!" Helen exclaimed. "He's been our friend forever, and he is Lady Wickenden's brother."

"I am well aware of his family history," Mama retorted. "It is irrelevant to the present discussion. There is nothing against Roderick Vale's birth, so far as I know, but they are a ramshackle family. Half of them are illegitimate and are yet foisted onto decent Society."

"You invited them all here, Mama," Gervaise pointed out.

"I could hardly exclude them by name from an invitation," Mama snapped. "Besides, it is not their fault. George Vale was a shocking old rake. Charming, though. Very charming." She fixed Helen with the fierce glare that had once reduced her to jelly. "I suppose this Roderick is charming, too?"

Helen said, "I find him so," and was appalled to hear the hoarseness in her voice.

"He makes a smart soldier," Mama allowed. "I hope he does not expect you to follow the drum."

"We have not discussed such matters yet."

"This is not the time or the place," Gervaise interjected.

"No," Mama admitted. "Well, let us go back to the ballroom. You may bring him to meet me."

"Phew," Gervaise murmured as they escaped their mother's presence. "That went better than I had hoped. For what it's worth, I think you made the right choice. I was impressed by the way he dealt with poor Eddleston's shooting. Quick, decisive action, and all without fuss."

For the first time in ages, Helen felt a genuine, spontaneous smile tug at her lips. "That is how he was at Whalen, too."

"Training and experience, I suppose."

"Will Lord Eddleston recover?" Helen asked, ashamed that her own petty anxieties had got in the way of something truly serious.

"Lampton says so."

She nodded, glad for him and for Lucy. "Gervaise?" she said

quickly as they entered the ballroom and he seemed about to go his own way.

"Yes?"

"You will not force this to be within the month, will you?"

His eyes hardened. "So that you can wriggle out of it somehow?"

It was what she had meant to do with Glover. Alice and the twins were already looking for heiresses. But such a scheme would hardly work for Roderick. Her stomach was in knots of anxiety and something very like desire.

"The sooner the better, I suspect," Gervaise said grimly, and walked away. As if he knew of that scene in the inn, of Roderick naked in the bed, in her arms, aroused and passionate.

She gasped and swung away, as if a change of direction could throw off the memories. She came face to face with Sir Julius Vale.

He was a formidable sort of figure, tall and broad-shouldered and somehow fierce, his good looks marred by a patch over one eye and a scar on his neck. And some old injury had lamed him. He too had an interesting face, and from nowhere, she had an urge to sketch him.

"I come to beg a dance of my newest sister," he said amiably.

"Of course," she said. There was nothing else she could say. She laid her hand on his offered arm.

"However," he added with a gleam of humor, "I think we might both prefer if we sat it out. A glass of wine, perhaps?"

Sir Julius made light, engaging conversation. She suspected he was adept at drawing people out and gauging their character— and gently probing hers to see if she would really do well for his brother.

She could see something of Roderick in his features and in his unexpected hints of dry humor. She could not help warming to him, and when other siblings drifted over in ones and twos, it entered her head that it might be fun to be part of such a family— so different from her own but no less valuable.

The time flew by. At one point she noticed Roderick sitting by her mother, no doubt being interrogated. He showed no signs of unease or annoyance. In fact, he smiled once. So did Mama.

Hastily, Helen dragged her attention back to Mrs. Maitland, whom she was now to call Felicia.

Then suddenly it was the last waltz of the ball, and Roderick was there. His siblings melted away, almost as if they had been saving her for him and left her now to his care. God help her, for there was no way out. He had invited her to dance, and everyone knew she was engaged to him.

She rose, accepted his hand, and walked with him onto the dance floor.

"I hope this evening has not been too much of a trial for you," he said, a shade awkwardly.

"It depends which part of the evening you mean."

The music began, and he took her in his arms. His closeness felt so good, shocking her back to life after the bizarre numbness of the previous couple of hours. And yet soothing and right. Dangerously right.

He said low, "I hope you do not actually think I brought Meg here."

"No. I suspect Glover did that," Helen said. "It was probably part of their agreement. Glover was meant to rescue me from the fake riot and win my devotion, or at least my hand and fortune. And in return, he either smuggled her into the ball or gave her his card of invitation. The servants would not have had time to study the names on each card, and there are no announcements at a masquerade."

A smile flickered across his face. "My thoughts exactly."

"I like your family," she said. "They are fun."

"I like yours, too. Even Braithwaite, when he thaws."

"You impressed him when Lord Eddleston was shot. I understand you disarmed the attacker and carried Eddleston inside."

"He is still in one of your guest bedchambers. In fact, I suspect Lucy has gone there to spend the last dance with him."

"The shot did not deter you," she pointed out.

"It appalled me," he said ruefully. "But the strength of the dreams seems to be fading. I might even be able to return to the army. Do you think I should?"

Startled, she said, "It is hardly up to me."

A frown tugged at his brow. "You have agreed to marry me. Every decision we make affects you. Of course it is up to you, at least in part."

She drew in her breath, fighting the urge to go along with the romance, the fairytale of the love match. She could not lie to herself. Or let him.

"Don't, Roderick. We both know it is a marriage of convenience. No more and no less."

His fingers tightened on hers. "Helen, Braithwaite might have determined the damnable timing of my offer, but not the fact that I made it. I fully meant you to be my wife, if you would have me."

"Oh, please!" She tugged as though she would pull free of him, then thought better of it. "Let us at least be honest with each other."

"I have no intention of being anything else."

"Except when it interferes with your honor," she said bitterly. "That is why you offered in the first place, and why you chose me over Meg at the unmasking."

"I would never have chosen Meg."

"No, because you are not ready for marriage to anyone. You told me as much, and it was perfectly clear at Whalen that I am not the wife you would ever seek." She stared into his eyes and tried to make her statement with flat dispassion. "You do not want me."

His reaction was not quite what she had imagined. Neither flummoxed nor sheepish, he gave one of his rare, sweet smiles and danced her backward. When they spun, he somehow held her too close.

"Do I not?" he said softly. "My dear innocent, wanting you

was never my problem. Keeping my hands off you was." His fingers moved subtly on her waist, while his thumb stroked her palm. Even through gloves, his caresses made her tingle.

Easy, so easy to believe him, because she *wanted* to. But if she were to survive this marriage to the man she loved, who did not love her, she needed the distance of honesty.

"You accept my terms," she blurted. "Or there is no marriage. I can still throw it back in my brother's face."

That did shock him. He must have felt her melting body, the heat, the need beneath his hands. But he heard her words and her tone. God knew what he saw in her eyes.

Then he surprised her. "I do accept your terms. I always will."

Chapter Seventeen

RODERICK, AT SOMETHING of a loss as to how to win Helen's trust back, at least learned one interesting thing from the twins before he left for the castle the following day. He met them at the breakfast parlor door as they skipped off to some mischief or other. But they paused to grin at him and congratulate him upon his engagement.

"Which at least means we don't have to look for heiresses anymore," Lawrence said.

"Heiresses?" Roderick said. "What do you want with heiresses at your age?"

"Not for me, silly, for Glover. So that he'd desert Lady Helen and show his true colors."

Roderick closed his mouth and swallowed. "Don't think me ungrateful, but—"

"Actually, it wasn't our idea," Leona said. "It was Lady Alice's."

"Was it, by God?" So Alice, the closest of her sisters, wanted this wedding. Did that mean he was just better than Glover in her eyes? Or that Helen loved him?

Once, he could have sworn Helen loved him. He had seen it in her eyes from the beginning, felt it in her kiss, and it had torn him apart, delight warring with guilt and gnawing unease at his own unfitness.

But Helen, for all her maturity, was only just eighteen years old. She was surely prone to fickleness. God knew he had been at that age. And in her case, how long could he have really expected her to put up with his hot and cold behavior before doubts sprang up? By any standards, he was a daunting specimen for any woman to take on.

And yet she was true and loyal. He wanted her love, but he was prepared to wait for it, to win it. Nevertheless, he was not entirely convinced that was the problem here. Was he just a coxcomb to imagine that she still loved him, that her doubts were in fact of *his* feelings? Was she afraid to open the door to her own and risk rejection, heartache? He could understand that only too well.

Antonia was right, he thought as he rode over the boundary wall between Black Hill and Braithwaite. He had indeed made a mess of this courtship.

What courtship? There has been none. That *begins today.*

SHE KNEW HE was in the castle, of course. Despite the place being full of somewhat lethargic guests drifting here and there, Serena and Maria set up a relay of communication traveling from the front hall to the studio, where Helen was trying to sketch a likeness of Sir Julius and seemed always to end up drawing Roderick with an eye patch.

"He's closeted with Gervaise in the library," Maria said, coming back into the room. "And all is quiet, so they are not tearing lumps out of each other."

"Did you expect them to?" Alice asked, looking up. At an old pianoforte, she had been playing odd chords and phrases of music, and then dementedly writing on her musical manuscript.

"No. I expect they're talking portions and dowries and other sordid matters," Maria said.

Helen caught her eye. "Is that what happened when you and Michael became engaged?"

"Sort of, I suppose. It was about looking after me, because Michael had no money."

"I don't think Roderick has either."

Alice frowned. "Then where will you live? Here, or at Black Hill?"

"I daresay I will be told in time," Helen said bitterly.

Her sisters exchanged glances.

Far sooner than she had expected, she was summoned to the library. Her sisters gave her bright, encouraging smiles. They had no idea why she was not happy. Alice at least suspected she was in love with Roderick, so her lack of euphoria must have appeared very odd to them.

Only when Helen pushed open the door, her heart beating uncomfortably fast, did she realize she had no idea how she should greet Roderick. *At least Gervaise will be there…*

Gervaise was not there.

Roderick stood alone at the window, his back to her, though he turned at once and came toward her. She felt as tongue tied as the child he thought her. Almost as she had been at the age of four when confronted by the splendor of the Prince of Wales in court dress, though for very different reasons.

He came to a halt before her, picked up her hand very gently, and kissed it. Flushing, she drew it free, though it still tingled where his lips had been.

"How are you?" he asked, surprising her all over again.

"I am well," she replied politely. "How are you?"

"Nervous. I have never been engaged to be married before. Shall we sit down? I'll tell you what your brother and I have been talking about."

Obediently, she went to the nearest sofa. He sat beside her, his back to the arm, so that he was turned toward her.

"Your brother is generous, so whatever happens to me or when, you will be independently secure. On top of that, he says that he will give us a house as a wedding present, which will remain yours in the event of my death."

She stared at him. "Oh, good."

"You don't want to know the legal stuff?" He sounded surprised, but only shrugged. "I'm sure his lordship will answer your questions should you have any, but these matters have some bearing on what we do next. If I rejoin the army, I may be posted somewhere it is neither advisable nor safe to take you—should you even wish to come."

You would go without me? Dismay warred with anger, but no words came out.

"I do not have to go back to the army," he said patiently. "I am happy to build up the guard business with Skelton. I think it will quickly become enough to live on. Besides which, there is another venture that might or might not come to fruition. Would you like to live in Blackhaven? In the town, if we can find a suitable house."

She found her voice at last. "Perhaps that would be best. Then you do not need to make up your mind at once, and if you do go back to the army"—*without me!*—"I will be close to my friends."

He nodded, as though that were at least one thing off his list of decisions to be made. "Your brother is still eager for a quick wedding. He is proposing a special license—well, a common license—so that we don't have to wait for the banns to be read. He is proposing next Friday."

"Friday!" she exclaimed in panic. "This Friday? That is six days away!"

"I know. Which is why I have to know what you want now. I am about to ride to the Bishop of Carlisle to obtain the license, and I have a few outriding tasks over the next few days."

"Don't let me keep you."

"Helen, I need to know what you *want*."

Why was he being so patient, so gentle with her? Why would he not quarrel, treat her like he used to as a friend and an equal?

"I *want* to paint pictures and go to Europe with Alice. It does not matter what I want."

"It matters to me." He raked his fingers through his hair, his only sign of anxiety. "You must know I will never stop you painting." He stopped and took a deep breath. "You spoke of honesty last night. So please give me an honest answer. I don't expect you to give me your reasons unless you care to tell me. But I do need to know this."

His eyes held hers, determined, steady, and yet surely behind all that calm was a tangle of desperate emotion. It made her silly heart leap.

"What?" she managed.

"Do you want to marry me?"

Her lips fell open in confusion, and a faint, rueful smile lurked in his eyes.

"Yes, I know we are engaged, and I am very happy for it to be so. I want to marry you, just as soon as you will have me. But I am aware, very aware, that you named me last night out of honor, to preserve me from the humiliation of being denied. Or to make it easier for me to avoid Meg! Either way, we were in an intolerable situation and got out of it as best we could."

He took her hand again. It jumped in his and was still. She still liked his touch. She liked it very much.

"I do not want you to throw me over, but if that is what *you* want, I will fight your brother, mother, and the rest of the town. We must do this because *we* choose to, whatever our reasons."

What are your reasons? She could not ask, not while holding back her own.

"So." He caressed her hand, and her pulse leapt. "Do you want to marry me, Helen?"

All the previous reasons for marriage stood. She did not really have a choice at all, and yet, with an aching heart, she was glad it was Roderick.

"Yes, I do."

He kissed her hand again. "Good. And do you object to Friday?"

"Is it not too quick? Encouraging the very gossip Gervaise was concerned to halt?"

He shrugged. "To most, we could easily have known each other before. There is no reason to wait. And besides, perhaps the certainty is best."

She gave a wry smile. "You mean get it over with?"

"No, just make a beginning," he said lightly. He dropped her hand and rose to his feet. "Then I shall get on my way and see you again in a couple of days."

A quick bow and he was gone.

THE NEXT ORDEAL was Mama. Helen and Gervaise were summoned to her private apartments for a discussion of the wedding.

"Friday!" the countess exclaimed, aghast, when Gervaise broke the news. "Don't be ridiculous. I have a house full of guests. How can I prepare a wedding breakfast in six days?"

She made it sound as though she, personally, would be slaving in the kitchen, rather than merely getting in the servants' way.

"The guests will begin to depart on Monday—even tomorrow, in some cases," Gervaise said. "And I believe Helen does not want a large party."

"It already seems a wretched hole-in-the-corner affair," Mama snapped. "She will have a breakfast suitable to her position." She glared at Gervaise. "What were you thinking of? They have nowhere to live, apart from here or that ramshackle place up at Black Hill which is full of Vales and cutthroats."

"Cutthroats?" Gervaise repeated in amazement. "Where on earth did you get that?"

"Everyone knows Sir Julius is employing the scaff and raff remnants of the army and navy."

"He is employing invalided soldiers and sailors," Gervaise corrected his mother, staring at her. "Men who fought and won the war for us."

Mama never accepted correction. She merely waved the matter aside and glared at Helen. "Well? Where *are* you planning to live?"

"In Blackhaven," Helen replied. "As soon as we find a suitable house in the town."

Mama's jaw dropped. "You cannot live in some mean little house—"

"It won't be mean, Mama," Gervaise intervened. "There is money to buy Helen a decent house, as there was for Maria."

Mama changed tack. "And Major Vale? Is he going back to the army?"

"Not immediately," Helen replied. "He is still on extended leave."

Mama stared at her with the uncomfortably penetrating gaze that had once made her confess all her sins. "Go away, Gervaise," she said. "I wish to speak with my daughter."

Gervaise obeyed. He knew there were matters brides had to discuss before their weddings.

Helen clasped her hands, digging her nails into her palms, while her mother gazed at her, frowning.

"I have married three daughters in love matches," she said at last. "Four if I count Eleanor. Even on days of nerves, disagreements, and downright quarrels, none of them ever looked as miserable as you."

Helen had no idea what to say to that.

The countess's face softened. "Helen, *do* you love him? Your sisters tell me it is so, but do you?"

Helen nodded. Somewhere, there was still pleasure in that, secret and precious.

Mama relaxed slightly. "Then what is it? Are you afraid of him?" Her eyes narrowed. "Has he taken *liberties*?"

Naked in bed, writhing beneath his caresses, wanton and eager...

"Not to the extent you mean."

Mama leaned forward and took her hand, forcing Helen to look at her. Her mother's love was fierce, but she had never doubted it. It had been the safest thing in her life.

"If you do not want this," Mama said clearly, "if you even have doubts about it, I will stop it."

And at last Helen could smile, even if a little tremulously. "I know. I chose him, Mama. I do want to marry him."

Her mother sat back again. "Then you have until Friday morning to tell me otherwise. After that, it will be…difficult."

FOR SOME REASON, the combination of her mother's support and her own defense of Roderick seemed to haul her out of her emotional slump. She would not go into this agreement like a helpless lamb to the slaughter. She would play her part and make her own decisions, beginning with finding a suitable house.

Of course, she could not do that on a Sunday, so she filled in the time by accompanying her family to church. There, the banns were read for Sir Julius Vale and Antonia Macy, and for Lucy Vale and Lord Eddleston.

In fact, one of the good things about those days before the wedding was getting to know Lucy. For two days after the ball, she spent nearly all her time at the castle keeping Lord Eddleston company. Naturally, she was curious about her brother's sudden engagement, though in such an optimistic way that it was impossible to take offense.

"It is you who has been so good for him, then," Lucy said as they strolled in the garden after church, making the most of some sunshine.

"Do you think so?" The words were out before Helen could help it. They made her sound pathetic, which annoyed her. "You find him happier?"

"Oh yes, definitely happier, calmer, less restless. Less…fraught." She hesitated. "He was different when he came home after Waterloo. Too serious, too…*boiling*. If you see what I mean. I think you have given him another reason to live and be happy."

Helen would have liked to take the credit, though she suspected it was merely time and new interests that were responsible.

"He has fewer nightmares," Lucy said, looking directly at her. "You do know about the nightmares?"

Helen nodded, and Lucy looked relieved.

"He hides at the top of the house so we won't know about them, but we still hear him. But I'm glad you know. He is…he *has been* a rather tortured soul."

"I know," Helen said quietly.

Lucy's eyes gleamed. "I'm told it's wildly attractive. Several friends have told me so." The smile faded. "But I don't want him to be tortured."

"Neither do I," Helen said.

"Good. Because the fun person he used to be is still in there."

On Monday, Lucy and Sir Julius came and whisked the recovering Lord Eddleston off to Black Hill. Helen and Frances went to Blackhaven to speak to the family solicitor. Mr. Worthing beamed at their request, wished Lady Helen every happiness in her forthcoming nuptials, and came himself to show them the available properties in the town.

Of the first four she saw, Helen considered only one. With the others, the rooms were too small, or there weren't enough of them, or there was no garden. Roderick liked the outdoors, so a house without a garden would not do, even with the beach close by.

"There is one more," Mr. Worthing said. "But it is rather old fashioned, and its owner recently passed away there, so it may not be where you wish to begin your married life."

"I don't mind old fashioned," Helen assured him. "But there

is no time for major renovation work."

"The building itself is sound," Mr. Worthing said. "It all depends on your ladyship's taste. And in its favor, Mr. Devonish's heirs are so eager to sell that we could obtain it for a very reasonable price, fully furnished."

"Mr. Devonish," Helen repeated, frowning, as the carriage moved on. "Why do I remember that name?"

"Probably because Serena and I told you his house was haunted," Frances said. "When we were children."

Helen sat up, suddenly much more interested. "Of course! Is it the one at the edge of the cliff, Mr. Worthing?"

"It is. Will that be a problem for your ladyship?"

"Goodness, no. I used to go up there with Maria and Alice so we could scare each other. But actually, I never really found it frightening. Mr. Devonish was a little eccentric, admittedly, but he had smiling eyes."

"The weather does batter it a bit," Mr. Worthing warned, "but the garden at the back is sheltered and sunny." He regarded the drizzle on the carriage window. "When there is any sun."

Helen knew as soon as she walked inside that she could be comfortable here. That she could make Roderick comfortable here. There was a bright reception room, a gracious drawing room with French doors onto a large, slightly wild garden, and a cozy dining room. There was also a smaller breakfast parlor and a room full of clutter that could be cleared out so that it could become Roderick's study or office. Upstairs were five good-sized bedchambers, and there was accommodation for servants under the eaves.

"You should not need many servants here," Mr. Worthing said. "Perhaps just a cook, a maid, and a manservant—as well as your personal servants, of course."

Helen found she was smiling out of the window at the view of the sea below. She swung around to Frances. "I love this house, don't you?"

"It has charm," Frances admitted. "And the furniture isn't

bad, even if it is old. I could see you here."

"Some of the rooms need brightening a little… I shall have to show it to Roderick first, of course, but I do like this house, Mr. Worthing. I like it very much!"

Chapter Eighteen

ODERICK RETURNED HOME on Tuesday, exhausted, but delighted to find a missive from his betrothed. He tore it open under the amused gaze of several siblings and then paused as possibilities hit him.

Was she crying off? He wouldn't blame her, of course, only… The rest of his life yawned before him, lonely and empty.

He blinked rapidly to dispel such foolishness. There was no point in mourning it until it happened. He read the letter quickly and didn't know whether to be relieved, amused, or disappointed.

"What does she say?" Aubrey demanded, grinning. "Is it a *very* soppy love letter?"

"Not exactly," Roderick said. It was in fact, a very businesslike letter, although her eagerness came through clearly enough. "She has found a house she likes and wants me to look at it as soon as possible." He hauled himself to his weary feet. "Which I shall do. I'll be back for dinner, Fliss."

While he would rather have seen the house with Helen, he was pleasantly surprised by it—both more gracious and less opulent than he had feared. The view was spectacular and the garden pleasantly wild. The house was not so large that she would rattle about it when he was away, or so small that she should feel cramped in it. Moreover, it had a pleasant *feel* to it. Old and comfortable.

Having returned the keys to Mr. Worthing, he rode up to the castle to tell Helen he approved. In fact, it was an excuse to see her.

He was shown straight into the elegant drawing room, where he found an unexpectedly domestic scene. Most of the castle guests must have departed, for the company consisted solely of family.

The dowager countess appeared to be dozing over her needlework. The earl was sipping tea and reading a newspaper, his wife leaning against his knees while sitting on the floor playing a lively game of cards with Ladies Serena, Maria, and Helen. Maria's husband, Hanson, was arguing politics with Lord Torridon, Lady Frances's spouse, and Lord Tamar was lounging on another sofa, sketching. Gentle music completed the scene, coming from Lady Alice at the pianoforte.

Everyone looked up when he was announced, and Roderick was delighted when Helen immediately jumped to her feet and hurried toward him.

"Roderick! Have you seen the house?"

It might not have been quite the greeting one hoped for from one's beloved after an absence, but he hid his disappointment by bowing to the room in general and greeting both Lady Braithwaites. Only then did he turn to Helen and hold out his hand.

"Yes, I have just come from there."

She flushed slightly, but gave him her hand and made no attempt to avoid him when he kissed it. "What did you think?" she asked eagerly.

Serena groaned. "Not more house!" she complained.

The younger Lady Braithwaite laughed. "Take the major into the garden, Helen—or at least to the orangery. You know how Serena only wishes to talk about her own house."

Serena stuck her tongue out at Eleanor without any malice and slapped a card onto the pile. "Ha!"

Roderick held the door for his betrothed, aware that the

dowager countess was watching him closely, though she made no demur.

"I like the house," he said, as Helen led him across the landing to another, smaller room, and out onto a terrace that sloped down to the lawn. The grass was damp, but the birds were singing, a blackbird among the chorus.

"Enough to live in?" Helen asked.

"Definitely. And I understand that we can move in immediately."

"As soon as Gervaise signs the contract. Which I shall make him do tomorrow. The walls and floors need brightening in a few places, but if you trust my taste, it can all be completed by Friday. Mama insisted on holding the wedding breakfast here, though I suggested the hotel."

"It is a small thing to give in on, and we shall be in our own house by the end of the day."

"That's what I thought." She cast him a small, fleeting glance as though finally prepared to risk it now that they had agreed on the important matters. Then her eyes lingered. "You look tired."

"I suppose I am. I have ridden a fair distance since I saw you last."

Her nostrils flared at a perceived criticism he certainly had not intended. "I'm sorry for dragging you out here—"

"I was not dragged," he interrupted. "I chose to come. Helen." He caught her hand, drawing her off the path and under a chestnut tree that shielded them from most of the castle windows. "My dear, what happened to my friend?"

Her gaze slid free and then came back to his with what looked like conscious courage. She did not pretend to misunderstand him. "She is still your friend."

"But she does not wish to be my wife? My lover?"

She flushed. "They are not necessarily the same thing."

Was that the worry eating her up, causing this damnable distance between them? "They have not been for me in the past, as you know," he said steadily. "But they are, and will be, from now on."

Her eyes widened. "Are you promising me fidelity, Roderick Vale?"

"I am. And rather insisting on it from you."

Her breath caught, and he wondered if he had made yet another mistake. Still, it was the truth, and it had to be said. And she did not draw her hand free, although he held it loosely enough.

He bent and kissed her cheek, and when she remained still, apart from the pulse jumping in her wrist, he softly kissed her lips. They parted at once, as though from instinct. But when he returned for a deeper kiss, she turned her head away.

"I want only you, Helen," he whispered.

Very lightly, he caressed the side of her neck, her nape, and she shivered. He could feel her body heat. If one of them only stepped a fraction closer…

She gave a nervous laugh. "Make your vows before God and Mr. Grant, Roderick. Come, we had best go back indoors. It's going to rain again."

And once more, she slipped away from him.

THE FOLLOWING MORNING, Roderick accompanied Aubrey into Blackhaven to enforce the drinking of the waters.

"You need another two hours of sleep," Aubrey said, surveying him critically as the carriage slogged along the muddy track to the Blackhaven road. "I will actually drink the damned waters without supervision, you know."

"Had a change of heart?"

Aubrey shrugged. "I've no idea whether or not they make any difference. Lampton says not. But I feel so much better here, I'm not prepared to change anything. So if I were you, I'd walk back to bed. Shall I get Hal to stop?"

Hal was their coachman, groom, and gardener, recruited by Julius from the hospital where he had been treated for an infected wound sustained at sea.

"No, I need to be in Blackhaven anyway. I have papers to sign and more printers and flyers to order."

"Your business idea is off to a good start?"

"Seems to be."

"Good for you." Aubrey's pleased expression changed to one of moody discontent. "Actually, I envy you. You have an independent purpose rather than just sponging off Julius."

"Black Hill is our family home and always will be. No one is sponging off Julius."

"Then why are you doing this guarding stuff?"

"To wake myself up, I suppose. I need to be busy."

"So do I now, since I don't have to lie on a couch all day."

Roderick regarded him more closely. He had been too wrapped up in himself recently, but he now he realized there was a kind of anguished desperation in Aubrey that he recognized only too well. Its cause and effect might be different in his younger brother, but it was no less real.

"I never thought to ask you," Roderick said slowly, "but you are very welcome to join Skelton and me in this venture. You would be an asset."

Aubrey's smile was both derisive and self-deprecating. "Hardly. Not really guard material, Rod. You couldn't rely on me."

"There's more to it than hard riding and looking threatening," Roderick said mildly. "There's observation, administration, being charming—and besides," he added, remembering an adventure a couple of weeks previously, "you were the one who captured the stolen horse."

"My one heroic gesture to prove I could. No, I wouldn't be reliable. And to be frank, Rod, it doesn't interest me."

"Pity," Roderick said. "You're an observant sort of fellow."

Aubrey wrinkled his nose. "Not much else to do when you're lying on a couch."

"Or sitting in drawing rooms, ballrooms, pump rooms…"

"Other people's lives are fascinating."

"You make them so," Roderick said, as a dormant idea began to re-form with new limbs. "I always enjoyed your letters. And I learned more about what was going on at home from your amusing epistles than I ever did from the girls' ramblings or Cornelius's concise reports."

Aubrey actually flushed slightly.

Roderick was glad his brother could still be embarrassed, even if just by praise. "I expect it accounts for your rakish successes."

"No, that is down to my good looks." Aubrey said, preening. "You must have noticed I'm the handsomest of the family."

"Well, you only *just* beat Felicia, but give it a couple of years and Leona will surpass you."

Aubrey threw his hat at him. Roderick laughed, but the idea rumbled away behind their banter and their glasses of water in the pump room.

"You are taking to the waters, too?" Aubrey said, surprised. "For exhaustion? Or stamina on your wedding night?"

It would not be stamina Roderick needed but patience, tenderness, and a good deal of insight—or luck—to pull down the barriers Helen had erected between them. Yesterday's moment in the garden had given him hope. She was not immune, but then was suddenly as skittish as a frightened kitten. Whatever happened to the girl who had so boldly asked him to kiss her at the assembly ball? He missed her.

"Sorry," Aubrey muttered. "Bad taste. You know I have every respect for her."

Roderick nodded and thrust that problem aside. He finished his glass of water and rose. "I need to be at the solicitors' office, but I shouldn't be too long. Do you know the print shop on Candle Row?"

"No, but I can find it. Why?"

"I'll meet you there in a couple of hours."

THE MARRIAGE CONTRACTS were signed and the title deeds to the house dealt with very quickly.

"I expect all my sisters to be in there by the afternoon," Braithwaite said wryly as they left Mr. Worthing's office. "Along with my wife and mother."

"I'll send my own siblings along to keep them company," Roderick said.

"Or to drag my family away. Helen has things she wants to do before you move in there." Braithwaite frowned. "The day after tomorrow. It is not long."

"You set the date, my lord," Roderick reminded him.

Braithwaite cast him a rueful look that was almost endearing. "Have I been an ass?"

"Perhaps you are too used to laying down the law and sticking to it," Roderick said, then relented. "But I am content with the situation if Helen is."

Braithwaite frowned. "I-I pushed her too fast. It seemed necessary."

"Perhaps it is."

"It wasn't fair," Braithwaite said flatly. A second longer he held Roderick's gaze. "For whatever it's worth, I am glad she chose you." He thrust out his hand, and Roderick clasped it.

"For whatever it's worth, so am I."

They parted in better understanding, and Roderick walked around to the print shop. Aubrey was already there, in the back of the shop, poking around the printing press and asking questions of Mr. Nimmo.

"Major Vale," Nimmo greeted him. "I trust your previous order was satisfactory?"

"Most satisfactory, thank you. I've come to order more."

"Certainly, sir." Nimmo was polite but hardly jumping for joy. A few flyers and business cards were not enough to save his business, his livelihood.

"Tell me, Mr. Nimmo," Roderick said, "do you have the capacity here to print a newspaper? Say, every fortnight to begin with?"

Nimmo blinked, eyeing his press. "I have the capacity but not the order."

"Could we sit down and discuss the possibilities of partnership? I have some money set aside which I can put into such a venture."

Nimmo looked stunned, and then a glimmer of hope appeared in his tired eyes.

Aubrey was staring at Roderick. "You want to produce a *newspaper* now? When the devil are you going to have time to do that?"

"I'm not," Roderick said. "You are."

Aubrey's jaw dropped.

"If you want to," Roderick continued. "You are the writer, the reporter of news. I can organize it and Mr. Nimmo can print it. If we can come to an agreement."

"I'll make tea," said Mr. Nimmo.

Aubrey swallowed. "Got any brandy?"

FOR HELEN, THE days since the castle ball had passed in something of a numb haze, through which very little penetrated. The discovery of the house did. And parts of her conversation in the garden with Roderick.

"Are you promising me fidelity, Roderick Vale?"

"I am. And rather insisting on it from you... I want only you, Helen."

The shocking touch of his lips... That haunted her, too, along with all his other kisses, and the growing closeness she had taken for granted before the disaster of Whalen and Gervaise's damnable ultimatum.

Only the house distracted her. Her entire family trooped around it shortly after midday on Wednesday.

"I like it," Serena said, twirling happily inside the drawing room. "It suits you."

"I told you," Frances said smugly.

Maria squeezed her hand. "You will be happy here."

"It is small and cramped," Mama pronounced.

"No it isn't," Alice said with a flare of temper that seemed to take everyone by surprise. "Only compared with the castle," she added, catching her mother's cold eye.

"It is a lovely house," Eleanor the peacemaker said. "And most importantly it means you will be close to us when we are in residence, and to your other friends. And the Vales are close by too."

Mama conceded the point and said she had no doubt Helen would make it handsome in time. As if on cue, the painters arrived and Helen shooed her family out to make way. She was half afraid they would intervene and overrule her instructions, convinced that they knew better. But in matters of color, Helen would bow to no one—except possibly Tamar—and she wanted this to be right, for herself as well as for Roderick.

She was almost surprised when they went. Perhaps they understood after all. Accordingly, she gave her instructions, approving the brighter wallpaper for only one of the drawing room walls and the elegant duck-egg-blue paint for the others. The dining room needed only a new coat of paint on the woodwork. The study was the other room that needed more work, so she set men to clearing it out, while the painters worked on the other rooms.

The tradesmen all worked hard through Wednesday afternoon and into the evening. Even so, they were already hard at work when Helen returned early on Thursday morning.

The bedchambers presented more of a quandary. She really needed Roderick to choose his room, and she didn't want to seize the one she really liked as her own. Two of the bedchambers had small dressing rooms, but one of them was at the back of the house, without the sea view that Roderick might well prefer. So she ended up just ordering them to repaint the woodwork in all the rooms upstairs, while she admired the drawing room and, with the help of the two servants Mr. Worthing had sent around for approval, set to rearranging, polishing and cleaning the furniture.

While she worked, she thought, not about the wedding tomorrow, but about the present and the recent past, those small moments of clarity during the week when she realized how important this new life, this marriage, was to her. Because it was to Roderick.

She had not liked that he was different with her now, treating her with kid gloves, like brittle china. She had wanted her friend back, which was almost exactly what he had said to her in the garden. But she acknowledged now that the very act of trying was more than he *had* to do. She was won. His honor and hers were safe. And yet he behaved as though he really cared. Just kindness? Maybe…

She engaged the maid and the manservant, who had been so helpful throughout the day, and a cook to begin right away. Leaving them scrubbing down the kitchen, she went back to admire the drawing room, which was now almost complete. The windows were open to dissipate the smell of paint, which made the curtains billow. She supposed the fabric was a little worn and faded, but they really looked rather good with the new colors.

It was time she went home, but before she did, she spread out the new carpet—a gift from Frances that had just been delivered from the new shop in the high street. The shade was perfect, the pile soft and luxurious. She placed it in the middle of the room, with the chairs and sofas on the edges, as she had already planned.

She was just adjusting the position of a small table when she realized footsteps were rapidly approaching.

She straightened as a man strode into the room.

"Helen," Roderick said in surprise. "You are still here."

His appearance cast her into a confusion of delight and embarrassment. Her heart was beating so fast, she was afraid her limbs would shake.

"What do you think?" she blurted, gesturing to the room as a whole, mainly to take his attention away from her.

He obliged, and she was gratified to see his eyebrows fly upward as he took it all in. "It looks like a completely different room. Soothing, comfortable elegance. I love the colors."

He could not have said anything to please her more, and she couldn't help smiling.

"Come and see the study. I thought you might want an office, if you keep going with the business."

"I think I will. In fact, I have another in the works too. I believe I shall sell out."

Only when he said it did she realize it was the decision she had wanted. Now they could choose when and where to go, and he would not risk his life or his sanity every time he left her. They could be together.

But for all your promised fidelity, will you love me?

He was amazed at the study, now warm cream and red with a desk, a pair of comfortable, unmatching chairs, and empty bookcases. "What on earth did you do with all the *stuff*?"

"Flynn put it in the attic. There's plenty of storage up there. Oh, Flynn came via Sir Julius, and I have engaged him, as well as a maid and a cook. You can meet them, if you like. Do you want to see the dining room and the bedrooms first?"

"Yes, I do."

It felt very strange climbing the stairs with him, like a prophetic vision anticipating many such trips. She shivered, her skin heating, and tried to redirect her thoughts.

"I don't know which bedchamber you would like, so I have left them more or less as they were," she said breathlessly. "The two at the front have the sea view…"

He made pleasant noises about the front room with the dressing closet, but surprised her by paying more attention to the other room.

He must want that one for his own…

The summer evening was still bright, and the lowering sun glinted off his shining, dark hair as he walked back and forth across the room.

"Correct me if I am wrong," he said at last, "but I think this would make an excellent studio."

She stared at him. "S-studio?" she stammered.

"For your painting. The light seems best. It is a little darker to the back, and of course there is no sea view there." He met her gaze and gave his rare, crooked smile. "I wanted to be sure you remembered your painting in all this flurry."

She wanted to cry. She could only nod mutely with gratitude and fight back the tears.

"Then we'll move the bed out as soon we have time. Maybe Flynn can do it while we are being married. I'll speak to him."

"Is that why you came?" she blurted.

"Yes." He seemed to be about to say more, but her legs moved without permission, propelling her across the floor to him.

She seized him by the arms and stood on tiptoe, pressing her lips to his with sheer emotion—because in all of this confusion, he had thought of her and her happiness, and understood the importance of her painting.

"Thank you!" she whispered, and fled before her emotion could embarrass him.

Chapter Nineteen

I F SHE HAD but known it, her emotion did not embarrass him in the slightest. On the contrary, it brought hope surging to the fore. Surely there had been more than gratitude in her kiss, however brief, and in her unshed tears.

He allowed her a moment to recover herself, then followed. He caught up with her in the kitchen, where she introduced the servants and he spoke to Flynn about the bed. Then they left the house that would be their home from tomorrow, and he handed her into her waiting carriage.

He took the opportunity to kiss her gloved fingers. "Until tomorrow," he said, smiling because suddenly he was looking forward to it more than he ever had to anything.

For some reason, it seemed to deprive her of breath, and then the horses began to move forward and he had to step back.

He had thought he was tired after spending the day guarding a man ferrying a fortune in jewels from a country house to a bank in Carlisle. But suddenly he had too much energy. He doubted he would sleep that night.

When he got home, his siblings seemed to recognize his mood and did not bring up the subject of the wedding, except to remind him of the early start. As though he could forget. As Julius retired for the night, he surprised Roderick by laying his hand on his shoulder when he said good night.

As they all drifted off, Roderick remained gazing thoughtfully out of the window. It was cloudy, as it had been for much of the summer, but there were occasional glimpses of the moon. Did Helen see them, too? Was she sound asleep, or lying awake and resentful at what she had been pushed into?

He had not noticed that Lucy was still in the room until she slid her hand into his and stood beside him. He remembered a similar occasion when they were much younger, when he had been on leave from the army and she a mere child. She had chattered away about her hopes and dreams, and he had been both surprised and delighted by the affection of the little sister he was afraid would barely remember him. But Lucy always remembered.

"And so you will be the first of us after all," she murmured dreamily. "Before me *and* Julius. I shall miss you, Rod."

He squeezed her hand. "Not for long. It—this—was never meant to be forever. And you are about to embark on the adventure of a lifetime, just as you always wanted."

"My Tyler is a good man to adventure with," she said. She always called him Tyler, the name he had given himself in jest, after the leader of the medieval Peasants' Revolt, Wat Tyler. "But I shall always be glad we have had this time at Black Hill."

"So will I," admitted Roderick, who could not, in fact, imagine having survived without it.

"I think we are all embarking on adventures," Lucy said. "The twins think so."

"The twins *make* it so," Roderick said wryly. "They made Julius and me go the ball, and they brought your Eddleston here. In fact, now that I think of it, everyone has been…distracted."

"Is that good?" Lucy asked.

"Oh, I think so," Roderick said. And just for a little, he believed in happiness.

WHEN SHE WOKE on her wedding day, Helen did not recognize the knot of nerves in her stomach. It might have been excitement or tension, or the knowledge that she was doing something *wrong* in marrying a man who did not love her.

Foolish. Lots of women married men who did not love them. In many cases, the brides did not care for their husbands either, so she was luckier than some.

Her family insisted on pampering her. Her sisters brought her breakfast in bed and stayed chattering while she ate it. Or at least tried to eat it.

"Wedding nerves," Serena pronounced, as she pushed the almost full plate away.

"I must say, you don't look like a girl who anticipated her wedding vows with a handsome soldier," Frances teased.

"I didn't."

Her oldest sisters exchanged glances. Then Serena leaned forward and whispered in her ear, "Don't fear that. It is adorable. *He* is adorable. And a gentleman."

Frances took the tray away, and Alice all but hauled Helen out of bed. She was bathed, anointed, brushed, and perfumed to within an inch of her life. Her favorite gown of green silk was dropped reverently over her head and fastened, and she barely noticed until she was asked to admire the finished product in the glass.

A beautifully coiffed version of herself gazed back, her expression dubious.

By then Mama was there too. "You will do," she said, "although I would have liked the time to dress you in a new gown."

"Oh, I almost forgot!" Serena exclaimed. "Look, we got you this delightful little hat!"

It was more of a confection than a hat, a ridiculous piece of silk and artificial flowers in the palest green to match her gown.

"Just *there*," Frances said, and Serena deftly pinned it at a jaunty angle. With relief Helen saw that it actually had a fine net veil, which she drew down with relief. She could hide.

"Shoo," Mama commanded. "You have yourselves to dress still, and the carriages will be waiting any moment."

And they all bustled off again, leaving her staring at the well-dressed stranger with her face and a painful knot in her stomach.

But no, Alice had not yet gone. She regarded Helen from the doorway, frowning. She half turned away as Helen rose from the stool, and then swung back.

"Why do you look like that?" Alice asked. "Are you still insisting you have been forced into this?"

Helen stared back. "I have. More to the point, so has he."

A flash of impatience swept Alice's face. "For God's sake, Helen, he *loves* you. Any fool could see that."

Heat rushed into Helen's face. Could it be true? The twins had said the same thing. "You cannot know that," she said hoarsely.

"Helen, everyone knows that. Except, apparently, you."

"He is a good and kind man." But kindness was not love.

"And he *loves* you," Alice repeated, and stalked out.

Helen gazed after her, her arm across her knotted stomach. *Then why does he not say so?*

THE LITTLE CHURCH of St. Andrew in Blackhaven was already filling up when Meg Maven arrived and, with difficulty, found a discreet seat in one of the rear pews. Of course, the whole town would turn out to see this bride, one of the earl's family. They did not know what Meg did. That the marriage would never take place.

She had known it since the castle ball. Her trick to entrap Roderick herself had misfired. In fact, she had been, as they said, hoist with her own petard. She had not expected the girl to stand up and claim him after it was blindingly obvious to the entire company that Meg, if not actually engaged to Roderick, was most certainly still on intimate terms with him.

But Roderick had claimed betrothal to Lady Helen, and she had gone along with it to save his face. It showed a spirit that Meg reluctantly admired, and it had certainly led to her temporary humiliation. Although the kind young gentleman had smoothly turned that into jest before ushering her from the premises. There was more to young Mr. Muir than met the eye.

In fact, there appeared to be more to Lady Helen, that milk-and-water miss, than Meg had first allowed. Helen had won that battle at the ball, but she had not won the war, for Meg knew Roderick would never go through with it.

He was not fit to live with people, let alone a sheltered, gently born young lady. He could barely sit still for longer than half an hour. He was eager enough for bed sport, and during it, Meg had enjoyed all his attention. But afterward…he could not lie still in bed, let alone sleep beside her. Apart from once, when he had clearly been in the grip of raging nightmares. His nerves were so wrecked, she knew he could not abide people around him for long. He only lived with his siblings because he had nowhere else, and even there, he lived at the top of the house, well away from everyone else, and seemed to spend most of his time outdoors.

How would he bear the intimacy of marriage? He could not, of course, and he knew it. It was true he need not share his wife's bedchamber, but Meg had seen the house people imagined the newlyweds would occupy. There would be nowhere for him to go to escape her.

But those were details. In fact, she knew Roderick had *never* had any intention of marrying Helen Conway. It was Meg who understood him and would put up with his bouts of madness, for the privilege of being a gentleman's wife. Helen did not need that from him. She did not need him at all. She could marry anyone she chose, and would do so—once Roderick removed himself from her vicinity. Which he would.

Meg settled in to watch the drama unfold. All the great and the good of Blackhaven were present. At least, she imagined they were, for she recognized many from the ball. The Vales, led by the lame, imposing figure of Sir Julius with his eye patch and a beautiful lady on his arm. The youngest sister Lucy, with a slight, elegant young gentleman at her side. The other brothers and sisters, all good looking, including a boy and girl so alike that they had to be twins.

She recognized Mr. Muir with an elderly lady and a darkly attractive younger one. Beside them were Lord and Lady Wickenden. Colonel and Mrs. Benedict. Mr. Winslow, the squire, and his family. A couple of splendid military gentlemen. She even thought she glimpsed the infamous Captain Alban, who had retired somewhere near here with his aristocratic wife.

Meg acknowledged surprise when Roderick walked in and Sir Julius rose to meet him. It gave her a nasty moment, until she realized that of course Roderick would never humiliate a lady by jilting her at the church. The Braithwaites would never let him. They would save face and their own pride, particularly Helen's, by humiliating *him*. It was the bride who would not turn up, who would leave Roderick alone and highly relieved at the altar.

The vicar, a remarkably personable man, greeted the supposed groom with a smile and a handshake. The three of them appeared to be joking together, until they were distracted by the arrival of the older and younger countesses, escorted by the sisters' husbands, who included an earl, a marquis, and a member of Parliament. The men acknowledged Roderick and Sir Julius in friendly enough spirit, but Meg, eagle-eyed, saw the dowager countess's cold glare.

Meg was surprised the old lady had troubled to turn up. But then she would have to preserve the myth of Helen jilting Roderick at the last moment. She settled down to wait, watching Roderick with appreciation.

He cut a very fine figure in his regimental uniform, tall, lean, and handsome in that dark, brooding manner that had first aroused her. The slightly wild yet hard eyes, the sharp blades of his fine cheekbones, the passion of his mouth… Too much man for little Lady Helen. Too unstable for her family, for anyone except Meg, to handle.

An uncomfortable memory intruded. In the foyer of the assembly rooms, slamming the door in the hope of sending Roderick into one of his nightmares, and scaring the girl off. Helen had glared at her, but somehow, she had led Roderick to privacy. She had not been frightened by what had looked like an attack.

Meg shifted position, thrusting the memory aside.

A stir of excitement around the door caused her breath to catch with excitement. This was it. The messenger to announce the wedding was "postponed." It might even be the Earl of Braithwaite himself, come to apologize to his guests…

And yes! There was Lord Braithwaite's tall, graceful figure. Only there was someone with him, on his arm, a young woman it took Meg several seconds to recognize as Lady Helen Conway.

Blood seemed to sing in her ears. Surely the girl did not mean to go through with it? No, there would be some stumble later, surely. All the more dramatic, but not good for Meg's nerves.

She turned her head to the front once more. Roderick's gaze was fixed on his approaching bride, a smile hovering on his lips.

Roderick never smiled.

A feeling of dread began to overcome Meg. As if in her own nightmare, she watched and listened to the short wedding ceremony that was binding Roderick to another woman. They each recited their vows in clear tones, and the vicar pronounced them man and wife.

They turned together and walked down the aisle and out of the church to the smiles of the entire congregation. Except Meg.

Stunned, she continued to sit where she was as everyone rushed out of the church after the happy couple. Absently, she rubbed her fingers over her heart. It hurt, and only now, when she could do nothing about it, did she begin to understand why. Roderick had married another, leaving Meg alone. But worse, much worse than that, she finally understood the reason she'd fought so hard.

Roderick was more than a means to an end, her path to gentility and the Society that would otherwise be closed to her. Somehow, she had done what she had vowed never to do. She had fallen in love.

And she had lost him.

Pain and grief overwhelmed her—until she discovered the saving splendor of anger.

MOST OF HELEN'S favorite people attended the wedding breakfast. Caroline Benedict—who hugged her with delight—and her husband and stepdaughter. Gillie Wickenden and her brother Bernard Muir, Mr. and Mrs. Grant, Dr. Lampton and his wife the princess, Lady Arabella and her husband, Captain Alban. All the Winslows, and Tamar's brother Lord Sylvester.

The uncomplicated happiness with which she would have enjoyed such a gathering at the beginning of the summer seemed to have vanished into the knot at the pit of her stomach. With a smile pinned to her lips, she went through the motions in a numb haze. Food was eaten, though she didn't think she had much of it, and toasts were raised to the happy couple.

Laughing, they all promised to gather again the following week for Sir Julius's wedding to Antonia Macy.

With a jolt, she realized she and her husband were leaving, and a wave of panic washed through her, dragging with it a sense of terrible loneliness. Like when Maria had gone to London with Michael, only worse, because now Helen was separated from Alice too, and going alone to the house of a man who did not love her.

The brush of his fingers on her cheek shocked her. She stared at him.

"Are you ready?"

Her smile ached but held. "Of course."

As they walked down the front steps to the waiting carriage, she said suddenly, "I wish we could walk."

"Of course we can. But you will be stopped every other step by townspeople wishing you well."

He had a point. She let him hand her into the carriage, felt another jolt of awareness as he sat beside her—her *husband*—and then they were moving, and she was waving out of the window at her brother and sisters and brothers-in-law. Her mother stood behind them, dignified and stern as always.

"They are not far away," Roderick reminded her.

She nodded.

"Helen?"

She looked at him.

"You can stop smiling now. If you want to."

She swallowed. Her jaw and lips trembled. "Sorry. It seems so odd to be leaving them."

"For your own home, which you chose and made beautiful in a matter of days."

"It is rather lovely, isn't it?" she said proudly, and that at least felt natural.

"I've always lived out of baggage, under canvas tents, or accepted whatever accommodation I was given. I've never had a home of my own before, let alone one to share with you."

A faint warmth curled around her heart. "I shall try to make you happy and comfortable there."

"I am happy." *Aren't* you? The words hung between them, but he did not ask them—which was a relief, because she did not want to lie to him.

Still, she could not help being pleased when he took her hand as they entered the house together for the first time. It was a warm house, old and soothing, as if with other people's contented memories. And she had never been so aware of a man as she was of Roderick. Her husband.

Violet, the smiling maid, served tea in the drawing room and departed, leaving them alone. For a little while, as Helen poured the tea, it was like playing at houses when she was a child. Only Roderick was nothing like her sisters, or even her brother. He was like no one she had ever known.

"Shall we see what they have done with your studio?" Roderick said at last.

She jumped up. "Oh yes! My things should have been sent over by now."

The bed had gone. So had the large chest of drawers and the dressing table. In their place was an older chest and tables she could happily spill paint and water on, and, in the center of the floor, an old chair and her beloved easel. Stacks of brushes, paints, paper, and canvases were piled on the tables, along with her sketchbooks, past and present.

"Do you think you will be happy painting here?" he asked.

She could only nod. Her throat felt too tight to speak.

"I'll go and find my own things," he said, and wandered off, leaving her blessedly alone.

And yet, almost as soon as he had gone, she missed his company. *Fool.*

Leaving the studio, she heard him rummaging in the large bedchamber at the back. She had known he would leave her the brighter room at the front with the sea view. It was kindness and chivalry.

Violet must have put everything away for her. There was nothing to do but take the silly hat off. At least it made her smile, because it was so typical of her sisters.

With her cushions and hairbrushes, childish ornaments and perfume bottles, the bedchamber was very feminine. There was nothing of Roderick's in here. She had known there would not be. Most married couples of her rank had separate rooms. Although she knew her sisters all shared bedchambers with their husbands whenever they stayed at the castle, and in their own homes. Perhaps Frances and Torridon had not, for a while, but now they did. Gervaise had his own official chamber, which he occasionally used to dress in, but everyone knew he slept every night in Eleanor's.

Her siblings had all made love matches. Hers was a marriage of convenience. One-sided love did not count. She had always known—indeed, she preferred—that Roderick would have his own chamber. She just hadn't expected it to make her feel so lonely.

Well, she had made her bed and must now lie in it. She walked briskly out onto the landing.

"What time would you like supper, Roderick?" she called. "I told Cook just something light."

"Good plan," he called back. "Seven?"

In spite of everything, there was a certain pleasure in dining alone with Roderick in their own dining room. With a glass of wine, she began to relax. They began to talk as friends once more, and the knot in her stomach started to unravel. She began to appreciate what she had in her marriage, to see a way forward for them. She even laughed more than once at his amusing tales. There was banter between them again.

After the meal, Roderick accompanied her to the drawing room, bringing his port with him. She was surprised to discover that the long summer evening was over and darkness had fallen. Someone, presumably Violet, had drawn the curtains and lit candles.

"This room needs a pianoforte," Helen said suddenly. "*That* is what is missing."

"I discovered a man in Carlisle who deals in secondhand instruments. We can probably buy one from him quite inexpensively. Come with me the next time I go, and we can choose one."

She smiled. "I will."

He took another sip of port. "I didn't tell you about my other idea, did I? About a Blackhaven newspaper, which Aubrey will run."

She grew quite animated in favor of this venture, offering help and new ideas until she realized he had not said anything for some time. He had leaned his head against the chair back, but his eyes were open, watching her, making her suddenly self-conscious and nervous. The knot in her stomach tied itself up again.

She rose. "I believe I shall retire. It has been a long day."

"Indeed. I'll light you up."

With quiet domesticity, she helped him blow out the candles in the drawing room, all but one, which he carried out of the room to light them upstairs. Her heart beat faster when he walked ahead of her into her bedchamber and lit the candles there, and her bedside lamp.

Then he set down his own candle and walked slowly toward her—lean, purposeful, predatory, as she had first seen him at the ball a lifetime ago. Her breath caught. Her heart was hammering again, and yet he had only come to say a civil good night.

"Mrs. Vale," he said softly, taking both her hands. "It is the first time I have called you that."

"It is the first time I have been that." And now, how to strike the balance between cool and cordial? She reached up and kissed his cheek, secretly loving the feel of his rough skin beneath her lips, inhaling his special Roderick scent.

But before she could bid him good night, he bent his head and kissed her lips. Warmth spread from her mouth to her whole being. Desire uncoiled in her stomach, only from that one brushing caress. And his closeness, the whisper of his breath. Soft, gentle kisses teased the corner of her mouth.

She tried to speak, to stop him, for this was not the way friends bade each other good night, but even as she parted her lips to speak, his mouth closed over them with much more purpose, enfolding her in sweet, delicious weakness. Butterflies soared and dived, and when he gathered her close, she knew what he wanted, because she longed for it too.

Chapter Twenty

A LARM BELLS EXPLODED in her head, making her gasp into his mouth. His fingers stroking her nape, his lean, hard body caressing her—all overwhelmed her with need. She knew that men "made love" frequently without the love. Roderick himself had confessed it to her, although until now he had at least saved her from that humiliation.

With a sob of loss and determination, she tore herself free, panting like a dog in the sun. Her whole body trembled, but somehow, she said clearly, "You seem to have forgotten that ours is a marriage of convenience."

His hot, clouded eyes gazed into hers without wavering. The silence stretched between them, and she thought he would never speak. When he did, she could tell nothing from his light voice. "I think we had both forgotten. Are you telling me now, I am, in fact, *inconvenient?*"

She had to hold herself rigid so that her knees did not give way.

"Yes," she said. "Good night, Roderick."

Something flared in his eyes that looked terribly like hurt, but then his lashes came down so quickly that she knew she must be mistaken. He even bowed elaborately, mockingly.

"Good night, Mrs. Vale," he said, and sauntered out, taking his candle with him.

He did not close the door, so she did it for him before sinking down on the bed and letting the tears come.

IT WAS A dull way to spend her wedding night, and when she stopped weeping, she acknowledged it. She could never give herself to a man without love, but did refusing him when she *did* love him make any more sense?

She sat up, suddenly disgusted with herself. Why was she being so wretchedly *passive*? If she wanted his love, she should be trying to win it, win him, not pushing him away like a spoiled child in a tantrum because someone had given her a faulty toy!

Why had she sent him away?

Because I wanted him to fight my foolishness! I wanted him to persuade me, convince me, love me... And maybe he does. A little. He might never have said it, but I have never asked...

The sudden clarity gave her much food for thought. So much so that she rose and began to pace the room as memories and possibilities bombarded her.

They had been pushed into marriage too soon. Roderick had more healing to do, and perhaps she had more growing up to do. Circumstances had been against them... Well, she and Alice had precipitated that, with a little help from Meg Maven. Helen had agreed to marry Roderick, and in truth life held no greater joy for her than to be his wife. No one was pushing her into bed with him. She wanted to be there.

So what was she afraid of? Being taken without love? Being a duty? Was it not up to her to make it more than that? To speak her own love?

At the very least, he was her friend who had gone out of his way to save her, both in Whalen and in the castle when she had almost made the worse mistake of accepting Glover. Separation from Roderick tonight achieved nothing except more misunderstanding. What they needed was to *talk*. If not tonight—after all, they were both tired, if not emotionally exhausted—then tomorrow.

And suddenly, she needed to tell him so, to give them both peace to sleep in and a kind beginning to their marriage.

She could have done better today and all of the six days leading up to this moment. But it was not too late to talk, to explain, to listen…

She hurried back across the room, swiping up one of the candles on her way, and left her chamber.

Although the rest of the house seemed to be in darkness, a glimmer of light shone beneath the door of Roderick's chamber across the hall. She hurried toward it, her heart drumming, and knocked.

To her surprise, the door swung inward and she realized it had not been fully closed.

"Roderick? May I come in? I don't want us to quarrel on our…"

There was no movement within. No voice bade her to enter or to go away. In fact, she knew he was not present. There was no *feel* of Roderick in this room. She walked in, adding her own candle's glow to that from the solitary lamp on his bedside table.

His things had all been put away. She wondered what he had brought with him, for there was no sign of whatever made him Roderick. Apart from the violin case propped in the corner shadow. And a cravat dropped on the still-made bed.

Did he feel as alone and at sea as she did? They should at least be comforting each other.

Where was he? Getting drunk in his study? Walking? It would be easy to walk to the beach from here…

She would look for him in the house, she decided, and then wait for him here in this room, to be sure they spoke—and not in anger or resentment or whatever had been going on in her foolish head.

But perhaps he was in the garden. She went to the window that overlooked it and pulled back the curtain. She saw the light at once, and her heart leapt because she had found him after all.

He stood beneath the window, illuminated by a light whose source she could not see. But he was not alone. He held a woman by both shoulders, intent upon her upturned, anguished face.

The face of Meg Maven.

RODERICK HAD LEFT his wife in the only way he could, with outwardly lighthearted acceptance of her dismissal. If there was mockery in his tone, it was aimed firmly at himself and his body's raging lust. And the emotional pain that went far deeper.

After all his self-lecturing, his determination to show only patience and understanding as he slowly wooed his young wife, he had rushed his fences.

But her body had melted against him. Her mouth had done more, much more, than yield to the passion of his. He had felt her urgency as if it were his own, and all his good intentions had flown out of the window.

She had been right to call him inconvenient.

It would not even have mattered so much had he not sensed her own grief, her own loss. She was denying herself as well as him, and he did not understand why. And so he had stared and stared out of his cold, empty bedchamber window, calming his lust and refusing to let in the demons of melancholy.

The evening had gone well until the end. They had been breaking down the distance their short engagement had some-how brought about, and time had flown by in delightful companionship, with just an edge of lust—on his part, at least. Because she was his wife. Helen Conway, his impossible dream of happiness, was his.

And like a randy schoolboy, he had let it go to his head. Or at least to his loins. She deserved better than that.

He wondered if she was still awake. Would it make things

better or worse if they tried to talk now? He had sensed her despair as he left her…

Something was moving in the garden below his window, distracting him. A woman with a lantern and an armful of something she must have dropped, for a moment later, she reappeared carrying only the lantern and walking swiftly to the woodshed at the side of the garden.

What the…?

She reemerged carrying chopped logs, returning toward the house. She was not Violet- or Cook-shaped. And in any case, it was Flynn's job to fetch wood for the fires, and this female was most certainly not Flynn! Something in her movement tugged his memory, his recognition. Something so ridiculous as to be impossible.

And yet he moved quickly, collecting a candle and striding from the room. On the landing, he noticed the light beneath Helen's door, but he could not hesitate now. This was insane enough to be urgent.

He moved smartly all the way down to the kitchen, straight through to the back door, which he unlocked and pushed open. He had to push hard, for there were piles of wood against it.

He raised his gaze from the wood to the woman frozen in the glow of his lamp and her own lantern. She was slightly bent, as though about to set the lantern on the ground. Or break it against the wood.

His blood ran cold, but he forced himself to speak lightly, almost humorously. "Meg. An odd time to make calls. Are you bringing me a wedding gift?"

She laughed, a curiously uncontrolled sound that grated because it held no mirth whatsoever. "I am. I hope you like it."

In the circumstances, a naked flame was a disadvantage. He blew out his candle and set it on the low table just inside the kitchen door, before stepping over the doorway. "Perhaps I would appreciate it more were the logs not already mine."

Her mouth, once so beautiful, twisted. "The logs are not your gift."

She swung the lantern high, but he was ready for her and seized her wrist while it was still in the air. Swiftly, before she could drop the lantern onto the dry wood, he wrenched it from her fingers.

"Seriously, Meg?" he said. "You would set fire to my house, risking the injury, the death, of my wife and servants? Have you ever *seen* people burned to death?" He had. Along with those who had survived the experience, they formed many of his nightmares.

With a cry like a wounded animal, Meg wrenched herself free. Roderick kicked the wood away from the door, scattering it, then turned and took her by the shoulders. For what she had so nearly done, he wanted to shake her, but there was something very wrong here, something very wrong with *her*.

"Why would you do such a terrible thing?" he asked.

"It's your fault," she burst out. "*Yours!* You used me and cast me aside. And now you marry *her*? How dare you?"

"How dare I marry someone else?" he asked, struggling. "We have been over that. We have both behaved badly, but don't pretend you ever loved me."

As soon as the words were out, he realized his mistake. This was more, much more than jealous rage devouring her. There was sheer agony on her face as she snatched up the lantern and fled, leaving him struggling with sudden self-awareness.

In spite of not wanting to, in spite of her selfish, mercenary, ambitious little soul, Meg had somehow fallen in love with him.

But then, somehow or other, lots of people loved him in lots of different ways—his siblings, his few old friends like Skelton who had survived Waterloo. Helen? Perhaps it was not so unbelievable that she might truly love him too.

He was not an unlovable man.

Something eased in him. He did not know if it was emotional or physical. It felt like both. Almost like euphoria.

And then a sudden cry of rage rent the air and a door

slammed like a gunshot.

PERHAPS IT WAS only an instant Helen stood frozen at Roderick's window, but it felt like an age of shocked betrayal. That he could go straight from trying to seduce her to an assignation with Meg Maven…

But no, that truly *was* ridiculous! Something was wrong, very wrong.

Meg wrenched herself from Roderick's hold, her face ugly with rage and anguish. Roderick appeared stern yet uncomprehending. Meg was shouting at him, though the words were indiscernible from behind the window.

Sheer instinct to help, to avert whatever danger threatened, propelled Helen out of Roderick's room and downstairs. The house had a side door, bolted on the inside, the key hanging from a hook right beside it. It was her quickest way to the back garden, so she set her candle down, threw back the bolts, unlocked the door, and flew outside, rushing up the side path to the back garden.

She did not even see Meg until it was too late. A pale, wavering light showed her the woodshed with its door wide open—and then, with a cry of rage, Meg flew out of the shadows, knocking Helen sideways and then shoving her so hard that she fell sprawling into the shed against hard logs that began to dislodge and tumble around her.

The door slammed shut on her, depriving her of any light at all, and then something crashed against the shed wall and a glow flared through the cracks. Flames!

My God, Roderick stopped her setting fire to the house, and now she means to burn me in here!

Roderick… Oh God, what has she done to him?

In a sudden fury of love and determination, she sprang to her feet and hurled herself at the shed door. Or at least into the thick blackness where she thought it had been.

She met no resistance whatsoever and flew through the door as if she had been catapulted. She almost lost her balance, but there was no time.

Roderick, his face a mask of desperation, sprinted the last couple of paces to the burning shed wall, a pail of rainwater in his hand, which he upended over the flames.

They went out with a hiss, plunging them once more into darkness—but not before Helen glimpsed Meg hurtling at Roderick, a log raised like a cudgel and aimed straight for his head.

Helen did not even think. She leapt, landing on Meg with such force that they both crashed to the ground. Helen could not breathe.

She was vaguely surprised that Meg did not fight back. A moment before, she had been like an angry, spitting beast of prey.

Urgent yet gentle hands were lifting Helen. Roderick crouched beside the still figure of Meg.

"Oh dear God," Helen whispered. "Have I *killed* her?"

"No," Roderick said. "But she's out cold and her head is bleeding. I think she struck it on a fallen log."

He straightened, reaching for Helen, and without thought she hurled herself into his arms, seizing his face between her hands and covering it with desperate kisses while incoherent words fell from her lips.

"I thought she would hit you, kill you, and I could not bear it—"

"*You* couldn't bear it? I thought she was burning you alive! How did you get out so quickly?"

"She didn't bolt the door," Helen said.

He blinked, as if stunned all over again, and then he began to laugh, and she was laughing too until his mouth, rough, desperate, and hungry, fell upon hers as if he would never let her go.

"I love you," he muttered against her lips. "That's all there is, all there has to be. I love you."

Enchanted, Helen had no idea how long the kiss would have lasted, had not another very different voice spoken close by.

"Embracing over the corpse?" Aubrey drawled. "Different, I suppose, but hardly *de rigeur*."

They fell apart, though Roderick kept his arm snugly about her.

"Aubrey?" he said. "What the devil are you doing here?"

It was definitely Aubrey. He carried a lantern, which he swung now over the still figure of Meg. She stirred, groaning, away from the light in her eyes.

"Long story," Aubrey said. "Shortened version, I saw her in church this morning. She looked mad as a bag of frogs, so we— the twins and I—have been keeping an eye on her."

Roderick glanced around as though he expected the twins to leap out from behind the woodshed.

"They're safely at Black Hill," Aubrey assured him. "I'm supposed to be the night shift." His voice changed and he looked, for him, almost shame faced. "Afraid I nodded off, and when I came to, she was no longer in the hotel. I came here on the off chance. What was she up to?"

"Trying to burn down the house," Roderick said.

Aubrey paled quite clearly in the light of his jerking lantern. "*What?*"

"I thought I had talked her out of it—she seemed calm and merely sad. Only then she caught sight of Helen, and it set it her off again."

Aubrey regarded the faintly smoldering, blackened patch on the wall. "And she thought burning down the woodshed would be annoying enough?"

"With Helen inside it, yes."

Aubrey's jaw dropped.

"She didn't bolt the door," Helen said quietly. "She did not mean me to die. I think it was just temper."

They both stared at her. "*Temper,*" Roderick repeated.

"Yes, well, we can debate that another day," Aubrey said, as Meg groaned and tried groggily to sit up. "Right now, I would suggest Mrs. Maven needs manacles and a doctor. Probably in that order."

Meg began to weep silently. It did not seem like mere remorse or pain or manipulation. It looked like sheer disintegration.

Helen said, "We should take her to the hospital. They have secure rooms there."

"I'll take her," Aubrey said, bending to help Meg to her feet. She let him, limp and unresisting. He frowned at her. "Try anything and I'll knock you out cold." He turned back to Roderick and Helen and tipped his hat. "Sorry your wedding night was disturbed. Good night!"

And he sauntered off, holding Meg by the arm, looking for all the world as if they were a pair of drunken revelers.

"Aubrey," Roderick called after them.

His brother half turned.

"Thank you," Roderick said, and Aubrey's teeth flashed in response.

Once they had poured some more water over the smoldering wood of the shed, they saw Aubrey and the still silently weeping Meg safely into the carriage. The horses set off at a fast clip. After a moment, Roderick and Helen turned as one and walked slowly back into the house.

"What a very…exciting wedding night," he remarked. "I doubt your mother warned you of such doings."

"Funnily enough, no," she said, her voice trembling.

He hugged her against his side, and she felt his lips in her hair. "Oh, my dear, I am so sorry. This is *my* fault. I never even thought of her pain. I never looked, even at the castle ball when it should have been obvious. I've been too wrapped up in my own troubles to see anyone else's."

She flung her arm around his waist, hugging him back, burying her face in his throat, breathing in his skin, his very essence. "No," she said fiercely. "You are right. It *is* an exciting wedding night. It could not be more so, because you said you love me."

He kissed her temple, tightening his arm around her. She wondered if he would dare repeat the words.

"I did say that." She could hear the smile in his voice. "I said I love you, and I do. And I will wait for you, however long it takes."

She looked up. "To love you back? Roderick, I loved you the moment I saw you."

"I know. I think it was the same for me, only I was slower to realize it. Being a selfish mess of a man. For the physical love, we may take all the time we need."

She stopped, at the foot of the staircase, and took his face between her hands. "We may. And if you wish it, I will gladly begin now."

Chapter Twenty-One

THEY STOOD ONCE more in the front bedchamber, facing each other. This time, Roderick had blown out all the candles and left only the lamp burning at the bedside. The glow was warm and friendly, unthreatening.

And this time, she had so much to say that her tongue would not be still. Nor would her fingers, which were unbuttoning his coat. "I was so hurt that you didn't want me at Whalen, at the inn."

He groaned. "My dear, I wanted you so much that my poor honor—and yours!—hung by the finest of threads! I could and should have handled the situation with more grace." He shrugged out of his coat and threw it in the vague direction of the upholstered chair. "At the very least I should have insisted on your having your own room. In my defense, I can only say that I still had a vague idea of taking you home that night. Except I slept like the dead. The waking nightmares tend to do that to me. I barely recall waking up in the night and getting rid of my clothes. It didn't register that you were there."

"I *did* make a big impression upon you."

"In such a state," Roderick said, "I would think of nothing but sleep."

He turned her gently and began to unhook her gown. When he kissed her nape, her whole back undulated with pleasure.

"What are you thinking of now?" she asked breathlessly.

"You. And you. And you."

She turned back to face him, her gown falling as far as her elbows. Something dropped around her ankles. Her stays? She didn't care. "I could not bear to be your duty, to be married for your honor or mine. I wanted to be loved."

"Oh, my sweet, you are," he whispered. "You are…" He bent and kissed her mouth with a tenderness that almost made her weep. It went a long time, so long that it came as a shock to realize she stood completely naked in his arms.

His gaze swept over her, devouring her, dragging fire in its wake. "You are loved, and beautiful, and mine."

"I took your gentleness and patience for politeness," she blurted. "I wanted your…*wildness*. I thought that was love."

"It is all love," he said. "Though how I expected you to know when I barely acknowledged it myself, I have no idea. Will you trust me to love you? To give you pleasure?"

She slid her arms around his neck, pressing as close to him as she could when his shirt and breeches were in the way. "I have all the pleasure I need," she whispered, and kissed him long and passionately.

His breath had grown ragged, his skin hot, his eyes clouded, as they had been at the inn. But his smile was wicked, and a surge of desire shook her whole body.

"Let us see," he said softly, lifting her in his arms, "if that is so."

She landed among the pillows on the bed, and an instant later he stretched over her, entirely naked. Somehow, she found herself hanging on by a thread to the conversation.

"If what is so?" she managed.

"That you need no more pleasure," he murmured, trailing kisses from her jaw to her throat, to her breast. "What about now?" He kissed her nipple, and she gasped, arching into him. "Or perhaps this?" His bold, caressing hand swept between her thighs. "Or this…"

It seemed there were many pleasures she had never even thought of, the aching, the sharp, the arousing, the desperate, and the sweet. And yet when he began to slide inside her, they all became one, driving and insistent until she could bear it no more and came apart in unique and boundless joy.

More than that, even through the wonder, she realized she had given him his own splendid bliss, and that was more stunning, more marvelous, than all the rest. This was pure happiness.

THERE WAS A sweet awakening at dawn. Roderick had not meant to impose on her again so soon, being careful of her almost-virginal body. But somehow, his amazing, innocent love took control, took him inside her, and then it was only gentlemanly to oblige her with a little more tender pleasuring. And receive his own.

At their second awakening, he was in more control. He had never found pleasure before in arousal that was not satisfied. He wanted to wait, to care for her.

She pouted, but not too much. Instead, she got out of bed and padded naked to the door, while Roderick watched appreciatively from the bed, his hands clasped behind his head. She listened, presumably for the sounds of servants, then opened the door a crack and gave a little crow of delight.

"Breakfast! They've left us breakfast outside the door. We must give them an increase in wages."

Roderick laughed and went to help. In moments, they were sitting in bed, sharing lukewarm coffee and toast and boiled eggs. He felt almost like a boy again, lighthearted with fun and banter. And whenever he looked at her, he was overcome with sheer love. His wife was passionate, loving, and vital, a constant source of surprise and delight.

And for some reason he doubted he would ever fathom, she loved him.

It was with reluctance that he said at last, "Perhaps we should get up."

"Why?"

"Well, I have a feeling Aubrey will appear with news of Meg. I wouldn't put it past him to barge upstairs in search of me."

Helen stared. "He wouldn't!"

"Maybe not," Roderick allowed, grinning. "But the twins would. Let me call for a bath for you."

While she bathed, he sat nearby in clean shirt and comfortable pantaloons, watching her and talking of wedding journeys, of places he had been, and those she wished to see.

"We cannot go yet, though," she remarked. "Sir Julius is to be married next week, and Lucy and Lord Eddleston the week after. And you have the newspaper to set up, and your business with Skelton to attend to. Perhaps we should wait until next spring?"

"Would you mind waiting so long?" he asked.

She smiled and climbed out of the bath. He found a towel to wrap her in. It was an excuse to cuddle her.

"No," she said. "I like to be here with you. I want to be home in our house for a little."

He had to kiss her for that, and so it was some time before she was finally dressed and they went downstairs together to partake of luncheon.

Halfway through, Violet appeared to ask if they were at home, because Mr. Aubrey Vale and Dr. Lampton had called.

"You had better show them in here, Violet," Helen said. "And bring some wine, if you please."

"Well," Aubrey said upon entering, throwing himself into one of the vacant chairs and gazing at Roderick, "don't *you* look like the cat with the cream."

To his annoyance, Roderick felt his face burn, but he held his brother's gaze steadily. "I am the happiest of men. Doctor, please sit down. A little wine?"

"Just half a glass, if you please," Lampton said in his curt way. "I can't stop."

"He saw Mrs. Maven," Aubrey said.

"Is she…ill?" Roderick asked.

Lampton frowned. "Yes, I think so." He took a sip of wine. "For what it's worth, I think it is temporary. Both Dr. Samson at the hospital and I have seen this kind of nervous upset before. Its root seems to be in severe emotional stress or anxiety of some kind. She needs complete rest—and away from Blackhaven."

"I have no quarrel with that," Roderick said wryly. "The further away, the better."

"The question is," Aubrey put in, "are you pressing charges?"

He glanced at Helen, and knew they agreed. "For what? Moving piles of wood around? We could charge her with assault against Helen, I suppose, but she definitely came off worse in the encounter. But if she comes near the house or near Helen again—"

"I don't believe she will," Lampton said. "I think she has realized how close she came to destroying her own life, which she has built up with such difficulty, whatever she did to yours. She needs time to rest and recover, and then go somewhere entirely new."

"Do you think she would do such a thing again?" Helen asked, as though unwilling to hear the answer.

Lampton considered. "I would doubt it. I gather her emotions took her somewhat by surprise. She is not used to it. The next time—if there is a next time—she will be better prepared. My wife is advising her to go to Brighton."

Roderick smiled. "Why not?"

Lampton drained his glass, stood, and bowed. "My thanks, and farewell. I shall see myself out."

"Thank you, doctor," Helen said, rising and going with him anyway.

When they were alone, Roderick found his brother smiling at him. "What?" he said irritably.

"If I didn't know better," Aubrey said, "I'd think you were

happy."

"I am, little brother," Roderick replied, raising his glass.

"And so am I," Helen said gaily, walking back into the room.

Aubrey smiled at her. He had a damned charming smile, did Aubrey, and he knew it. "Three down," he observed.

"Are you next?" Helen teased.

"Oh, I doubt it," Aubrey replied, unexpectedly rueful. He raised his own glass to them. "But I know one of us will be!"

Epilogue

Paris, two years later

THE COMTESSE DE la Ravanne's reception was billed to be the last truly fashionable event in Paris before the nobility and anyone else who could afford it left the city for summer.

Roderick, never a great lover of such social events, was exceedingly nervous of this one. But he could not allow Helen to know it. So he smiled at her lazily from the opposite carriage seat and pretended not to see her fingers twist together in her lap.

Tonight, her portrait of the comtesse would be unveiled. And, for all intents and purposes, this would be her first Paris exhibition, for several of her others works would be on display. To be praised here tonight would be a huge boost to her reputation—and, no doubt, her commissions. To be reviled, or even dismissed, would be a definite setback.

More than that, it would *hurt* her. Roderick wished he could form up all the dilettante guests of the evening like a troop of soldiers and instruct them. But she would never forgive that. Apart from anything else, such behavior would prove *he* had no faith in her. And he did. It was malice and jealousy he would shield her from.

The carriage turned into a wide gateway behind several others, and a few minutes later was able to stop at the front steps. A liveried footman opened the carriage door and let down the steps. Roderick alighted and handed Helen down.

Her gloved hand was shaking. He placed it on his arm and walked with her up the steps to the house.

"You and Alice organized the exhibition in Whalen without any support at all," he murmured. "There is no such pressure here."

"You know that was different. It was only Whalen."

"Only Whalen, where the people are not cultured enough to know about art?"

She flushed. "Some of them do."

"Some of them here will, also," he said, and she smiled at him, squeezing his arm in gratitude.

"It is easy to get such things out of proportion."

"I know."

Their arrival caused a bit of a stir and some blatant staring. Helen took this in her stride. After all, though she had never had that London Season she dreaded, she had always been used to attention as the Earl of Braithwaite's sister.

The comtesse welcomed her with delighted kisses on both cheeks, and greeted Roderick in similar fashion. Her gaze was admiring, flirtatious, but fortunately she was more seriously in love with Helen's portrait of her to make any serious efforts at seduction.

A footman offered them champagne, and Roderick took a glass for each of them. When Helen accepted one, he raised his glass to her. "You are looking particularly and beautifully *interesting* tonight."

She smiled, at least a hint of genuine amusement behind her nervousness. In fact, it was the truth. She looked superb with her artistically ruffled hair, gowned in shades of shimmering green silk, with a thick, twisted gold necklace and matching bracelet, both with dangling garnets that provided a delicious and becoming contrast.

Her dress had grown bolder in the almost two years since

their marriage, but somehow it was never other than tasteful. As if she was growing into *Helen*, inside and out.

They mingled among the other guests, nodding to acquaintances they had made over the last couple of weeks. When Roderick was sure she was comfortably in conversation, he excused himself and walked among those inspecting the pictures hung on the walls of the salon.

"Skelly," he murmured to Captain Skelton, who had brought the paintings from England and was now responsible for guarding them as he moved unobtrusively among the comtesse's guests. Much fitter than two years ago, he no longer needed to be coddled by North or Roderick and took on his full share of the business.

"All right and tight," Skelton said, deceptively casual as he watched paintings and guests and servants. "Much admired," he added, guessing Roderick's worry.

Of course, praise was not universal. Roderick overheard a few derogatory or dismissive remarks.

"Some bored, aristocratic Englishwoman with nothing else to do, showing off her schoolgirl paintings…"

"She only gets any attention at all because she is Lord Milord Tamar's sister-in-law."

"Insipid, don't you think? If she had any true talent, she would paint in oils."

He spotted Lord Tamar, who caught his eye and winked. He was keeping his distance to prevent emphasizing his connection to Helen, though he was clearly proud of her. Roderick made his way back to Helen's side.

She was in conversation, her French obviously holding up better than his. He could understand more than he spoke, and since he did not interrupt, no one noticed his presence at first.

"And your husband, madame?" an effete gentleman of middle years inquired. "He permits this…activity?"

Helen's chin tilted. "Of course. He encourages me."

"I suppose it must make up for lack of children," a woman

said spitefully.

"You are misinformed, madame," Helen replied. "We have a son who is a year old."

Roderick's heart melted with pride and love at the mention of Jules, who was with them in Paris.

"And is your husband a great appreciator of art?" the effete man inquired.

"Indeed he is," Helen replied with pride of her own. "Of all forms of art, including music and literature. He runs a newspaper and publishing business, among other things." She became aware of him standing beside her and smiled. "My husband, Mr. Vale," she said, taking his arm, just as the comtesse called the company of guests to order.

"The moment we have all been waiting for. Madame Helen Vale's stunning portrait of my humble self!"

A servant removed the covering and a sigh whispered around the salon. Several people stepped closer. One or two stepped back.

"The devil," observed the effete man. "I have to say, I thought your landscapes were rather good, but I did not see how a portrait would stand up in such a medium. Madame, you amaze me. Never have I seen such definition, such character, in a watercolor portrait. It truly is Madame la Comtesse in all her beauty and foibles of nature."

"And vulnerability," someone else said, peering closer. "How on earth did you see that, never mind paint it?"

"Practice," Helen said lightly. "You are both too kind."

Other artists were there, examining her technique, glancing occasionally at the comtesse with something like surprise. One or two congratulated Helen with genuine admiration. She accepted the compliments graciously, for their praise meant a good deal to her. However, only when a path was made for Tamar to inspect the painting did she hold her breath.

He approached it slowly, as carelessly handsome as ever, inspected it up close, and stepped back again before he turned smiling to congratulate the comtesse—and then he walked up to Helen to give her a loud kiss on the cheek.

"Well done," he said, and switched to English. "In fact—pardon my French—bloody well done!"

The evening was an undoubted success, and Helen was bombarded with requested commissions.

"If you are happy to come to England in the winter or next spring, I shall be happy to accommodate you," she replied to each.

Inevitably, their faces fell. "You do not stay in Paris?"

"No, I am on my delayed wedding journey. We are going to Vienna and Rome, Venice and Florence, and wherever else takes our fancy."

They had already been to Brussels and driven out to the old battlefield of Waterloo. It had brought back a lot of pain, a lot of ghosts for Roderick, but he thought he had finally laid them to rest. He would never forget, and the nightmares still occasionally woke him. But his present life was so full of love, fun, and interest that he pointed himself firmly toward the future to keep it that way.

"You wish us to come to London? In winter fog?" was a frequent, dismayed response to Helen's condition.

"Oh no. Come to Blackhaven. We only have sea fogs there. The landscapes you were admiring are all of Blackhaven."

"Then you go back to *domesticity*?" someone asked with more disappointment than spite.

"No," Helen said, taking Roderick's arm, and he knew it was time to leave the reception for their own apartment, their own child, and their own blissful bed. "We go home to joy."

But, in fact, joy was something they carried with them, always.

About the Author

Mary Lancaster lives in Scotland with her husband, three mostly grown-up kids and a small, crazy dog.

Her first literary love was historical fiction, a genre which she relishes mixing up with romance and adventure in her own writing. Her most recent books are light, fun Regency romances written for Dragonblade Publishing: *The Imperial Season* series set at the Congress of Vienna; and the popular *Blackhaven Brides* series, which is set in a fashionable English spa town frequented by the great and the bad of Regency society.

Connect with Mary on-line – she loves to hear from readers:

Email Mary: Mary@MaryLancaster.com

Website: www.MaryLancaster.com

Newsletter sign-up: http://eepurl.com/b4Xoif

Facebook: facebook.com/mary.lancaster.1656

Facebook Author Page: facebook.com/MaryLancasterNovelist

Twitter: @MaryLancNovels

Amazon Author Page:
amazon.com/Mary-Lancaster/e/B00DJ5IACI

Bookbub:
bookbub.com/profile/mary-lancaster

www.ingramcontent.com/pod-product-compliance
Lightning Source LLC
Chambersburg PA
CBHW060354310726
48976CB00003B/815